THE

AEON

CHRONICLES

BOOK 3

April M Woodard

DISTANT WORLD PRESS

For information, contact:
P.O. Box 2020
Villa Rica, Georgia 30180
http://www.aprilmwoodard.com

Cover design by SHANNANTHOMPSON ART
Edited by Tiffany White www.writersuntapped.com

ISBN: 978-1-7322490-3-5

First Edition: February 2020

Distant World
PRESS

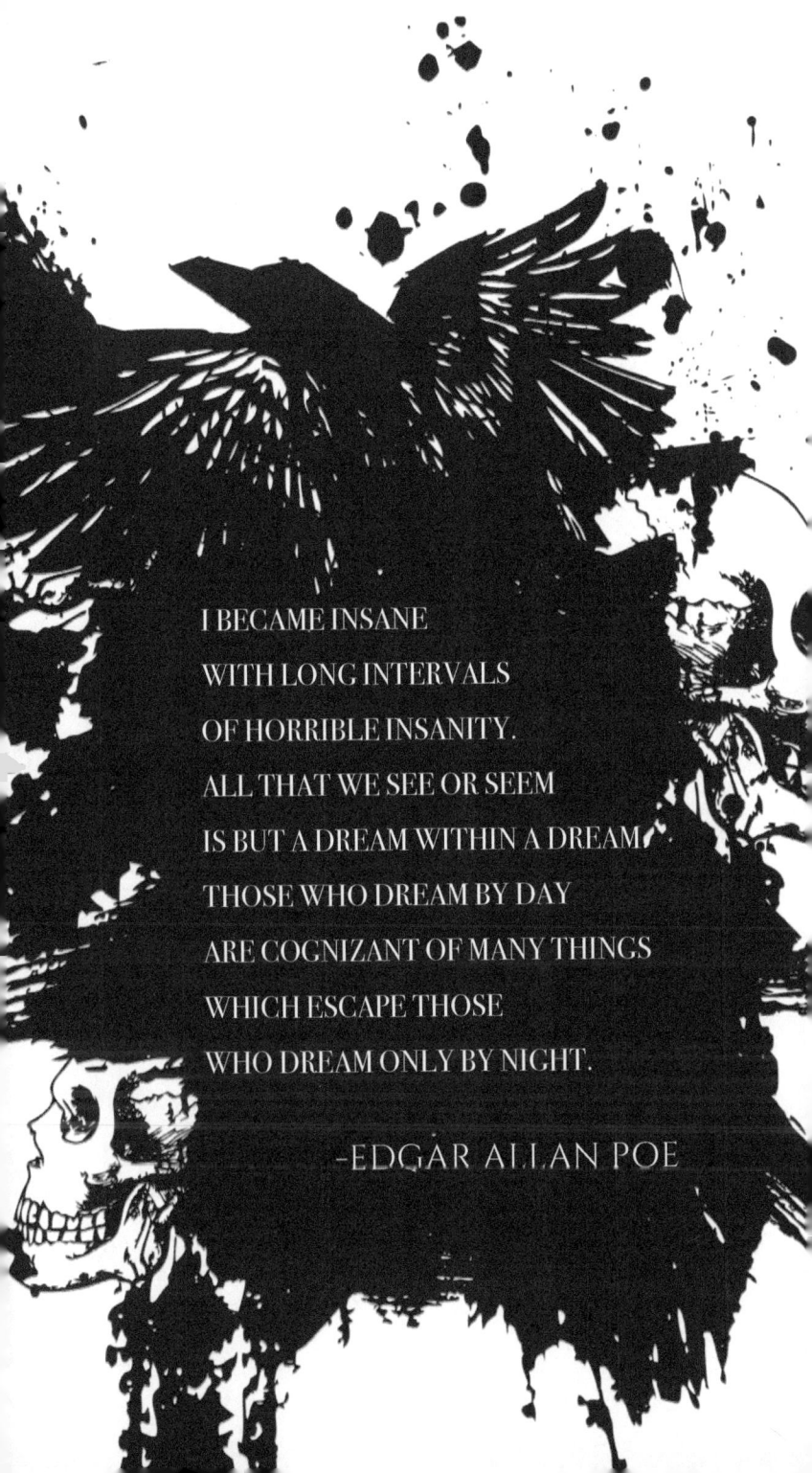

I BECAME INSANE

WITH LONG INTERVALS

OF HORRIBLE INSANITY.

ALL THAT WE SEE OR SEEM

IS BUT A DREAM WITHIN A DREAM.

THOSE WHO DREAM BY DAY

ARE COGNIZANT OF MANY THINGS

WHICH ESCAPE THOSE

WHO DREAM ONLY BY NIGHT.

-EDGAR ALLAN POE

ALL WET

TUESDAY, 9:23 P.M.
LAS VEGAS, NEVADA

AVEN leaned away from the stone pillar the moment he heard Kitten's heels hammer the marble tile. He hadn't been sure she would come. She had ignored his phone calls, never replied to his texts—except the 911 he sent over an hour ago. He knew he deserved the silent treatment, but after seeing a vision from his past life, he had to tell someone, and that someone was Kitten.

He glanced at his watch and then up at the statue temple, wondering if this golden idol was one of his ancestors.

When Kitten rounded the corner of the eighteen-foot waterfall, Aven couldn't help but beam with pride. She wore the Prussian blue georgette gown he had bought her in Greece.

Maybe fate is on my side after all.

The second Kitten set her gaze on him, Aven knew she wasn't in the mood for compliments. She came to the edge of the shallow pool and crossed her arms, glaring as if they had already been arguing.

"What do you want, Aven? Nick's waiting for me in the casino."

"You were right," Aven said, leaving the rotunda to descend the steps. He paused at the water's edge, holding back a clever grin.

"That's a first." Kitten narrowed her eyes. "About what?"

"That you're not my wife, but I can't help being protective over you. If you get wrapped up in the drugs again and OD, I—"

Aven wet his lips, thinking about the time he had seen Kitten after four years of being abroad in Britain. He'd been with some of his graduated college associates, showing them around Vegas for a good time.

When he walked into the gentleman's club, the announcement of "Kitten" caught his attention. He hadn't seen her in years, but there was no denying it was her. No matter the smeared kohl eyeliner or how her ribs extruded from her skin, he'd known by her singing voice.

The moment she exited backstage, he had paid the manager a month's rent to have the private VIP room. He kept his face hidden in the shadows as she knelt at his feet. When she went to unzip his pants, he stopped her and spoke about things only they would have known from their childhood. The moment Kitten's doe eyes glinted in recognition, he threw her over his shoulder and toted her to a driverless cab.

"That's why you called me here?" Kitten rolled her eyes. "I'm not using."

"If I find out you are," Aven said, now looking at Kitten's well-fed but slender figure, "don't think for a minute I won't take you to a driverless cab half-naked and lock you in my bathroom to wean you off the drugs again."

"Are you finished with your lecture now?"

Aven tipped up his chin and grinned. "Yes."

"Good." She spun around, heading for the hotel. "I'll see you in the morning."

"There's something else," Aven called out, taking a few steps across the pool. He hoped she'd turn around to see him walking on water, but she stormed away much too quickly. He increased his strides across the pool and called out her name.

"I'm not in the mood to hear more whining about what you did to Claire," she told him, not bothering to look over her shoulder.

Aven's forehead wrinkled.

Claire? So she did listen to the voicemails. She's jealous?

"You remember that time we were dancing, and I lifted your feet off the ground?" Aven asked, catching up to her.

Kitten stopped and turned. She glanced at the temple where he'd been standing and then at his damp trail of shoe prints. She didn't ask how he had made it across the pool without getting his pants wet. Which was exactly what Aven had wanted her to do.

"It was a really good trick." She met his gaze with scrutiny. "Even for a twelve-year-old."

"What if it wasn't a trick?" he asked, wrapping a hand around her waist. He took her hand and swayed them left to right to the soft music coming from the speakers.

Kitten glared. "What are you doing?"

"Close your eyes."

"Aven."

"Pretty please?"

Kitten let out a groan but did as requested, and Aven closed his eyes too.

He two-stepped them around the concrete dance floor and concentrated on the air beneath his feet. When he was confident he could support Kitten's weight, he bent his knees slightly to ascend an invisible staircase over the Apollo pool.

Twirling the two of them in a circle, Aven opened his eyes and never took them off her doll-like face. He held back from tracing her pouty lips, from running his fingers through her platinum-blonde hair. He had no desire to tap her button nose, to tease her about her ears like he had when they were kids. Instead, there was a feeling, one Aven had only felt around Claire, and it fluttered in his stomach like the flight of thousand monarch butterflies.

"Can I open them yet?" Kitten asked, clearly still irritated.

"Something happened to me while I was away. It's somewhat of a dilemma," Aven said, drawing her close. "I was going to tell you right away, but seeing you in that dress, I find myself faced with a whole new conundrum. Maybe it's me. Maybe it's you. Maybe I'm finally seeing everything I've ever wanted. It's been standing right in front of me this whole time, and now I can't help but wonder . . ."

When Kitten's lips parted, Aven didn't waste a second before kissing her. His mouth became greedy with each sweep of his tongue, tasting the hint of an apple martini. One hand explored her curves; the other clutched her hair tightly at her neck. There was nothing but air to press her against, no way to grind his hips. He cursed himself for floating. He wanted her, all of her.

It became clear that the feeling wasn't mutual.

Perhaps the way he groped her that made Kitten shove him away. Aven didn't have enough time to figure out why. He was too panicked by her scream.

Somehow during the plunge, he managed to grab Kitten's hand. He drew her into his arms and against his chest before he turned, making sure the pool below hit his back. The impact of their fall stung much more than he anticipated, but what stung worse was the wet smack across his face when he surfaced.

"Don't you EVER do that again!" Kitten demanded with a strangled voice. She coughed, sweeping her wet hair from her face.

"What?" Aven asked, rubbing his cheek. "Make you fly?"

"Kiss me like that!" she hissed and swam to the shallow end of the pool.

"Katharine, wait."

"If Nick had seen that—"

"I don't care about Nick or what he sees."

"You should. You know how angry he gets. He'll take it out on me."

Aven remembered back to the time she had covered her arms despite the blistering heat during an event years ago. He took her to the side, drew up her sleeves, and rushed off to confront Nick the moment he saw the bruises. That was the first time he and Nick had been in a scuffle. The problem was, it hadn't just happened in front Kitten, but in front of every member of The Circle. That following afternoon, Aven was put on probation, and Nick was sent back to Italy.

"I'll kill the bastard," Aven promised, wading to Kitten at the pool steps. "If he lays another finger on you—has he?" He twisted her around to make her look her in the eye. "Katharine, I swear if he—"

"He hasn't."

Maybe she remembers that night too. Maybe she knows I really would kill the prick. Family or not. I'd cut the bastard's throat.

"You don't belong to Nick," Aven said, cupping her face. "You belong with someone who's good to you." Aven lifted her chin and fixed his gaze. "You belong with me."

In an instant, Kitten's eyes filled with fury. "Are you fucking kidding me right now?" She splashed water in his face.

Aven splashed her back. "Are you not going to admit you have feelings for me?"

"Don't make things complicated, Aven. You're going to ruin everything."

"We can try." Aven drew her back to him by her waist. "If it doesn't work out, we can go back to—"

"Try with someone else," she snapped, wrestling out of his grasp. "Because I'm not going to be a rebound for a few weeks, only to be dropped the moment Claire calls."

Aven's heart sank to his stomach like a lead weight. He hurt everyone he cared about. Claire, Kitten, his mother. Will. He'd destroyed every relationship he ever had. He once thought it was only with people he had spent the night with, never to see again, but now he knew that wasn't true. He had lost Claire. He couldn't lose Kitten too.

"She's not going to want me back," Aven tried to assure her, "not after what I said. And I can't tell her my new secrets."

"There's more than the flying trick?"

"Mm-hmm." Aven grinned and slipped his fingers through her wet hair at the nape of her neck.

"Aven," Kitten warned. "I swear if you kiss me again—"

"I just want to show you what I can do," he said, holding back the urge to kiss her again. "Mind Walk with me."

Kitten averted her gaze to Aven's lips. Their kiss. It caught her off guard. She hadn't realized he made them float in the air until they were falling. No telling how long they had hovered.

What's so secretive that you can't tell me out in the open?

When Aven's hands warmed at her neck, Kitten held his gaze and counted back from ten. The second she blinked, she found herself in a blank space in Aven's mind.

As expected, Kitten now stood in a room wall to wall with white. Aven stood before her in a dry suit, holding her hands.

"I want you to think of all the dreams you've had of us together," he instructed, squeezing her hands gently.

"Aven," Kitten groaned.

"Dreams that were not of this life, but another. It looked much different, more beautiful."

"I don't have dreams," she reminded him. "You took them away."

It was true. The mind manipulation Aven had done on her years ago convinced her brain not to dream. It had been his way of protecting her from Nehia, from the torture he endured. Without dreaming, there was no way for the demon to taunt Kitten with her a troubled past or her own guilt. Like hypnosis, a Mind Walk could alter one's thoughts. The Circle had used this tactic for centuries to control CIA agents, people in power, but most of all, the masses. But unlike those within the brotherhood of The Circle, Aven had never used his gift of Persuasion for evil; at least, that's what Kitten hoped.

"The dreams from before that Mind Walk," Aven said. "They're still in there. Concentrate."

As Kitten thought of the wonderful dreams of her childhood, the white walls became clouds. When the fog cleared, Kitten stood on a stage in a golden amphitheater, wearing a glittering ivory gown. She peered down at the full house and searched the faces. When she found Aven's in the front row, she made him her focal point and sang to the heavenly tune of the symphony.

She couldn't believe the sound that came from her mouth or the applause when the music stopped. Aven stood among her adoring fans, clapping, shouting "bravo," and whistled through his fingers. She thanked the crowd, and Aven helped her down the steps of the stage, walking her away toward a white light at the end of the aisle.

Sunlight warmed Kitten's face as they entered a colorful courtyard. She was in awe of the preparation for the festivities about to begin. She turned to Aven, ready to lead him to a cart adorned in handmade instruments, but to her dismay, he wasn't by her side any longer.

Thorny vines weaved their way along the path in front of her, climbing blocks that built stonewalls on all sides of her. She was in a beautiful garden now, following the briers that bloomed with roses at her every step. They led the way to a fountain where she found Aven seated, tucking a girl's stray hair behind her ear. Her breath hitched seeing that girl, seeing Claire with a crown upon her head and a beaded braid that Aven twirled in his fingers. He tugged Claire gently toward him and leaned down to kiss her parted lips.

With a gasp, Kitten opened her eyes, breaking free of the illusion. She shivered, finding the blue pool waters up to her waist. "I don't like these mind games," she told Aven.

"It's not a game. Not this time."

Kitten's gaze darted from the steps over his shoulder to the path leading back to the hotel. She had to get away from him. She had to ignore what she saw, what he made her see.

Why is he torturing me?

"We knew one another long before we were kids, Katharine," Aven said, lifting her chin to make her look at him. "What you saw was a memory. You know I'm telling the truth because it felt like it was real."

Yes, it had felt real. Somehow more real than reality itself. Everything had been so vivid, so crystal clear. Emotions in that place were exaggerated, as well as smells and sounds. It was as if she had been given some kind of potent hallucinogen, had been high on a wonderful trip. But seeing Aven kiss Claire at the fountain, Kitten began to question the authenticity of the wonderful scenes.

"I don't know what I feel," she lied. "And neither do you. Whatever that was—"

"Katharine?"

Kitten clenched her teeth at Nick's voice and turned cautiously to face him. "Nick," she said, sweetly. She swept her hair to the side, although there was no way to make herself look presentable. "Aven dropped something in the pool. I was leaning over to look for it, and I slipped." She gave an innocent shrug, hoping her lie would appease him.

By the way Nick's eyes narrowed, she could tell it clearly hadn't.

"I'll go home and change." She told him and got out of the pool.

"Care for a swim?" Aven asked, splashing Nick's dress shoes.

Nick wrinkled his nose as if the pool was filled with rotting garbage before he turned his back, grumbling obscenities in Italian.

"You're always so dramatic," Kitten accused Aven. "Are you really this starved for attention?"

She wrung out her dress and eyed the pool, seeing her heels waving from the bottom of it.

Great. Guess I'm walking barefoot. That's coming out of your account, Crey.

"No, I–" Aven began, but she cut him off.

"Forget it," she snapped. She was done talking to him. Done being the girl that ran to his side the moment he called.

I am NOT some clingy, one-night stand, Aven Crey.

She lifted her dripping dress and walked along the side of the pool, heading toward the valet parking area. Her heart was still racing. Part of it was from Nick's dirty looks; the other was from thinking about Aven's kiss. She licked her lips, still tasting him, still hearing that light moan he made. She had heard it so many times before, had wanted for so many years to be the one to satisfy his need.

A want pulsed between her thighs, but she kept walking, cursing the length she had felt against his hip. It was all she could think about now.

"Months ago you would have found the humor in this," Aven shouted and playfully splashed her. "Being around Nick is making you dull."

Kitten stopped in her tracks, shivering at the droplets that beaded down her back.

She hated the words she knew she must say, but if she didn't, she would always be stuck as the friend to entertain in his shenanigans.

"Find someone else to be your assistant," she told him, not looking back.

"You can't quit without giving a two-week notice, you know," he teased.

"It's in the mail," Kitten announced and disappeared around the corner, tapping an alert to the valet service that she needed a driverless cab at Aven Crey's expense.

A MISS

"BODIES are still being found beneath the rubble as talks of war between China, Russia, and the United States continue. Conspiracy has not been squashed. Fingers are pointed, issuing blame, quoting, 'the quake was a "catastrophic attack," rather than the wrath of Mother Nat–'"

Claire jabbed her thumb into the TV remote. She was sick of the news, sick of seeing the never-ending reports of the aftermath that had occurred over the past few days. New York was not the only area that had been hit. All the surrounding states along the East Coast had been significantly affected. It was always the same report, always the same sad story. Families were searching packed hospitals for their loved ones in New York. Looters were stealing out of cars, breaking into stores, and burning flags in the streets of Harlem. Coney Island had been shut down. Martha's Vineyard was vacant of tourists.

With a sigh, Claire glanced at the magazine table in front of her. Lying there was a book she'd barely read, an empty greasy-stained pizza box, and crumbs that trailed to a crumpled bag of potato chips next to a dripping carton of ice cream, now filled with soupy cookie dough remains.

The inn had been trashed by carelessness, but Claire didn't care. No one would be traveling here now, not after the news had slapped caution tape along the eastern coastline. It wasn't only the fear of another quake. No one had the money to travel now. The stock market had crashed, and the United States was facing the worst economic collapse of the century.

Claire winced at the bruise on her forehead as she swept her greasy hair back, silently cursing the ladder that had attacked her at Will's house a few days ago.

"Scan," she ordered the TV.

Channels blinked like a strobe light until they stopped on one according to her preferences. Seeing a tropical island with white sandy beaches and lapping waves of bright blue, Claire relaxed and leaned back in the chair. She thought of the angel from her dream, wishing she could dream of him again. She needed comfort from the warrior's embrace. She needed his hope. But that dream wouldn't come. Not until her next birthday.

Staring at a tranquil ocean, Claire pictured those light blue eyes looking deeply into hers again. Those eyes then came with a face. Will's face. Again she felt the patter of rain on her shoulders, the touch of his warm fingers grazing her skin. All the feelings from their moment in the pouring rain came over her again. It took her out of her misery, took her to an escape, but only for a moment.

The channel flipped automatically back on the news with an urgent message.

"We are live here in Brooklyn," a news announcer said. "As you can see behind me, there is extensive damage left from the quake that hit only a few days ago. Phone towers are still down, and officials are asking everyone to be patient when trying to contact your loved ones."

When the feed panned to the streets, Claire frowned, watching the citizens fight one another in desperation for survival. Those who could afford to fuel their cars were bickering with others in line waiting for a turn at the charging outlets. The scene jumped to other people who stood in line for assistance from NATO before the news then broke with a photograph of another businessman who had jumped from the Four Season's hotel after he had lost everything. The newsfeed zoomed in on the reporter and then an unkempt homeless man, standing by the blurred-out brain spatter on the sidewalk.

Claire thought she had seen this homeless man before and rubbed her wrist as an image of him tugging her arm flashed in her mind. With a shake of her head, she broke free from the illusion of an ashy campsite and watched the homeless man hold up his cardboard sign. Sloppy handwriting in permanent marker came into focus as the camera zoomed in on his warning.

THE END IS NEAR

The footage cut to an aerial view of worship centers across the world, where masses of people gathered. The feed jumped to another aerial view of Rome, then the pope, who was speaking. A closed caption below him translated his words.

Despite our religion . . . |
Despite our color or creed . . . |
We must unite as one to save humanity.

Prayers chanted in Italian filled Claire's living room, but they were soon hushed as multiple live feeds popped up. One screen was of all the sacred monuments in different countries where people gathered, another of muted mouths, pleading to their gods to save the world from pain and suffering, and last, the firefighters searching the rubble in New York for any survivors.

"TV off,"

The screen went black.

Leaning her head to the side, Claire stared at the letter on the side table with distaste.

Foreclosure. There was no way to save the inn now. Not that she cared. The inn had been her mother's dream.

Balling up the letter as if it were her mother's death certificate, Claire threw it across the room. She curled up under a blanket in her dad's La-Z-Boy. She hadn't slept in days, and it showed. Purple crescents rimmed her lower eyelids. Her hair was greasy and tangled. Her face had broken out from the smorgasbord of sweets and junk food she'd eaten.

She wondered if it had been her poor diet that brought on the nightmares. According to the health channel she had watched earlier that day, stress and poor eating habits affected a person's sleep significantly. A heavy sigh flared her nostrils. No matter the attempt to distract herself with the TV, she was unable to get the frightening images of the dream out of her mind.

In her recurring nightmare, Claire had been looking for her mother and brother among the rubble in New York left by the quake. Before the dream ended, she always heard the cry of a baby, her newborn nephew. She clawed through the rubble until her fingernails bled, frantic to find him, but never could. Instead, she would wake to her own wailing.

All Claire could think about was her dead family. When she wasn't thinking of them, she thought of Aven and what he said before he left her at Will's.

She also thought about Will and how her heart ached at the guilt of leaving only a note as her goodbye. She thought about texting him, thought about what she would say, but she knew the grieving process. She was going through it herself. Now was not the time to apologize.

Closing her eyes, Claire hoped that sleeping during the day would keep the nightmare away. Soon her heavy lids sealed shut, and the pleasant silence was soon replaced with the sound of soft lapping waves.

A bubbling surf kissed her feet. Salty air wisped the ends of her long tresses. Palm trees swayed in a warm breeze.

A siren broke the serenity.

Claire startled awake and snatched her phone from the side table to answer the call.

"Hello?" she croaked.

"Claire. It's Mrs. Harlow. Are you still coming to the vigil? I wanted to have those photos of your mother to put on the board before tonight."

Crap. I forgot.

"Yes, of course. I'll be there shortly."

It was about a thirty-minute drive to the worship center, no longer called The Cathedral of St. John the Baptist. It was a beautiful center, apart from the renovations. The outside was still magnificent. The blue and white steeples, trimmed in gold, reached to the sky, making the church look more like a castle than a place of worship. On the inside the stained-glass windows depicting saints had been replaced, and angelic statues had been removed, but the beautiful architecture still remained.

Claire's favorite part was the ceiling. It was arched and decorated with ornate light fixtures that hung from golden-sculpted fleurs. As a child, she would stare at the blue-painted sky of stars before falling asleep in her mother's lap during service. She would give anything to be cradled in her mother's warm arms right now.

"Be careful, sweetie," Mrs. Harlow said. "There are cars stalled on Abercorn. You should take Liberty Street and park there."

"Yes, ma'am. I'll be leaving in about five minutes."

Kicking off the blanket, Claire grumbled as a cool draft chilled her skin. She rubbed her arms and then her eyes, telling herself she could attempt to sleep again before tonight's vigil service.

Making her way into her mother's deserted bedroom, Claire ran her hands along the patched quilt her grandmother, GG, had made. She missed her grandmother deeply, missed her wise words in times such as these.

"We must endure through the pain, even when we are angry or upset," her grandmother had said one night when Claire was only five and learned that her kitten had been put to sleep due to distemper. *"Things happen out of our control. Some, for a purpose bigger than you and I could ever understand."*

Claire couldn't believe in her grandmother's words right now. It was hard to as a child, but even more so now with what she saw on the news.

How can people dying happen for a reason?

Letting out a long sigh, she picked up the picture frame on the nightstand and bit her lip. The photo had been taken a year before her father's death, before photo labs closed down, never to print again.

In the photo, Claire stood wedged between her mother and father. Lapping waves froze in time behind them as sunlight cast an orange glow on their faces. Claire rubbed her stiff neck as if she could still feel the sunburn from that day. She now wished she hadn't rolled her eyes when her mother mentioned reapplying sunscreen. Now she thought of every snappy reply, every harsh word she had ever spoken to her family throughout their lifetime together.

Tears rolled down her cheek as she took the picture from the frame and tucked it in the back pocket of her jeans. Mrs. Harlow had asked for a five-by-seven. This photo was only a four-by-six.

Once in the stale and dusty attic, Claire sorted through several photo albums. She grinned wide at the happy moments capturing her childhood. Christmas, birthdays, and every vacation had filled these yellowed pages. She paused at a photo of her parent's wedding and eyed the size.

Claire knew Mrs. Harlow and the congregation would appreciate seeing this happy memory to reflect on. After all, her parents had been married in that very same worship center and attended every service faithfully.

Noting that this picture had been taken before the renovations of the church, Claire studied the stained-glass window. A golden hue shone from the saints and angels that smiled down on them, and Claire wondered if there really was a Creator.

I hope they are at peace Beyond the Veil. Wherever that is.

Between putting away the albums and stacking up the boxes, Claire wiped her tears until the flood couldn't be controlled. She cursed the quake, cursed herself for being so selfish taking her family for granted. If only she had stayed with her mother and not gone to Vegas, if only she had been there when the quake had happened. She could be Beyond the Veil with them.

Dead, but with them.

They're gone. Your father, your mother, your brother, his newborn...

Deafening screams lit a fire to Claire's throat as she flung the albums one by one across the attic.

"You could have saved him!" she cried, pelting plastic bins. She growled, going to the box marked "Christmas" and launching it into another stack. Glittering balls spilled across floor, rolling to one of the bins assaulted by her fury.

Seeing her father's station-wear uniform, Claire fell on her knees and pressed it to her face. She inhaled his faint scent, soaking it with her tears.

GG said you'd be there for me, she said to the Creator. *But you've taken away everyone I love. Why? Why leave me alone? What was the purpose?*

No answer came. None ever did.

Claire entertained the idea of going downstairs to the bathroom and ending it all. At least she could be with her family again. And if there *was* no afterlife, at least she would be in a never-ending sleep. She wouldn't have to suffer. Not anymore.

How selfish, her inner voice chided. *What about your other relatives? They just lost your family, and here you are, thinking of a way to bring them more pain? Be another story on the news?*

"I can't do this," Claire whispered to her dead father, hoping what GG had told her was true. She wondered if her father could somehow speak to her, give her a sign of what to do.

"Please," she begged him. "Say something."

Waiting for his answer, Claire watched the settling dust sparkle in the sunlight from the window. There wasn't a voice, no words from her father, but there was a sign glinting at her knees.

Moving her father's folded plaid shirts away, she found the cover of a leather book, bearing a symbol she knew she had seen before.

A warrior. His gauntlet. A symbol.

Claire traced the infinity overlapping the letter "A," then the embossed wings above and below the Omega, wanting to say what the symbol stood for, *who* it stood for. It was on the tip of her tongue, at the very edge of her foggy memory.

Visions of that same emblem came again. She now looked down at it as she stood on a lush rug in a cozy Tudor home. The inlaid symbol glittered from the shiny crystal floor. She could feel a warm presence at her back now, then the weight of a strong comforting hand on her shoulder.

Claire winced at the pinch in her palm and loosened her grasp, realizing she had been clutching the charm on her necklace much too tight. The book glinted again, but this time from the brassy lock that bound the pages shut.

Fumbling with her necklace, Claire unclasped it and slid her skeleton key charm into the lock with clammy hands. She sucked in a shaky breath, closed her eyes, and turned her wrist.

Click.

At the sound, Claire opened her eyes and the book. She blinked once, then twice to wet her dry eyes, but then several times as the strange writings that blurred into words.

'Many are called, but few are chosen. It is I, the maker of the heavens and earth, who has chosen you.'

Claire slammed the book shut.

Stop it, Claire, she scolded herself. *You were past all this. It's not real. It's a metaphor. Your mind is trying to help you cope.*

Then how can you read the book? a voice asked softly.

I'm delusional, Claire countered. *And my dad always collected strange things. This is just some weird ancient book like all the others. It has nothing to do with me.*

And the key? The voice asked with that same soft tone.

Maybe he gave it to me because he thought it was cool, Claire told it. *It's just a coincidence.*

Is it? The voice questioned.

Whenever the voice spoke in her mind, Claire felt warmth accompanied by it. It faded the more she tried to convince herself the voice hadn't been real. A cold draft met her neck as she doubted. She traced her fingers over the cover again. The emblem shimmered at her touch, as did the strange symbols and letters in a matching gold beneath it. Claire squinted her eyes to read, and to her surprise, the text blurred into a legible title.

THE WORDS OF ARAMIS

The silhouette of a face came to Claire's mind in an instant. It was shrouded in a bright light, and she couldn't make out the man's features clearly. She could tell he was very tall, that maybe he was smiling down at her. She relaxed her tense shoulder, comforted, but then the image fled.

She thought about making an appointment with Dr. Seresh like her mother had suggested. She didn't want to end up like her Grandmother Grace.

GG read this to you for a reason. Or did you forget? The voice gently, but sternly noted.

Claire strained to remember her early childhood. A memory surfaced, one of her grandmother, GG, reading to her in bed during a thunderstorm. It was a story about a princess, one that had to make a choice.

Save the Outcast or follow her destiny.

At that time, books like the one she was now holding were considered to be radical, but they had not yet been outlawed. When news had spread that GG had held a small study session to talk about the book with a few close members of her congregation, they turned her away at the door of their Worship Center the following week.

Claire was about the age of ten when she watched the police haul her grandmother away. GG went quietly. She didn't fight; she had only smiled at Claire and told her to be strong. Later that evening, her mother explained their family's medical history. Psychosis. It ran on her mother's side, and unfortunately her father's too. They told Claire if she ever had any ideas like her grandmother, or had any episodes, it was best to keep it to herself.

'Schizoaffective Disorder'. That was the diagnosis they had given GG. It had been the same they had given Claire at the Counseling Center after she had explained seeing a smoke monster the day of the house fire. The following year, her parents were sent a court order to send Claire to a local clinic to be 'Deprived'.

A shiver ran down Claire's spine, thinking back to how frigid the steel gurney had been the day they took her right to bear children. It reminded her of the Psych Hospital GG had died in.

The day of her grandmother's death, Claire had walked into the icy hospital room, seeing GG lying in a bed, hooked up to an IV and machines. She was skin and bones, a drugged-up lifeless imitation of who she had once been. The doctors had informed her parents in hushed voices that her grandmother had been suffering from Dementia, and that her mind was too deteriorated to recognize any of them, that it was best to go ahead and 'put her to sleep' to save their pockets. But the moment Claire touched GG's arm, her eyes had flung open, and she had squeezed Claire's hand tight.

'I'll see you again.' GG had said, 'Beyond the Veil with air miss,'

Air miss...I'll miss you?

Not 'A miss.'. . . Aramis.

At the ring of the doorbell, Claire gasped and snatched up the book. She climbed down the ladder and hid the illegal item beneath her dad's lazy boy chair before answering the door.

"Claire Grace?" A carrier asked handing her a tablet.

"That's me,"

"Sign please."

As Claire scribbled her signature, the carrier toted a large rectangle package to her doorstep. She thanked him and dragged the cardboard box inside the house, hoping the tip she had given him wouldn't be charged to her bank account until Friday.

Upon opening the box, Claire's brows rose and her mouth parted, seeing a canvas, covered in a vibrant array of galaxies and stars.

Abbie's painting.

Claire vividly recalled the little girl's curls and her sweet smile as she found the talented child's painted signature in the corner. Abby had commented about Claire's light during the gala, that Will had a light too, but that Aven only seemed to brighten when he was with Claire.

Flushing with heat, Claire found an origami rose, taped to the back of the canvas. She knew who it was from, but feared to read the words in calligraphy folded in the creases.

A gift for the Queen of Hearts

He was lying. He was pretending to care about me.

But that doesn't make sense. Why would he have sent this if he had been pretending?

He was loaded, Claire. Money to burn. Literally.

She couldn't call Aven, not even to thank him. She didn't want to hear his voice, didn't want to feel that rejection again.

But Aven hadn't painted this beautiful scene, Abby had. No matter if it were a reminder of the wonderful and heartbreaking time she had spent with Aven, she would keep the breathtaking artwork.

Where the paper rose had been taped, was a stamp with the name of the foundation and a code to scan to access their website. Finding Cynthia, Abby's mother, in the websites directory, she made the call and drummed her fingers on the kitchen counter. The phone rang several times before a sullen voice answered a heartbreaking greeting for voicemail.

"This is Cynthia Tate. I'm unable to get to the phone right now. If you are calling about donations, please send them to The Las Vegas Autism Foundation in lieu of flowers for Abigail. Thank you."

Claire's heart stopped at the sound of the beep and her gaze was glued to the painting as a startling thought raced through her mind.

In lieu of flowers . . . Abby is . . .

Claire's heart sank when she found the memorial posted online for Abigail Tate in the news feed.

A PRECIOUS LIFE TAKEN TOO SOON

Claire wondered if it was one of the seizure's Cynthia had spoken of that had taken Abby's life. She pictured a possible scenario of the little girls last moments alive, what it would have looked like if Abby had gone into a grand mal seizure. She could see Abby foaming at the mouth, her body jerking uncontrollably, her mother cradling her, helpless to do anything to stop it.

Claire flinched when her phone blared a ringtone.

"Yes, Mrs. Harlow," Claire answered in a shaky voice.

"Yes, ma'am. I'm on my way with the photo now."

FOR SALE

FRIDAY, 10:24 A.M.
JOHNS ISLAND, SOUTH CAROLINA

WILL saved his mother's room for last, having been unable to go in it since her death. After guzzling down his third cup of coffee, he washed out his mug and headed for her room and the last few boxes left in there.

His body ached for sleep as he plodded up the steps. The past few nights, he'd awoken in a cold sweat hearing the beep of machines and Olivia's footsteps down the hall. No matter if Olivia and all the medical equipment had disappeared from sight, he still mindlessly went into his mother's room to check on her. Finding it empty, he had slunk back to his room and silently let the tears fall until sleep took him. But even when sleep came, the nightmares still woke him all hours of the night, and he found himself stumbling to his mother's room to check on her again.

With the stack of boxes cradled in his arms, Will made his way down the hall, heading for the barn until Blue barked. The sheepdog was at the studio door again. She had been sitting there day after day, scratching and whining. Will didn't understand why she insisted on entering. She had never been allowed in the room before. The Australian shepherd breed was known for shedding, and when he used to paint, Will had kept her locked out, unwilling to risk rogue merle hair flying up onto a drying canvas.

That was when Aaron would take her out and play fetch. That's why she liked Aaron more.

"Blue, you know you don't go up there."

Blue snapped a raspy bark and scratched at the door that was now splintered with peeling wood. He let out a heavy sigh, knowing it would have to be replaced before the realtor came to take photos. He hated that he was selling his childhood home, but he had no reason to stay. Not anymore.

"Fine," he huffed and sat down the boxes to take the key from the top of the doorframe.

Blue wagged her tail with glee, and the moment the door opened, she rushed up the steps, barking wildly as if to say "follow me!"

Will shook his head but did.

Topping the last step of his studio, his mouth parted and his brows furrowed at the mess before him. Paint tubes were scattered about. Canvases were tipped on their faces. A ladder lay on the floor next to Blue.

She yipped at it.

The earthquake.

Will paused while reaching for the ladder, finding a red paint splatter on it.

He looked down, seeing more splatters on the floor and got down on all fours to study it. Crusts of the crimson stained his fingertips at the touch of the dried dribbles.

Not paint. Blood.

Blue stooped down beside him and whined.

Claire.

Adrenaline shot through Will, and he jumped to his feet, taking his phone from his back pocket and thumbing through the names. His racing heart skipped a beat when he thought of her beautiful face, then squeezed when he remembered she left without saying a word.

At least not to my face. Why didn't she wait until I came back? What was she doing in my studio?

A million questions raced through his mind. He wondered if she and Aven had broken up or if she was with him. He thought about calling Aven but was still upset he was a no-show at their mother's burial.

He was there. You saw him. Was Claire in the cab I saw? Was he taking her to the hospital? Was she injured?

Will stared at Claire's number. He cared for her, worried about her. There was an unexplainable need to protect this girl he hardly knew. But it was more. There was something between them. He knew it. It had been the way she looked into his eyes as they stood in the pouring rain. Something had happened in that moment. He wondered if she felt it too, questioned if she had been curious about how he got to her so fast to catch her fall from Snow's saddle. When they had sat on the porch after Aven stole the mustang, he thought about telling her everything. But being a weapon for the government wasn't exactly a conversation starter.

The mustang was my little brother's. He was drafted. Not me. I enrolled in World War E to protect him. We were picked for a special project. Given a secret serum. It made me superhuman. That's how I survived the bullet wound you saw on my shoulder. My body can heal itself.

"That's a miracle," she would say.

And then I would say that I used to believe in miracles. The AA fridge magnet is a whole other story. Let's just say I was numbing the pain, but it takes a lot to get me drunk. Like, a lot. I pretended to be dead until I found out my mom was sick. You know about the letter, about Aven, but what you don't know is that when I found you, my whole world got turned upside down—not in a bad way—I think I'm in love with you, because you remind me of this angel I dream of . . . no not that kind of dream, well sometimes, but—

Will groaned.

It wouldn't have gone well.

I should have kissed her. Maybe she wouldn't have left if I had. Maybe she would have stayed . . . for me.

Blue barked, drawing his attention back to the canvas. Will sighed heavily, shoved his phone into his pocket, and propped the art against the wall. He took a step back and crossed his arms, critiquing the beautiful scene he had painted years ago. It could never be as vibrant as the dream, never as beautiful, but it was as close as he could get to being back in heaven.

He knew it was somehow connected to the recurring dream of the wave and the beautiful angel he always sketched during sleepless nights. He could never forget her face, never forget the way he felt around her in the dream. Deep down, he wondered if Claire was somehow incarnate of that angel.

What if she is? What if she was the one who was supposed to save me from myself?

Soon, Will was in his mind, watching through the eyes of his dream-self, going through the motions of that very dream that spurred the depiction before him.

He sat in a courtyard, sweeping azure, deep purple, and gold across the tight linen before brushing in the bright yellows and shades of white portraying the warmth of the glow he felt from the bodies passing him. Each bright aura said "good day" or "blessings to you" without a word. Joy wasn't the word to describe how he felt sitting in this place. No words could ever explain its serenity. Only colors, and these colors were his unwritten poetry.

One aura in particular stood behind him, beaming so bright that it warmed his neck and made Will pause from his work. He cleaned his brush and wiped his fingers with a rag before he swiveled, but there was no one to greet him. There was only a hint of inexplicable admiration and awe that still lingered, leading his gaze to a white-hue-lit trail that led to the library nearby. As he packed up, ready to wait for whoever had been standing behind him to exit the library door, a black haze dimmed the scene.

The dream always ended there, and Will had never been able to go any further from that moment of waiting for that white light of joy to return to him. There had been other scenes, other dreams he painted and sketched. One of a waterfall, one of the angel floating in the ocean, another of the two of them embracing as a monstrous wave came to swallow them whole.

Blue gave a piercing bark and Will's eyes fluttered as he came back to reality.

"Did she come up here?"

Blue tilted her head, raising a furry brow.

"I should check on her."

Blue replied with a raspy bark and a wag of her tail.

"But first," Will said, covering the canvas in the drop cloth nearby, "this needs to be put away."

Blue sneezed in protest.

"We're going to the cabin," Will scolded. "This whole place will be underwater in–"

Will couldn't finish his words, but he said them in his head.

. . . In a matter of months? When?

He didn't want to admit that his dreams about the East Coast flooding had bothered him for years. It was why he kept in contact with Jeremiah every day, checking the USG until his mother fell ill. But the moment the New Madrid earthquake hit a few days ago, the moment he saw a similar scene on the television, Will couldn't help but believe his premonitions were coming true. He had seen the future. And if that were true, what he saw coming was much worse than what he had seen on the news.

The events of the vision started with a massive quake. It appeared dark, cold, maybe fall or winter. He waited for one phrase, and that phrase had yet to scroll across the newsfeeds.

A Quake Felt around the World.

Swallowing his fears of what was to come, Will toted the six-by-eight-foot canvas to the barn. He didn't know why he bothered packing everything up. It was going to be destroyed.

Because it's what the realtor said she wanted.

She had instructed Will on the renovations. Packing things up was the last on the list. He had given the walls a fresh coat of paint, installed the new automatic faucets and toilets. Other than the upgrades, the house was to be bare, simple. Will had no qualms about it. Not really. He had, however, grieved painting over his and Aaron's growth chart on the front doorframe. He passed the still wet doorway, making sure not to brush against it.

He glanced at the for-sale sign in the yard, only to focus back on the barn when guilt churned his stomach.

You know what's going to happen. Why would you let a family move in? They'll die here.

Or you could be crazy and delusional from the drugs they gave you in the war. Look what InfiniCorp did to Aaron.

He set his eyes on the beat-up Mustang that had been totaled in the car crash after he and Aven's bet at 1919. He should have insisted that he be the one to drive and not Claire. He still didn't understand what he saw.

An angel? I thought angels helped people. Not make people plow into a tree.

Again, Will thought about Claire. He worried about her head injury from the car crash, and now, a new injury from his ladder. His fingers itched to grab his phone from his pocket, and he shoved the canvas against the wall.

It would have been a natural instinct for most people to dodge or brace for impact of the box that fell from the shelf, but Will wasn't like most people and caught it with ease. He studied the scribbles of thick permanent marker on the box, but the word was hardly legible.

Attic?

He had fixed up the attic and moved the boxes to the bar when he returned home after the war, after he came out of hiding.

Curious, Will flipped open his pocketknife and sliced through the duct tape, finding a picture frame halfway rolled in bubble wrap inside. He squinted at the image through the plastic, ignoring the random pops at his touch. Dust glinted in the rays of sun coming through the wood slats as he held up the photo. It was like a sign, as if the universe was shedding light on this very moment, whispering that this was the beginning of something big.

In the family photo, Will stood beside Aaron with an arm wrapped around his neck. Will distinctly remembered they had been horsing around, his mother chiding them.

"Boys," he heard her say again. *"Stop being teenagers for a minute and smile."*

Aaron held up a set of keys but made a screwed-up face like a bug had flown into his mouth. It hadn't been a bug; it had been the jab of Will's finger poking him playfully in the ribs.

Aaron's birthday present, the Mustang sat behind them; glossy from the fresh coat of wax Will had lathered on that morning. The classic car had been passed down to Will after his father's death. He never drove it. Not once. He liked his beat-up pickup truck, and having Hannah as his girlfriend back then, he hadn't needed to impress the ladies with a nice ride. Aaron, being shy however, had needed all the help he could get.

Putting the photo frame gently on the seat of the lawnmower, Will took out another carelessly wrapped frame. It wasn't another family photo. This one was of his deceased father.

Murderer, Aven's voice echoed in his mind.

No. His dad wasn't that. He was a good man. He was doing his job.

Rummaging further down in the box, Will found some of his dad's mementos. There was his old police badge and a few awards from his service, a tattered New York baseball hat, and a college T-shirt with grass stains. These were all the items Aaron held onto as a boy. These were all the things his mother hadn't had the strength to put away.

I did that for her.

Looking at the flap of the box again, Will realized the permanent marker scribble wasn't the word "attic."

This had been his own handwriting—his very sloppy, very drunken handwriting.

Will found more photos of his father serving—group shots with Caleb, his father's best friend, some of them playing cornhole in the front yard, others of them drinking beer in a backyard at a barbecue. His father hadn't been a murderer, but he had been a liar.

His father, Adam, had been an undercover agent working for the CIA. That information had been divulged in the letter his mother had written Aven. That had been the secret she kept, the reason she left her oldest son, why she and Adam had lived in hiding. Their whole life story had been a lie so that they could live only to die by the hand of the same company they had been hiding from. The same company Will had signed a contract giving permission to be experimented on.

InfiniCorp.

Something gold, glinting in the bottom of the box, drew Will's attention back to it. It was the last item buried in the haunting memories, the last painful reminder that everyone he loved was gone. He withdrew the leatherbound book and froze, seeing the embossed emblem.

This was the book he'd seen in Vincent's parlor, the same one locked behind glass that he stared at with curiosity.

The golden emblem shimmered as he held it up, wondering if he could read the foreign text again. When he was about to give up and pack everything away, a voice called to him.

Look again, it whispered.

Will stared long and hard, and before his burning eyes threatened to blink, the symbols shifted.

THE WORDS OF ARAMIS

"It will unlock the truth," he heard his mother say again.

Will put in the skeleton key from his key ring and turned it. At the sound of the *click*, he slowly undid the latch and opened the cover, only to find page after page filled with the same numbers and same strange symbols.

Will squinted his eyes, waiting in anticipation to find out the truth he had unlocked, but the text didn't change.

"This is insane."

Leaning against the lawnmower, Will rubbed his scruffy face and flipped through the book. A photograph slid out from inside and drifted to the floor.

Picking it up, Will stared down at his doppelganger. He had the same build, the same dirty blond hair. He stood dressed in a Navy Seal uniform beside a woman who looked unbelievably similar to Claire. Beside the woman was another male, dark-skinned, in the same military uniform. They were huddled together on a sailboat, surrounded by tall green mountains and with a vibrant half-rainbow behind them. Flipping over the photo, Will tried to make out the date. It was illegible, having been smeared by a water stain, but the names in cursive, were clear.

William Carpenter
Leviticus Robinson

Evelyn Grace

Grace...
It's not possible... is it?

SECRETS SAFE

AVEN was about to give up, about to strew everything in his uncle's safe across the room. There was nothing other than old coins, useless paper money, and outdated documents in folders. There was no information chip as his mother had led on. At least, that's what he thought until his fingers grazed the edge of one.

A breath of relief left Aven's lips. He snatched up the tiny information chip and then froze when he heard his cousin's voice.

"Nick tells me you decided to take a little swim the other night," Vincent teased. "He also informed me that you threw Katharine in the pool."

Aven slammed shut the safe. "Nick needs to mind his own business and stop treating Katharine like she's his trophy wife." He turned to face his cousin. "She's *my* assistant. And I didn't throw her in the pool. We were having fun. Which is something none of you snobby elitists know anything about."

"Looking for something?"

"Not anymore."

"And what could possibly be in Father's safe that wouldn't be on InfiniCorp's computer files?"

"A secret. Apparently, our family has many of them."

"You think Father kept secrets?"

Aven held up the chip. "Obviously."

"Were you told of the information on it?"

"Not exactly," Aven said, heading for the door, "but I'll soon find out."

Vincent blocked Aven with his hand and looked at him sidelong. "Perhaps you should open it up here."

"You don't know the passcode." Aven smirked. "Do you?"

"I don't need the passcode," Vincent stated, slipping his hands back into his dress pants. "I know all there is to know about the Ancient Ones."

"Then there's no need to open it up here," Aven quipped and attempted to walk out again.

"We don't keep secrets from one another, Aven."

"Is that so?" Aven snapped, spinning on the toes of his black biker boots. "The Genesis Project. Is there a reason you kept that dark little secret from your soon-to-be partner?"

"I've had that file on my computer for years," Vincent said.

"Hidden in code after code," Aven countered, "buried in dirt, just like the bodies you put six feet under."

"You know the trials are risky."

"I doubt the lab rats were informed of the side effects."

"I'll tell you whatever you need to know. All you have to do is ask."

"How about you tell me how long you knew my mother was alive?"

"Father thought it best to withhold such information. I was respecting his wishes."

"And the fact that you were in command of Genesis Project Six? Was keeping that from me in my best interest as well?"

Vincent narrowed his gaze. "Ask the question, dear cousin."

"Did you or did you not order Aaron Carpenter, my half brother, to murder his own unit?"

Vincent appeared unfazed by Aven's harsh tone. He walked to a cabinet and took out a bottle of brandy.

"Decades ago, the CIA funded InfiniCorp for The Genesis Project. They had been working on new experiments, having done away with the old ways of inhumane LSD and electroshock torture. My father, and yours, had been given the funding to continue with trials using their own ways. But by the end of Project Genesis Four, the government found promise in the soldiers' newfound abilities, spurred by the serum, and drew up a new contract. So our fathers signed, agreeing that they would test the newly initiated CIA agents' conformity. "

"Compliant super soldiers," Aven said. "The next big thing in military advancement. Worth millions more than the weapons traded on the black market to our enemies, I'm guessing."

"Precisely."

"Why were the trials continued after The World Peace Treaty?"

"You and I both know there is never an end to war. It continues, just as it will after these new talks of putting differences to the side."

"They thought they could just take in more soldiers? Mind Control them to do their will?"

"That was accomplished with Genesis Five. With Genesis Six, there was a new purpose for the trials."

"And that was?"

"Did you know that your mother was the very scientist who created the formula for Solace? With her help during Project Genesis Five, InfiniCorp legally owned the rights to the discovery of the century."

Greedy bastards.

It didn't surprise Aven how calm his cousin's countenance was over the subject, how his voice was so void of empathy.

Murderers have none.

The Creys. King of corpses. A lineage that built their throne with the bones of their victims and drank their coagulating blood like a fine wine.

A homicidal psychopath. That's what Vincent was in Aven's eyes right now: a cold-blooded killer without an ounce of remorse.

InfiniCorp had killed thousands of sons, daughters, mothers, and fathers. Aven had seen the numbers, had become sick scrolling through page after page of their names. Each cause of death had been labeled in InfiniCorp's favor. All suing court cases by remaining relatives had been quickly dismissed.

"Our empire was on the cusp of ruling the world," Vincent went on, "but there was one thing your father desired, one thing he couldn't let go."

"My mother," Aven answered flatly.

"You, Aven. He couldn't let go of you."

Because I'm a freak, or because he cared about me? I guess I'll never know.

Vincent took a sip of his brandy and walked to his desk. "After your father was killed, my father continued with Project Five until his untimely death. During World War E, I approached the government for a contract for Project Genesis Six. The field test with the Carpenter boys was the last of that project before we made Solace available to our buyers."

"So it was payback?" Aven asked. "Taking Adam Carpenter's life for my father's?"

Vincent smiled. "Unintentionally. Leave it to fate to make things right."

Aven took a step forward, holding back the urge to slap the glass out of Vincent's hand. "That wasn't fate. That massacre was planned. By you."

"They signed the form. They knew the circumstances. That is, if they read the fine print."

"You made them think they were on a secret mission to diffuse some old land mines but led them into the desert and executed them. Were you surprised when Will showed up at the gala? Or did you think his ghost had come back from the dead to haunt you?"

"Those who didn't follow commands were to be terminated." Vincent shrugged. "Simple protocol."

"I guess dumping the bodies in the Pacific didn't exactly get rid of the evidence of your failed experiment, now did it?"

"If there's one thing I'm good at, it's cleaning up a mess. Just like I cleaned up yours." Vincent came inches from Aven's face. "The only reason you weren't given the death penalty, dear cousin, is because I am very good at what I do. You accuse me of being a killer, but if you take a good look in the mirror, you would see the only reflection staring back is your own. If I had *wanted* Mr. Stryde dead, he would be."

Aven's eyes narrowed. "You knew Will was alive."

"I did."

"You've been keeping tabs on him this whole time. Why?"

"The project is still in effect. We need to study him."

"You didn't study enough of his little brother?" Aven asked, swallowing the bile rising in his throat. The footage had been too hard for him to stomach. His half brother, and Will's only known brother back then, had been carved apart like a Thanksgiving turkey only hours after his death.

Vincent lifted his chin. "Mr. Stryde is part of our control group."

"There are others? How many?"

"He is the last. The others, well, let's just say they weren't so good at keeping a low profile."

Vincent finished off his glass of brandy and went to pour another. Taking a sip, he took a step back and glanced up at the framed keys lining the wall. "The young lady, Ms. Grace. Did she come back with you?"

"It didn't work out between us."

"She's with Mr. Stryde, then?"

"Maybe. Why do you ask?"

"You know from the documents that the control group was also given the serum."

Aven shrugged. "Will's got some abilities. So what? If he's using them, it's only to run a smelly farm."

"He's unstable, dangerous. With his PTSD, there's no telling when the switch may flip."

Aven thought of how Will had always been so distant, how he kept to himself these past years. In the files, there had been detailed information on soldiers that had been in Project Four.

They had acted the same, hiding away until they had gone crazy. The masses would never know that the "mindless acts of violence" had actually been InfiniCorp's fail to control their agents. Mass shootings, assassinations, and serial killers, even the lesser murders in small towns had been the doing of the most powerful company in the world.

But knowing this, knowing that these soldiers had once been just good ol' boys, Aven didn't think Will was dangerous.

He could have kicked my ass in that bar parking lot, but he held back.

"He's not going to hurt anyone," Aven insisted. "Especially Claire."

"Bree has seen the future regarding Ms. Grace," Vincent began. "If you had come up to the party as I had requested the night you met her, her fate may have been prevented. But now the chain of events foreseen has been put in motion, and there's no stopping what's coming."

"What did she see?"

"Death and destruction. You would know of such things if you attended the séance sessions."

Aven rolled his eyes. "You can have your enlightened orgies. I don't need your whoring psychic to warn me of a possible future. Now that I have this," Aven held up the information chip, "I can get my answers."

"As you wish, cousin. But as you know, once you unlock Pandora's box, there's no closing it again."

"And as you know"—Aven nodded to the genuine Grecian artifact Vincent had bought at an auction—"it was a jar," he reminded and walked out of the room.

5

BREAKDOWN

FRIDAY, 11:44 A.M.
TYBEE ISLAND, GEORGIA

CLAIRE white-knuckled the steering wheel of her hunter-green jeep, holding back her tears. The visit to the worship center had been an emotional roller coaster. Everyone had gathered around her, said they were praying for her, that her family was at peace on the other side.

The congregation spoke of how the world was ending and how all people, all beliefs, and all races needed to come together, now more than ever. Claire was full of mixed emotions. Not only over the blending of contradicting beliefs but the government's close involvement. To Claire, it was all about control, a push to unify.

It wasn't only that. If it were true, if the world was ending, she had missed out on so much. She never had the chance to get married, to find someone who would love her despite her inability to have children. She was alone, and no matter how many angels the church members said surrounded her, Claire couldn't feel them. If the world was ending, she would face it alone.

Will's alone too. You left him like that. Left him without a proper goodbye. What if it's destiny after all? Maybe he needs me just as much as I need him.

The symbol of his hood flashed in Claire's mind again. She remembered her dream about the warrior. She strained to see his face, for it to be revealed. Past the amber glow, she could see the hero's handsome features clearly. It was Will, and she knew he was somehow connected to her visions and dreams.

She glanced at the passenger seat where the book she found was stashed away in a canvas bag. She thought about her grandmother and the stories she read from the book. They had been stories about the Creator, about a war between angels, about the princess who chose to go on a mission and help save those who had fallen for the lies of Seraph, and the warrior who had protected her.

Claire snatched up the book and flipped through the pages. A huff escaped her lips when she found what she expected.

Or maybe . . .

Squinting her eyes, Claire fixed her gaze on the mysterious text, believing that somehow it was possible this book held some kind of magic, answers from the Creator himself hidden in a secret code.

Like magic, the numbers shifted into a word.

Forgiveness.

Claire threw the book in the passenger seat and muffled a scream that erupted from her throat.

"Forgive who? You? Why do you let these horrible things happen?" she shouted.

When she was finished sobbing, she grabbed her phone from the dash and held her thumb above her therapist's number.

They'll put you on the drugs again. They'll stick you with needles. They confine you in a room. You'll be alone. All alone with no one to come to visit you.

I'm already alone.

You're not, a voice whispered.

Will's exact words came to her, the same ones as when she stood in his brother's room. She had told him she didn't want to be a burden. "*You're not*" had been his reply.

In our darkest moments, he will carry your burdens, she heard her father say.

It was a quote about the Creator, about faith, about trusting her maker. She knew that even when fear and doubt were bearing down on her, she had to be strong.

Daring to glance at the book once more, Claire sucked in a sharp breath when she saw a familiar face poking its head out from the edges. She stared at the picture of the woman who stood between two men in uniform.

GG.

She recognized the young dark-skinned man, Levi, to her grandmother's left. As a child, Claire had played with his granddaughter, Serena, while GG and Levi sat at the kitchen table reading a book with numbers and symbols.

They had told the young girls that one day, they too could read it.

Seeing the man on GG's right, Claire held her breath, finding that the stranger held an uncanny resemblance to Will.

"Is this some kind of sign? What do you want from me?" Claire pleaded through her windshield to the sky. "What am I supposed to do?"

Forgiveness, the voice whispered.

Will's mother came to Claire's mind. That was the very same word she had spoken to Claire before she passed. Claire had never understood what the word meant until now.

"This is crazy," she said to herself, heading in the direction her gut led her to go.

SERENA

FRIDAY, 12:30 P.M.
SAVANNAH, GEORGIA

TO Claire's surprise it wasn't Levi who answered the door, but a little boy with light brown skin and earthy-green eyes.

"Hello," Claire greeted with a small hand wave.

"I'm not supposed to talk to strangers," the little boy stated.

Claire smiled at the child who appeared to be a few years older than Abigail, maybe eight. "I'm not a stranger."

The boy raised a suspicious brow. "Prove it."

"Right." Claire cleared her throat. "Um. Is Leviticus Robinson here?"

"Leviticus Robert Robinson! What have I told you about going to the door?" a young woman about Claire's age scolded.

When she glanced up, she pressed a hand to her chest. "Claire?"

"Serena," Claire mumbled.

She cleared her throat, trying to regain her nerve. She hadn't thought Serena would live here, but it appeared she did. She glanced at the pink unicorns and fluffy clouds on Serena's purple scrubs. Claire remembered Serena always had a thing for purple. She had worn a purple tutu during dance class while Claire wore pink.

The purple reminded Claire of the lavender lacy shawl Serena had been wearing the last time she saw her. Serena had pulled it over her shoulders, shielding herself from the pouring rain under a black umbrella. Everyone had been under a black umbrella. It matched the color of mourning, the attire expected for a funeral.

Claire had been angry, grieving the loss of her father, not to mention edgy from the medication she'd been taking for her broken ankle. She spat harsh words at Serena as she left the cemetery. Her mother chided her, but Claire hadn't cared. Back then, Claire was certain Serena had been the one to blame for her father's death.

Years had gone by since that day. So much time had been spent in therapy where Claire had to speak about her resentment. Her resentment soon turned to guilt. Her harsh words couldn't be revoked.

"So you were telling the truth," the little boy said, still in a suspicious tone.

"About what?" Serena asked.

"She said she wasn't a stranger," the boy answered.

Might as well be.

"Claire's a friend," Serena said, appearing slightly uncomfortable. "We used to play together when we were little."

"I'm sorry," Claire said. "Are you heading to work?"

Serena glanced down at her scrubs. "No. Just got off my shift a few hours ago. I haven't had time to change. Do you want to come in?"

Claire nodded and walked into the house. It looked and smelled just as she remembered. The kitchen was to the right with the same white round table. Two chairs were pushed underneath it, one strapped down with a plastic red booster seat. Claire stared at the torn firefighter sticker on the side of it until Serena called for her son.

"Come in here and draw on your tablet while I talk to my friend . . . Levi?"

The little boy shot off into the living room to the left and jumped on the plaid couch. Claire recalled the time when she and Serena had been scolded for doing the same. But Serena didn't scold her son. When a squeal followed by laughter came from the faded cushions, Claire couldn't help but smile.

Serena roared like a dinosaur, twisting her face into silly exaggerated expressions that made Levi giggle.

An ache swelled in Claire's chest as she watched them play. She would never have a son to tickle, to play silly games with like that. Not after what the psych hospital did to her. She was thankful she hadn't called Dr. Seresh.

That would have been a mistake.

"Draw a picture, baby," Serena instructed. She straightened the cushions and walked into the kitchen to the coffee machine. "That boy wears me out."

"Leviticus. Is he named after your grandfather?" Claire asked as Serena pushed a button on the machine.

"He is. Coffee?"

"Yes, please," Claire pressed her lips together before she dared to ask. "And Robert?"

Serena slowed her hasty pace from reaching in the cabinet and lowered two mugs to the counter. "I named him after your dad for saving my life . . . and Levi's."

Claire looked at the little boy who was now playing with a fire truck in the living room floor. The toy wailed as he drew up the ladder and placed a fireman on top. "Ma'am! Don't panic! We're here to save you!" he shouted.

"Levi!" Serena called. "Sirens off, son."

Claire cringed. She always did when she heard that sound.

Levi turned off his toy and hopped up when he met Claire's watchful stare. He went over to a desk and pointed at a picture frame. "Paw Paw's in Haywi, but Maw Maw couldn't go. She died."

Claire got up to see which of the many photos he was pointing to.

"I'm sorry to hear that," Claire said softly.

The boy smiled. "She's an angel now. Paw Paw will be an angel soon too."

Claire gave another sympathetic look until a face caught her eye. Bending over, she found a photo of Mr. Robinson and his wife in their early sixties, smiling as they danced at what looked like a wedding anniversary.

She looked at all the other framed pictures, finding one with her grandmother and him together. Again, the same man that looked like Will was in the photo with them. In this picture, they weren't by the ocean. They were in a desert. Her grandmother stood sandwiched between the two men in a nurse uniform, the men in matching military attire. This time their smiles were not so bright. Something appeared to hinder their happiness.

"Ha-why-ee," Serena pronounced. "Why don't you draw something for Claire? She'd like that," she instructed her son as she handed Claire a cup of coffee.

"Your grandfather is in Hawaii?" Claire asked, watching the little boy scribble on his tablet.

"Maw Maw died a few days ago," Serena said, picking up the frame. "Paw Paw had planned to take her to Oahu to surprise her for their fiftieth wedding anniversary, but she passed suddenly in her sleep. So he had her cremated, paid the guy in charge of the crematorium to give him her ashes, and told me to watch the house so he could fulfill his promise to take her to The Royal Hawaiian Hotel. Maw Maw sure did love the ocean. He's gonna do one of those sunset lantern ceremonies they have there every year."

"That's really sweet," Claire said, giving a genuine smile.

Serena put a hand on Claire's arm. "I'm sorry to hear about your mama."

"How did you know?"

"Saw her face on the news. How are you doing?"

"To be honest, I feel like I'm losing my mind," Claire admitted, dragging a clammy hand down her face. She pointed to the photo with her grandmother. "This picture. Do you know the man next to GG?"

"Never met him. Looks like he served with Paw Paw."

"Do you know where Levi was stationed when this was taken?"

"We could always see if that's on the back. People did that back in the day with these paper pictures, didn't they?"

Claire forced a smile as Serena picked up the frame, took out the picture, and flipped it over.

"It's in some kind of script. I can't read it."

"Cursive?" Claire took the picture and squinted, trying to make out the handwriting. "They were all around twenty years old. The place this picture was taken in was . . ."

"Nada?" Serena asked, pointing.

"Nevada," Claire whispered before she realized her hand was shaking.

"Claire?" Serena asked, leaning down to make eye contact. "Are you okay?"

As if time had slowed, Claire watched a droplet of her coffee slide down her hand and onto the carpet, but then time sped up and she gripped the mug tight with fluttering lashes. She opened her mouth to apologize, but Serena had already rushed off to grab a towel before she could speak.

"Don't worry about it," Serena said. "I've got it."

"I'm sorry," Claire mumbled as she sat at the kitchen table and wiped her hand on her jeans.

"It's okay." Serena laughed. "Nothing a little spot cleaner won't fix. Coffee is nothing. Try cleaning up grape juice." She tossed the towels into the sink and unbuckled the booster so she could sit.

Claire stared at the crumbs Serena had swept onto the floor from the chair. She wasn't sure how she would apologize, how she would begin such a conversation.

"At Dad's funeral," Claire managed. "I'm sorry for what I said. And then at school. I was avoiding you. I thought I was avoiding my grief . . ."

"If I could go back in time, I would. It was my fault. He got me out. He saved me," Serena said, her face showing her remorse.

"No," Claire held back her tears. "He went back in for me."

"I never saw you at the party."

"I was upstairs," Claire admitted. "That's why I was on the roof."

"So the rumors Tyler spread about you two—"

Claire shrugged. "There's truth in rumors."

Serena leaned in and lowered her voice. She glanced to her son in the living room. "The guy was a prick. Everyone knew that."

Claire let out a soft laugh. "Yeah. That's what Laura says."

"You still hang out with Laura Weatherford?"

"Can't get rid of her."

Serena laughed. "I heard she went into the boy's bathroom and punched Tyler in the nuts after he said all those things."

"She did?"

Serena shrugged. "That was the rumor."

It felt good to laugh, but it didn't last. Guilt crept up Claire's spine when she thought of whose fault it was that her dad died. It wasn't Serena's. It never had been.

"If I hadn't been at that party—if I hadn't gone upstairs . . . I made a mistake, and it cost me."

"I know what you mean." Serena pointed her chin toward the living room. "That's why I'm a single mom working double shifts at the hospital. But our mistakes can become miracles. At least that's what Paw Paw always says. That the Creator can turn everything around with just a prayer."

Claire thought about her mistakes, and then, without any warning, Aven's face came to her mind. She had given back the bracelet he gifted her to remind him of his choice, to remind him he had made the wrong one.

Maybe he didn't. Maybe this was how it was supposed to be.

"Can you forgive me, even after all these years, for what I said to you that day?" Claire asked.

Serena smiled and took Claire's hand. "As Paw Paw says, 'Forgive trespasses, as the Creator forgives ours.'"

"I'm done!" Levi shouted. He ran into the kitchen with his tablet and held it up to Serena's face.

"Oh, good job, baby. Do you want to tell us about what you drew?"

Levi laid the tablet on the table and pointed to the pink doodle. "That's her," he said, glancing at Claire. He then pointed to another doodle figure in orange, and then another one in yellow. "That's Paw Paw with the knight who tries to save him, but Paw Paw dies."

Claire and Serena looked at one another with brows raised, but Serena quickly leaned down and tickled her son. "Did you unlock the password on the TV controls again? I've told you the History channel is not for kids."

Levi giggled and ran off into the living room.

"Sorry. I'm not sure he understands death. Maw Maw was the first person he ever lost."

"It's okay," Claire said, studying the drawing that looked eerily similar to her dream.

"Kids." Serena shook her head.

"Speaking of kids," Claire said. "I know this sounds strange with books being illegal and everything, but do you still have that book your grandfather read with my grandmother when we were little?"

"What book?"

"The one with numbers and weird symbols."

"Oh," Serena said, drawing out the word. "I remember that. No. Can't say I do. The police came over and checked the house for contraband last month. They didn't find anything. Paw Paw must have gotten rid of it ages ago."

Claire stared hard at the coffee in her mug. Every year, every house, especially those closest to the city, were searched by FBI agents making sure no one held any illegal goods. You could buy it off the black market if you wanted to risk getting arrested. That's why they shut down all the e-commerce shops online. If you didn't have a permit, you couldn't sell.

Do I have his book then? Or did GG have one too? Did the agents never think to look up in the attic?

"Do you want something to eat?" Serena asked. "I was just about to fix lunch."

"Oh, um, no thanks," Claire said. "I've got to be going. They're holding a vigil at the worship center tonight. I'm supposed to say a few words. I should go home and write something for it."

Claire stood and went to the door. Serena followed, as did her son, who hopped up with his action figures in hand.

"Do you mind if I come and pay my respects tonight?" Serena asked sheepishly.

"No, not at all," Claire assured her. "It would be nice to have a friend there."

The soft, yet firm hug Serena gave surprised Claire, but she embraced Serena back.

"I'll see you tonight," Claire said and glanced down at Levi with a smile. "I'll see you again soon."

"Here," Levi said, offering his figurine. "He's my favorite."

Claire took the plastic knight from Levi and stared at it.

"You looked scared when I showed you the picture," the boy said.

"Oh, no, I wasn't," Claire lied.

"Were too," the boy argued.

"Levi," Serena chided.

The boy looked at his action figure. "The knight can't save Paw Paw." He looked up at Claire. "But he can save you."

FLUFF BALL

SATURDAY, 2:00 A.M.
LAS VEGAS, NEVADA

KITTEN cursed under her breath as she tripped over the clothes on her floor. She had thrown them from her closet and drawers, then piled them up, thinking of toting them to the dumpster to burn them. They had all been bought with Aven's money.

Pretty gifts for shitty apologies.

It was hard giving him the silent treatment again, but it had to be done. She needed her space, needed time to think about if she was going to move on. The confession at Caesar's Palace hadn't been the breaking point for her. It had been the Mind Walk where she had seen Claire and him together.

Another bang came from the door as she flipped on the lights and wrapped her silky robe across her chest. She rose on her tiptoes to peek through the two-way mirror on the door, but the moment she heard Aven's voice calling her name from the other side, she gnashed her teeth in fuming anger.

This better be good.

"What the fu–" She cut herself short, finding a fluff ball in the crook of Aven's arm.

"Why haven't you been showing up for work?" he slurred. The moment she met his bloodshot eyes, she could tell he was utterly intoxicated.

"I quit," she reminded him.

"You can't quit!" Aven's voice echoed in the hall as he stumbled back.

Kitten took hold of his shirt and steadied him. "Hush! You're going to wake up my neighbors!"

"As if I give a shit!"

"Are you trying to get me kicked out of my apartment?"

"Hold this."

Kitten took the tiny kitten that meowed, wondering what the poor thing had been through on the way to her apartment.

"What are you doing?" she asked as he held his phone to his ear.

"Buying your apartment building so I can YELL ALL I WANT!"

Kitten held the little kitty close as it startled at Aven's voice.

"What the hell is your problem?" she asked, jerking him inside.

"You. Why didn't you tell me you're going to Italy?"

"Because what I do with Nicoli is none of your business."

"None of my busi—how's it not my—" Aven hiccupped and braced himself against a potted plant as he stumbled into the apartment. It slid off its pedestal, dumping dirt as it thudded on the carpet.

He squinted an eye at the mess, wobbling back and forth. "Fuck."

"You're paying for that."

"I want to go. I love Italy. Wait—" Aven stumbled back against the wall. "Nick?" he said like the name was a bitter taste in his mouth.

Kitten smiled. "Yep."

"I should fire you!" Aven bellowed, swinging his finger.

The kitty meowed again, clawing to get out of Kitten's grasp.

"Lower your voice. You're scaring this baby to death!" she scolded Aven. "You want some milk?" she asked the kitty and kissed the top of its soft furry head. "Jade, you have company," she announced and headed to the kitchen.

A pure white cat with bright green eyes pranced into the living room at Kitten's call. It stopped in its tracks and hissed at Aven before turning the corner. Finding a new feline in her path, Jade cautiously sniffed the newcomer.

"We're going," Kitten informed Aven as he leaned against the doorframe. "He said he has some work to do for Vincent first. A few more days and we'll be in Venice."

Taking the creamer from the fridge, Kitten poured it into two small dishes. She sat them far apart, unsure of how Jade would react to the newcomer during treat time.

"I'm not paying you to elope with that Casanova, pose"—he hiccupped—"poser."

"I'm not. I'm going on a vacation. I have paid leave, don't I?"

"The contact"—he hiccupped again—"the contract spess-spec-i-fies," Aven reworded with emphasis, "that vacation leave is only paid as long as it isn't taken with some *asshole* who wants to use you for his ego."

"Asshole." Kitten laughed. "You're one to talk. And what's up with all the swearing?" she asked, watching the kitty lap up the cream. Like a mother hen, she stooped down, petting Jade the moment she finished. She barricaded the two for a few seconds until they both got a good sniff.

When Jade licked the kitten's milk-covered chin and then its ears, Katharine smiled.

"I knew you'd like that little ball of fluff," Aven noted as Kitten straightened. He swiped a bottle of water from the fridge and chugged it down, and then another. He didn't bother to pick up the empty bottles as they tumbled from the counter and bounced on the floor.

The cats flinched and then pawed them, making a game as they rolled away.

"She has beautiful blue eyes," Kitten admitted.

Aven's stutter and slur seemed to have been somewhat cured by his water intake, and he spoke clearly. "Just like yours."

Kitten's heart skipped a beat, but she didn't meet Aven's gaze, no matter the heat burning into her. "What's her name?" she asked.

"Kitten." Aven wiggled his brows.

Katharine crossed her arms and gave Aven a look. "Kitten?"

Aven shrugged his shoulders "I thought it only appropriate. I didn't want my encounters to think I was crazy for calling out 'Kitten' randomly every morning."

"And why would you do that?"

"Well, it's not like I'll have a *kitten* around once you elope with that buffoon."

Kitten laughed. "Buffoon? Wow. How much have you had to drink?"

Aven counted on his fingers with one eye shut and dropped his hand after the count of three. "He *is* a buffoon. Not even that good looking. And his charm is a complete ruse."

"And yours isn't?"

Aven's brows rose as he placed a hand on his chest. "Am I *not*," he slightly slurred, "naturally charming and devilishly handsome?"

"You're an ass," Kitten told him. "Coming here piss drunk."

He reached into the fridge for another bottle of water and drank it down. After letting out a throaty sigh, he nodded to the cats as they played. "Jade likes her."

Kitten knew Aven was trying to change the subject, that he didn't want to admit he had been drinking an absurd amount of liquor.

"That's because Jade likes everyone except you," she quipped.

"You know that's not true," Aven said. "Jade liked me just fine before Nehia showed up."

"What do you want, Aven?"

Aven bit his lip as if he was thinking over how to say what was on his mind, then looked her in the eyes with that serious stare. "To show you something. Something I can't show anyone else."

"I think you showed me enough at the pool."

"This one is a special secret."

"Oh, I feel so privileged. Another secret to keep for Aven Crey," Kitten said, voice thick with sarcasm.

"I thought you liked keeping my secrets."

"I don't."

A clever grin pulled at Aven's lips. "You'll like keeping this one."

"Then tell me. You have"–Kitten glanced at her phone sitting on the kitchen counter, noting the late hour–"thirty minutes."

"It's not something I have to tell you. It's something I have to show you. I doubted that after the last Mind Walk you would let me try again, so I've figured out another way."

"Is that so?"

"Mm-hmm. I know from experience what it takes to jog one's memory." Aven opened the French doors to the balcony and walked outside. He stood on a chair and put his hands on his hips, looking down at Vegas below.

"Well?"

When Aven placed a foot on a chair and his other on the table, Kitten's heart leaped into her throat.

"Aven—"

"It's the only way."

"What are you doing?"

"I told you."

The moment Aven stretched his foot to the balcony railing, Kitten rushed toward him and jerked back his black leather belt in a panic.

Something flashed with a wave of familiarity.

In her vision the sky was dark and filled with smoke. Fireballs rained down from the heavens. She could hear waves slapping the rocks below. And Aven, he was about to fall off the balcony, but it wasn't her balcony—somehow she knew it belonged to him.

The vision fled as Aven crashed into her. They rolled through the French doors into her living room with Aven landing on top of her.

"What the hell is wrong with you?" Kitten groaned, shoving him off. "Are you trying to scare me half to death?"

"So you do care about me." Aven winced, favoring his head.

"Of course I do, you idiot." She punched him in the chest. Hard. "But you didn't have to prove it by doing something so stupid."

"If you care what happens to me, then why did you ignore all my voicemails? You know I can't take care of myself without you."

Kitten gave a heavy sigh, folding her legs beneath her. "Because I'm mad at you."

"Because I kissed you?"

"Because you kept going on and on about Claire. 'I broke her heart, Kitten. She'll never forgive me, Kitten. Boo-hoo, I'm a terrible person,'" Kitten mocked.

"I didn't know who else to talk to. You're my best friend, Kat."

Kat. He hadn't called her that since they were kids.

Kitten let out a frustrated growl and jumped up. She paced her living room and shook her head. "I can't do this anymore. I need you to give me some space."

Aven snorted, coming to his feet. "I give you space."

"Not enough that I can date. I'm always so busy taking care of you that I never get to do that anymore."

"Fine." He shrugged. "Date."

A bit of hope and relief came at Aven's words, but they quickly dissolved when he added, "Anyone but Nick."

"I'm not your girlfriend. So stop acting like you own me."

"You're right." Aven's brows knit together as he closed the space between them. He cupped her face gently, fixing his stare. "You've always been so much more."

Kitten's knees grew weak at the soft caress of his thumb at her cheek.

"I don't own you, I don't want to," he said in a husky breath, "but your heart, that's something that will always be mine."

Maybe it was the drunk talking, the soft spot Aven sparingly let out, but it was his truth. Aven was always so vulnerable when he had too much to drink. No matter how much Kitten didn't want to admit it, she liked seeing this side of him. Not the childish boy she wanted to punch in the face, but the part of him that admitted his feelings. But she couldn't let him see how much his sentimental gaze or touch affected her and slipped away from Aven's grasp.

"Friends take care of one another," Kitten stated, "and that's what I am. Your friend. *Only* your friend."

"Is this your way of telling me you don't want to be more than friends?"

More than anything. But if you broke up with me, I wouldn't survive.

"Fine." Aven crossed his arms and shrugged. "Don't admit you're in love with me. We'll be 'friends,'" he air quoted. "But friends don't walk out on one another, and they don't ignore phone calls."

Guilt crept into Kitten's chest, prickling her shriveling heart like a thorny cactus. Maybe the silent treatment had been a bit much. Maybe she held a grudge over the fact that Aven had fallen head over heels for Claire. But she couldn't help it. Kitten had loved him since they were kids, and it only took one night for him to be completely enamored by some girl that wasn't even his type. Not that he had a type.

Katharine picked up the meowing kitten and scratched under its chin for a distraction.

"I'll take care of"–she petted the patches of orange fluff, thinking of an appropriate name–"Dinah for you. Go to a bar, bang an encounter, and sleep off the buzz," she said, walking him to the door.

"And when can I come to get my kitten?" Aven asked in his witty tone as he crossed the threshold.

Katharine didn't know if he was talking about her or the cat, but answered, "When I say you can," and shut the door in his face.

8

THE GENESIS PROJECT

AVEN balled his fists as he crossed the threshold of Vincent's front door, not bothering to thank the butler. Anger fueled every step he took as he climbed the stairs and stomped down the hall. Everything he had read on the chip was swimming in his head. The files were all about his family's history and the crimes they had committed over the centuries. All the questions he had planned to ask his mother were answered, just as she said they would be.

His uncle's digital journal had hundreds of pages of juicy information. There was enough dirt to blackmail every world leader that had ever been in power. The evidence of InfiniCorp's faulty experiments was also documented. What struck Aven odd was that most of the information on the chip was a fable about a war between the Creator and one of his Seraphim. Along with that tale was the Crey's family genealogy, listing "gifts" that had been given to his ancestors from the joining of Seraphim who had left their habitation in the heavens and seduced women. The children birthed were hybrids, and Aven's name was included in this genetic family tree of half-human, half-god like creation.

"Vincent," Aven shouted, banging on his door.

Vincent opened it and gave Aven a once over. "You're not dressed for brunch."

"That's because I'm not going."

"The sultan of Brunei is expecting us, and you know how I feel about being punctual," Vincent said, retrieving his suit jacket from his closet. He walked out of his room, and Aven followed him down the black marble staircase and into the study.

"How long have you known what I am?" Aven demanded.

Vincent glanced up. The dancing flames of the fireplace reflected in his eyes, making it appear as if the flames were coming from inside him. "And what are you, dear cousin?" he asked, going to the liquor cabinet.

"Half human, half devil."

"You know, as well as I do, there's a difference between devils and what we are. However, you've entertained a few, have you not?"

"How long have you known our ancestors are fallen angels?" Aven demanded.

Vincent poured a glass of blood-red wine and took a sip. "The Ancient Ones did not fall—they were demoted and are sorely misunderstood. The stories passed down from the Truth Keepers are merely fairy tales. Our story is the real truth."

"Sounds to me more like Aalok was the one in the wrong."

"Do you not live as you please? Walk a life without consequence? That is all our descendants ever wanted; that was all that our makers required of us."

"Our makers." Aven licked his lips, scowling. "So it's true, then? The Circle is still doing human sacrifices because our *makers* require it in exchange for knowledge?"

"It's true." Vincent took another sip of his wine, and Aven watched him, disturbed with how calm his cousin appeared.

"Not just any sacrifice," Aven added. "The blood of children."

There had always been rumors of the rituals, but Aven had shrugged it off years ago, assuming it was a way of the past, that conspiracy theorists had dreamed it up to put the Circle in a bad light. Now he knew otherwise. According to the file, a ritual was performed only a few days before his uncle had died, and what happened during that ritual made Aven drink two bottles of bourbon in less than two minutes before he had the stomach to read on.

Glancing at the wall paintings and catching a hint of iron in the air, Aven wondered if it was in fact wine that Vincent was drinking.

"What else did you learn about our ancestors?" Vincent asked.

"When the red planet is again to the west of the sun, humanity will face utter destruction."

"Not all of humanity. Just the weak."

Aven glared. "Sounds rather insensitive."

"Survival of the fittest. Those who do not evolve, perish."

"People. Will. Die," Aven bit out.

"Everyone dies," Vincent said all too calmly.

"How long has the Circle known about this planet?"

"For over two thousand years."

"Then why hasn't the world government prepared for it?"

"Because there's nothing we can do to stop it."

"So they're just going to let people go about their lives, unaware their days are numbered?"

Vincent slid a hand into his pocket and narrowed his eyes. "Can you imagine the mass chaos if this information got out to the public? The anarchy? It's human nature to act like dogs to survive. What you see on the television is only the beginning. If people knew, they would have no reason to care. There are already packs of them in the cities wreaking havoc. With news of doom and gloom, they'll be tearing one another to pieces without a second thought. The High Council unanimously agreed not to cause alarm."

Aven averted his gaze to the flames dancing in the fireplace. "All to keep the peace."

"Do you recall my meeting with the pope a few weeks ago? He gave a message at the Summit that was broadcast all over the world."

"Yeah, sounded like he had lost his mind, talking about interdimensional beings coming to save us."

"For centuries our makers have warned of war, of disease, and each time it was the Oracle who delivered this message. We have always announced the future through those with respectable titles—kings, popes, presidents, yet our message is dismissed by ignorance. It is of their own stupidity that they will be wiped out. Only those who truly listen to the gods shall be saved."

Aven scoffed. "How merciful of the gods to save their own kind."

"It is indeed mercy, for if humans knew the truth, they could not stomach it. It's better this way." Vincent walked to a glass case and placed his thumb to the scanner. Taking out the book, he gazed at it with sentiment, tracing his fingers over the gold emblem. "A few months from now, the shift will occur, and a new era will rise."

"You got this information from Bree?" Aven asked.

"She is the Oracle, Aven. You would do well to listen to her."

"And you believe her about this prophecy?" Aven asked.

"Yes, just as you choose not to."

"How do you know these entities, these so-called gods speak through her? For all we know the demons could be playing games."

Vincent looked at Aven. "Has our Oracle ever been wrong before?"

Aven swallowed. No. Bree's predictions had never been wrong. She was the one who gave the warning of WWE. She had prophesied the recent earthquake. It was Aven who had dismissed her gift, but now he knew he could not deny that she had some dark and divine connection to the other side.

"The world doesn't have to end," Vincent said, handing the book to Aven. "Aalok wants to save us, all of us. Even those who are willing to convert."

Aven looked at the gold emblem, and as if he were imagining it, the numeric script below it shifted, forming what he thought were words.

"Can you read it?" Vincent asked, leaning down to get Aven to look at him.

Aven blinked and handed the book over. "You know I can't."

"Hm. Father thought perhaps one day you could."

"And why is that?"

Vincent replaced the book in the glass. "Because you're a half breed."

"That's right. A mutt. Isn't that what our grandfather called me? Why he tried to have me killed."

"Half one of us, and half one of them."

Aven tilted his head. "Them who?"

"Your mother was a descendant of the very bloodline of Aramis himself. He breathed life into his chosen, molded them with his own hands, and made them into flesh."

"And you know this how?"

"Your father tested her blood. There is a specific gene in their DNA. It is unlike any other, similar to ours. It was in the files, but perhaps you stopped reading once you found out what you were?"

Aven had. He had jumped right out of his chair, hopped into his red Corvette, and sped to Vincent's mansion to confront him. He had been full of rage reading about the sacrifices, the demented practices of the secret brotherhood, but what had enraged him the most was the footage of two brothers in a desert being shot.

"That's why he kept your mother around," Vincent continued. "A Truth Keeper can decipher these pages."

"Did she?"

"No. She refused. Even with your father's gift of Persuasion. That part of her mind was locked, so to speak."

"And he wanted her to read the book because? . . ."

Vincent fixed his gaze on Aven. "A Truth Keeper and only a Truth Keeper can tell us when the Creator will destroy the world."

"And you think that timeline is in a book?"

A pleasant smile formed on Vincent's lips. "I've been awaiting the day we would have this conversation. Now that you know, you can be initiated into the Inner Circle. They will be most pleased to see what gifts the gods have bestowed upon you."

Alarm shot through Aven, but he didn't let it show. "What gifts?"

Vincent crossed his arms and tilted his head with a devious grin. "Come on now. Don't be shy."

Aven shrugged. "I don't know what you're talking about."

"That's right," Vincent said as he went to his desk and pulled a letter opener from the drawer. "You love to play games, just like when we were boys."

Before Aven could blink, Vincent flicked the letter opener with absolute precision.

The world slowed as Aven held up his hand, and the letter opener stopped a fourth of an inch from his palm.

Vincent chuckled, clearly pleased. He crossed his arms and leaned against his desk. "Grandfather was wrong about you, after all. If only he had seen your potential. Persuasion can be taught, but true power is given by Aalok himself."

Aven pushed the air with something deep inside of him, aiming the hovering letter opener to drive like a nail into the wall, but Vincent caught it without looking.

"If I have these gifts, why did my grandfather want me dead?" Aven asked.

"The Inner Circle has always kept our bloodline pure. Any breeding outside of our people is forbidden, unless by a bonding of marriage, and unless there are no children born from the bonding. Your father was the first to break the code of our Brotherhood, and no matter how many other children he seeded to women of the Inner Circle, the Council was unsatisfied. It was agreed that you should be terminated. But my father, being obsessed with your mother, just as your father had been, begged the Council to let you live—as long as they acquired something valuable in return."

"The formula."

"At first the Council had hoped your mother would agree to read the book, but when she offered something much more valuable, the Council was satisfied."

"Solace," Aven said, knowing it had the power to cure all diseases, prevent them even.

"Not only a cure," Vincent said, "but a serum that can control a Truth Keeper."

"Did my father use it on my mother?"

"He did, but even with the Mind Walking and his gift of Persuasion, she wouldn't read. Such a mystery." Vincent sighed and stared off into nothing while spinning the letter opener in the air over his palm. "He could control any soul he came into contact with, and yet your mother was immune to his gift."

"Has a Truth Keeper ever been Persuaded before?"

"No. On the contrary, it's been the other way around."

"How so?"

"Ah, that's right. You didn't read on. If you had, you would have seen the last journal entry. The part where Jimmy admitted to talking to your mother about the Creator. He was ready to get on his knees and beg for forgiveness. Seems Truth Keepers are quite persuasive themselves."

Aven took a few steps forward, ready to hear more. "Was my father in danger of being convinced to side with her?"

"Your father didn't keep a journal. His secrets were his own."

"Did he know where my mother was when she left and went into hiding?"

"No one did. At least not until the night your brother came to find you."

The breath in Aven's lungs left him all at once. "Will's a descendent."

"A pureblood. From a long line of Truth Keepers."

"That would mean his brother was as well. How were you able to control him if my father couldn't control my mother?"

"All the soldiers' strengths were enhanced, except Aaron Carpenter's."

"Solace didn't work on him?"

"It did. Quite well, actually. Now I know the key characteristic I'm looking for."

"And that is?"

A clever grin slipped across Vincent's lips. "Complacency."

Aven narrowed his gaze. "You're going to use Solace on another Truth Keeper."

"I've been altering the formula. I may have found a way to get any Truth Keeper to do what I ask, regardless of their innate abilities. All I need is another field test."

Aven laughed. "Well, you're out of luck. Will's *not* compliant."

"If I remember correctly, there were two Truth Keepers you brought to the gala, were there not?"

It all made perfect sense now. This was why Aven had seen Claire's halo. She was a pureblood, a descendant of Aramis.

Aven licked his dry lips. "How did you know she was one of them?"

"I've been gathering the glasses from every event and testing the DNA," Vincent said.

"Maybe it was someone else's glass."

"I retrieved her glass myself. I knew she was different the moment she walked through the door."

Aven swallowed to soothe his itchy throat. Whatever his cousin had planned, he hoped it didn't involve the sick rituals he had seen on his uncle's files.

"Claire and I aren't exactly on talking terms right now," Aven admitted.

Vincent slipped a skeleton key from his pocket and stared at it with longing. "I'm sure you can Persuade her to give you two another chance. When you have reconciled, bring her to me."

"And if I don't?"

"Then, dear cousin," Vincent said, tossing Aven the key, "the blood of humanity is on your hands."

9

HACKER

SATURDAY, 11:35 A.M.
JOHNS ISLAND, SOUTH CAROLINA

"JULIAN, guess who it is?"

Will watched the baby on a changing table razz his lips.

"Hi, Uncle Willy." Jeremiah said, waving Julian's tiny hand wrapped around his finger.

"How's everything going?" Will asked.

"Little dude is crapping up a storm. Forget the six-pack of beers next time you come. I need diapers."

Will glanced at Julian as he cooed. "Should you be cussing around him?"

"Dude, he's a bebé."

"Right."

"The cabin ready yet?"

The cabin, also known as, 'the safe house', was an off the grid bunker in Montana, hidden beneath a rundown shack. After the quake, Will and Jeremiah had watched the news in the waiting room at the hospital while Julie visited with her family. Will and Jeremiah both agreed they should get the bunker ready, just in case shit hit the fan. And by the way the United States and Russia talked about war, it could very well hit—and hard.

Since Jeremiah and Julie had just come home from the hospital and were delirious from lack of sleep, Will had offered to get the cabin ready alone.

"Yeah, just gotta stock up on rations and replace some solar panels. After that we can move on in," Will said. "But hey man, no rush."

"Have you seen the news?" Jeremiah asked. "Shit is bad and no one even knows it."

Will tried to ignore how much Jeremiah swore around his son and reminded himself why he had called.

"Hey, when you get Julian situated, I need you to look someone up."

"Another asshole?"

"No." Will sighed. "Not another asshole."

"Still can't believe your bro ditched your mom's funeral. The dick could have at least given you some money to pay for the headstone. That girl ever call? Explain why she left?"

"No, but she left a note saying she was sorry for leaving."

"You should call her."

"I don't think now is a good time to ask her out. She's probably worried about her family. Her mom was visiting New York during the earthquake."

"Well, they're still finding bodies. Can you imagine the smell?" Jeremiah made a face. "Probably a lot like the mierda este niño dropped off."

"Jeremiah."

"Who do you need me to look up?"

"Evelyn Grace and Leviticus Robinson. I found a picture of them in an old book my mom gave me before she passed."

"A book." Jeremiah shook his head. "You're treading on dangerous ground, man. You should burn it."

"I can't," Will admitted, but he wasn't about to tell Jeremiah the reason why.

"Why not?"

"Because it's special and no one can open it without a key."

"A key? What kind of key?"

"A skeleton key." Will took his key ring from his pocket. "I've never seen one like it before and—"

Claire's necklace flashed in his mind.

How is this possible?

Will watched Jeremiah place Julian in the swing and then fall into his rolling chair at his desk. A screen share appeared on Will's tablet, accompanied by the sound of the rapid clicks of a keyboard.

"Grace, you said?"

"Yeah."

Photos and information filled the shared screen, and Will leaned in to look at it.

"Evelyn Eleanor Grace was a nurse during World War III. She married Peter Grace and had one son, Robert Grace, who was married to an Amanda Clark . . . grandchildren, two . . . Ryan and Claire."

When Claire's senior photo scrolled across the screen, Will's eyes went wide.

"And Robinson?" he asked Jeremiah.

Claire's picture was replaced by a military photo of a man with dark skin and deep brown eyes.

"Vet, served two tours, lives in Georgia."

The screen scrolled down to show a more recent photo of Mr. Robinson, now in his late seventies.

"Address?"

"122 Winchester Dr., Savannah."

Will ran his fingers through his hair.

Claire lives in Tybee. He lives in Savannah. Should I ask Jeremiah to look her up too? Should I stop by and check on her?

"Robinson doesn't have anything to do with this InfiniCorp stuff, does he?" Jeremiah asked with narrow eyes, rocking back and forth in his seat.

Will looked at the screen, seeing the InfiniCorp logo on Mr. Robinson's brown leather gloves.

"No," he answered truthfully. "I've just gotta ask him some questions about my grandfather."

"That important?" Jeremiah asked.

"Yeah, that important."

Jeremiah typed again, paused, and then said, "Well, he's not home. His wife just passed away, and he was last seen at Daniel K. Inouye International yesterday at twelve hundred hours, boarding Hawaiian airlines."

"Hawaii?"

"Affirmative."

Will was silent for a moment, staring at the double screens. Just the idea of flying to Hawaii to find this guy and ask him questions about a book sounded crazy.

"Do you know what hotel?"

"Do I need to give you a mental test before we shack up at the cabin?" Jeremiah teased.

Yes. Because I've lost it. I'm reading numbers that somehow make words.

"I'm fine," Will lied. "It's just something I feel like I need to do."

"The Royal Hawaiian, room 233," Jeremiah said.

"Can you book me a room?"

Jeremiah groaned, throwing his head back. "Fine. But you gotta bring me like five packs of diapers and wipes when you get back."

"Deal."

A DEMONS

WRATH

SUNDAY, 5:32 A.M.
LAS VEGAS, NEVADA

THE tires of Katharine's pink Porsche screeched to a halt as she whipped into Aven's driveway. She had been in a deep sleep an hour ago until an urgent text had woken her.

She busted through Aven's front door and flew up the steps to his room. "Aven!"

No answer, save the squeak of her sneakers as she skidded to a stop after flinging his bedroom door open.

She covered her mouth as her jaw dropped open.

Blood. It was everywhere: on the sheets, the nightstand, Aven's phone, and on the floor. Drops of it trailed to the bathroom, and Kitten followed it, finding a naked body beneath a scarlet-tinged pool.

Kitten kicked a bloody knife across the onyx tile as prickling panic itched her skin. She screamed Aven's name over and over again and struggled to lift his lifeless body.

"Wake up!" she demanded and drained the tub, surveying the cuts on his chest, then the ones on his wrists.

Whoring bitch.

Blood streamed down Aven's wounds, off his palms, and down to his wrinkled fingertips.

"AVEN!"

No response.

"Wake up, you stupid boy!" Kitten shouted as she slapped his pale, cold face.

Aven's eyes flung open, and he sucked in a sharp breath. He gripped the tub and snapped his neck left and right.

"Hey, it's okay," Kitten said softly. "It's me."

Aven ignored her. His wide eyes darted, looking for the demon who had possessed him. She had stripped him naked, drawn a watery grave, and had slashed his body to drown him in his own blood. This was her way of showing her power over him. This was her way to get him to be subservient again.

The hour of dawn sounded in the bedroom with a shrill call.

Glancing at her designer watch, Kitten assumed Aven's clock had been turned back a few minutes, most likely by Nehia.

Aven's lashes fluttered. "Katharine?"

"You're okay. It's over. I'm here."

Aven glanced at the lacerations on his wrists. "Shit."

"Can you get up?"

Aven's jaw tightened as he nodded.

Kitten had seen him naked many times before, had studied the tight abs and muscles leading to his glory every chance she got, but this time, she didn't. She only wrapped a towel gently around his waist and led him to his bed.

"Where's the first aid kit?" she asked, grabbing another towel from his bathroom.

"Downstairs."

She looked at the cuts again. "You're going to need stitches."

"I won't," Aven argued as they descended the steps.

Kitten sat him down at the bar in his kitchen and rushed off in search of the first aid kit.

"She's mad at me," he said.

"You think?" Kitten scoffed, slamming a cabinet after retrieving the kit. "What did you do to piss her off this time?"

"I tried to control her."

Kitten rolled her eyes and flung open the kit. "You're such an idiot."

"You won't need the gauze."

"You're right. I need to call a doctor, dummy."

"Kitten." Aven glanced at his arms, and Kitten followed his gaze as he lifted the towel from his arm and wiped the blood away.

The wounds had healed as if they had never been there at all.

"What the hell?"

Aven smirked. "What the hell indeed."

"Are you playing mind games again?" Kitten demanded.

"I tried to tell you."

"Tried to tell me what?"

"I'm not exactly . . . human."

"Come again?"

"Using my lines now?" A playful grin spread across Aven's face. "Are you hinting that you would like me to show you what else I can do?"

"I'm hinting you'll get a punch in the face if you don't explain what the fuck is going on."

"I'm part angel." Aven held up his finger. "Correction. *Fallen* angel."

Kitten blinked. "Fallen angel?"

"Descendant of one."

"How?"

"I'm pretty sure you know where babies come from."

"This is insane," Kitten said, shaking her head. "You're insane."

"Everything was on an information chip I got out of my uncle's safe. I've gone through all the files, learning about my ancestors, what they did, what they do, who they are, where they hide. You have to stay away from the Circle, Katharine. Stop going to sessions. Stop practicing magic."

"What? Why?"

Aven's eyes wandered to the dip of Kitten's cut-off sweatshirt. "Those beauties are quite suitable for the tip of a blade."

"What are you talking about?"

"Oh, just murder." Aven shrugged. "Does Nick play with knives?"

"Aven, enough already."

Aven leaned on the bar, clasping his hands together. "Nick is from a long line of Seducers. Bree is an Oracle, as you know, Vincent's her protecting knight, and everyone in the Inner Circle is a blood-sucking sadists."

Kitten stood with her mouth gaping open before she blinked. "Are you on drugs?"

"No. And neither are you. That was the mistake Nick made last time. That's why he left. He screwed up. You were supposed to be clean."

"This is by far the most unbelievable story you have ever made up, Aven Crey."

"You two have fooled around, but he's never–" Aven jabbed a finger in the air, squinting. "You're still a virgin."

Kitten let out a sarcastic laugh. "Did you forget where you found me after you came back from Britain?"

"If I remember correctly, the choices on the Prancing Pony's à la carte menu didn't include 'dipping the wick.' Not to mention the neon sign with the words 'No entrance' and 'No refunds.'" Aven tilted his head and rubbed his chin. "It still doesn't make sense why they charged more for a hand job than the flick of the tongue. Takes longer? Gotta get them off and out to make room for the next pitiful soul, I suppose."

"Aven," Kitten groaned.

"Besides the broken bastards at Prancing Pony, besides Nick, who have you entertained? And don't say that college kid whose sweatshirt you wore like an 'I've had sex badge.' You didn't let him stick you either. That one-night stand was a one-hit wonder after five measly minutes of foreplay."

"It was a lot longer than five minutes, and how the hell would you know, anyway?"

"The first time you mentioned your encounter, I found the guy and told him I was your boyfriend."

"Wait. You're the reason Josh wouldn't answer my calls?"

"You're high maintenance. I did him a favor."

"You're such an ass!" Kitten slapped his arm. "He was a sweetheart!"

Aven's smile faded, and he stared at Kitten a long moment. "They only sacrifice virgins."

Kitten's eyes flicked to the floor. "Nick told me he wanted to wait. I mean before, he said it was about my age but—Italy." She met Aven's gaze. "I thought he wanted to make it romantic."

"Oh, what's more romantic than screwing you on an altar and plunging a dagger in your heart?"

Kitten's stomach bubbled, and acid rose in her throat.

"They'll drain you, drink your blood, and chant praise to their gods. It's what sick demented bastards do, Kitten. And that's exactly what they are. Psychopaths with no empathy. It's in their genetic code. They don't feel emotions. Not like normal people."

Kitten shook her head. "I don't believe you."

"He doesn't love you. He's been planning this for years, waiting for the right opportunity."

"No."

"Rome is where they gather. It's quite the event. I've seen the footage."

Kitten furrowed her brows. "Of what, exactly?"

"Of Meagers being sacrificed,"

"Meager? What? Like a beggar?"

"Meagers are domestic herds to the Inner Circle. Anyone not of supernatural making is livestock. The more livestock and land you own, the more reputable you are. The sacrifices are how they conjure their gods and gain insightful information, or make requests, or hell, even something as simple as getting bets in their favor. Ah. See? Now we know why Nick likes the horse races."

Kitten flopped into the bar chair across from Aven and held her head. Her brain throbbed in her skull. Aven may have been one to play around, but she knew he was being serious. That's what scared her. It wasn't that he somehow had the magic ability to heal, that he could fly. It was the fact that he was telling her that her life was in danger.

"They chose you because you have no one but me," Aven explained. "No close family, no relatives. No one would question if you disappeared." He took her hands from her face and squeezed them gently. "I need you to stay away from anyone involved in the Circle. Don't go to any more sessions. That's how they gain your trust. They convince people to join, make them believe they can do magic. But it's only the unseen entities, the demons, that give that illusion."

"I think I'm going to be sick."

"You've been fooled, little Meager. A sheep led to the slaughter."

"What do I do?"

"There are two options. One. I could do you now, taint you so that you're no longer a viable sacrifice."

Kitten glared.

"Or two. You leave everything here in Vegas behind and hide with me until the end of the world."

"The end of the world?"

"It's coming. Sooner than you realize."

"Like the apocalypse?"

"Mm-hmm."

Kitten jumped from her chair and paced the kitchen. "How am I supposed to believe any of this?"

"I'll show you everything I've seen."

Kitten stopped pacing. "A Memory Lapse?"

Aven got up and took Kitten's hand, leading her into the living room. "It's not pretty,"

Kitten had done a Memory Lapse with Aven before. It was how he had caught her up on his time spent abroad in Britain, showing her all the places he had visited in Europe. It was like a Mind Walk, but different. A Memory Lapse let you walk through a person's memories. You couldn't change or alter the past. You could only watch the vivid sequence as if you lived it too.

"How far back in time are you taking me?"

"However far my mind wants to take you."

Kitten let out a breath. "Okay."

"You're sure?"

"Yeah." Kitten shrugged. "I need proof that your story isn't some ploy to keep me away from Nick."

Aven placed his hands gently around Kitten's head and leaned in, inches from her face. "You're going to get one nasty headache."

"Just do it already."

Aven drew in a controlled breath through his nostrils and fixed his gaze on Kitten's. As he exhaled, she relaxed, letting the warmth of his hands at her temples sooth her. When grogginess set in, she let her eyes close.

Kitten walked down a glaring white hallway until a white door appeared before her at a dead end. When she opened it, she found herself at the gala again. In this particular part of Aven's memories, Kitten watched herself dance with Nick, but this time, she could feel Aven's emotions. He was disgusted with Nick, but more with Bree as he spoke with her. Their conversation was about an angel, about Bree insisting Aven remember his past life. She called him—

Serus.

The name sparked something in Kitten's chest. She then watched Aven's drunken night at the bar in South Carolina, the figure in the red robe with black wings coming down like lightning, how it felt spinning in the Mustang and the way it slammed against the tree.

Kitten fell deeper into the Memory Lapse, watching Nehia show him a strange scene of a familiar balcony and a deal made with a black-winged male. He looked almost identical to Aven with the same black hair and smirk. She felt the sting of the feather as Aven cut his arm, saw something unexplainable seep through his skin as the blood pact was fulfilled. She watched through Aven's eyes as the angel flew away, and then the scene faded into darkness until there was a blank space.

Skipping the blank page, Kitten saw his tearful breakup with Claire, the hateful words he said, felt the regret aching in his chest. She saw him standing in front of his mother's casket. All his past emotions flooded her. She almost fell out of the Memory Lapse, but her focus moved to the ground-shaking earthquake, the bobbing cab, and the way Aven Persuaded the cab driver. She felt his desire for the cigarette. Kitten had never smoked before, but the need for nicotine overtook her. What she craved more was the power Aven conjured to hover the lighter.

Time sped past the Caesar's Palace pool kiss and Aven retrieving the chip from the safe. It didn't slow down as he raced his motorcycle home and plugged the information chip into his laptop. Files and documents popped up in multiple windows. They were of InfiniCorps' involvement all over the world, Uncle Jimmy's journal entries, and page after page of a book about the Ancient Ones and the Crey's genealogy. They scrolled too fast for Kitten to read, but she knew every word as if Aven's remembrance of them were her own.

Finally, the pace of the memories slowed as Aven focused on footage of the Inner Circle walking through a subterranean passageway. Red-robed figures circled around an altar as a naked man in a goat like horned mask, moved in rhythm on the woman beneath him. He lifted a glinting blade and plunged it into the woman's throat, cutting off her guttural scream.

SERVENT GIRL

CHOKING on a gasp, Kitten came back to the present from the Memory Lapse and fled to the kitchen. She puked in the sink, gagged, and puked once more.

"Katharine?"

Kitten held up a finger for Aven to wait and reached into the fridge. Screwing off the top of a water bottle with trembling fingers, she tilted it up and drank down an aspirin in two large gulps. Aven had been right. One nasty headache throbbed in her skull.

"And you thought it was jealousy," Aven teased, leaning against a black marble column.

"That doesn't prove Nick is some sadist seducer. He wasn't there."

"No, but it does prove I was telling the truth. And if I was telling the truth about what you saw, then you should believe me when I tell you Nick is deeply involved."

"Angels. You're related to angels? And that blood pack. Aven, what the hell?"

"I'm damned because of the deal I made. But you don't have to be. You still have a chance to overcome it."

Kitten rewound Aven's memories until a girl from his past life and present came in clear.

She snapped her gaze to Aven. "Claire—"

"Needs to stay as far away from me as possible." Aven said as he headed for the decanter in the sitting room.

"But if she's a Truth Keeper, then she can help you. She was trying, and you pushed her away."

"She can help others who actually deserve a chance at redemption. I can only hope Vincent doesn't go looking for her," Aven took a drink, "or Will. He thinks I'm going to bring her to him, but I won't. I'm going to disappear, and you're coming with me."

"When?"

"A few weeks."

"Do you think your brother is with her?"

"I hope. If anyone can keep her safe, it's him."

"Do you know where the other soldiers are?"

"They're working for the Circle or in bags in a freezer."

"So the world is ending, and you're just going to wait around for it to happen? What if what Vincent said was true? What if we could stop this?"

"Once he gets what he wants, he'll kill her."

"Then expose the Circle. Show the world what they've done with the file."

"The world government is under their control. We'd be burned at the stake by the Meagers."

"What about the Truth Keepers? Can't they stop them?"

"Most of them don't even know who they are. And they won't. Not until it's time for them to stand up against Aalok."

Aalok. The name rang like a bell in Kitten's mind.

"He's coming back," Aven said, "and when he does, the world will be converted."

"Like his attempt before," Kitten said, still not believing all that she knew to be true. Maybe it wasn't. Maybe it was. Whatever it was, it was from Aven's head.

Aven finished off his drink and set down his glass. "And according to what my uncle had in that file, it might be possible that even the very ones chosen to testify against him could be swayed. The Persuader of Persuaders shall return, and he is coming back to rule. Not just the Meagers, but all."

Kitten peered up at Aven meekly. "Do you think I'll be Persuaded?"

Aven furrowed his brows and stared at her for a long moment before he said, "I want to show you something, something you wouldn't let me remind you of when I came to see you the first night I was back from South Carolina."

Kitten gave him a wary gaze. "What?"

"Your past life."

"You've seen mine too?"

"We were together once. Much like we are now. You were, shall we say, my servant girl."

"Was I a stupid Meager back then, too?"

"No." Aven gave a sweet smile and caressed Kitten's cheek. "You were faithful."

Kitten swallowed as Aven closed the space between them.

"Let me show you who you were," he said in a hushed tone. "Through your own eyes."

"I don't think I can do that again,"

"Please. For me."

Kitten took in a deep breath and stared into Aven's eyes a long moment before she blinked.

There were no halls this time, only a door waiting for her entrance. When she walked through the door, she found a room of black and red. A book lay on a bed of red velvet. She went to an oblong mirror, finding the reflection of someone that looked like her but wasn't. This girl was more than beautiful. So much more than any makeup tool could conjure. Her eyes were bright, and no blemishes or wrinkles marked her skin, other than the ones lining her forehead as she frowned.

A whispering wind and a shouting voice came from the veranda doors. As if on instinct, Kitten rushed to the balcony and jerked Aven back from the ledge.

"Hey!" he yelled as he stumbled back. "I was getting a better view."

"You were about to kill yourself!" Kitten said, realizing now she had said those words before.

"Ha! As if it matters. We're all going to die anyway."

"This is no time to be irrational."

Aven's laughter turned to sorrow, and soon he quietly gazed at the ocean for a long moment. "Everything is coming to an end. I have lost the one that I love, disgraced myself before Aramis, and been a fool . . . a fool to believe that I could be happy."

"Serus."

Kitten marked this name in her mind. It was Aven's name, and somehow she knew hers was Aerith. She was indeed his servant. It was like history had repeated. She clenched her teeth, somehow knowing the next moment had never truly been forgotten.

"Why aren't you screaming and running like everyone else?" Serus asked.

"I had to see you," Aerith said.

"You had to see me?"

"I-I needed to tell you something," she admitted, sheepishly.

"Then say it!" Serus slurred. "We are moments away from destruction!"

Aerith fidgeted with her hands. "I just wanted to say that although it may feel like no one cares for you . . . there are those that do."

"We care for so many, and yet they leave us." Serus sighed, bowing his head.

"Some are still faithful."

He turned and stared at her for a long time before he spoke. "Do you think love is eternal, Aerith?"

Kitten felt her past-self gulp down a knot in her throat. "Of course I do."

Serus smiled faintly, then looked up at the stars through a space between the clouds.

"My only prayer is that I'll see her again, just one more time, just one more chance to prove how much I love her. I'd take back everything I did if I could just hold her in my arms."

Kitten somehow knew he was talking about the Truth Keeper, about Claire—or Sophie, rather.

It pained Aerith deeply, feeling Serus's desperation, his hope that he would somehow find the Truth Keeper again in his next life. Kitten now knew he had.

"I'm glad you're here, Aerith," Serus said.

Kitten knew the heartbreaking words that would come next, how Serus had brushed her off. No matter how much she wanted to say something, to change her painful past, she couldn't. Because this wasn't a Mind Walk. It was a Memory Lapse.

"Seems I'm almost out." Serus hiccupped and raised a half-empty bottle, shaking it significantly.

The scene faded into black, and Kitten opened her eyes, finding Aven wiping tears from her cheeks.

"I'm sorry," he whispered. "I was so blind. You were always there for me, just like you are now."

Kitten took a step back and shook her head. "You were in love with her. You're still in love with her."

Aven tilted his head down. "There are many forms of love, Katharine. The love I have for Claire is deep, but so is the love I have for you. You loved me back then, and you love me now. And I'm finally seeing what's been right in front of me this whole time."

Kitten met his soft eyes as hers welled with tears. "You'll never be able to let her go."

"I already did."

At his words, Kitten parted her lips. She was ready for his kiss, ready to accept him, to admit that she had always loved him.

But Nick's ringtone blasted in their ears.

"Nice timing, Psycho Lover Boy." Aven scorned.

Kitten wiped her lower lids, hoping her mascara hadn't smudged, and took her phone from her pocket. The moment she read the message, she frowned. "I have to leave,"

"Don't go to him," Aven pleaded, following her to the door.

"I need some time, Aven."

"But do you understand now? Can you see that you're just as much a part of this as I am? I don't have a choice, but you do."

"A choice to do what?"

Aven's throat bobbed as he scrunched his face. His eyes seemed full of pain, of regret, as he said, "To escape the terrible fate that awaits me at death."

NEW JOB

SUNDAY, 9:00 A.M.
LAS VEGAS, NEVADA

AVEN had given Kitten a chance to appease Nick but told her to meet him for lunch at Paula's after. He didn't want her to drop Nick. It would have caused suspicion. She would have to wean the suckling leach slowly. The moment Kitten walked into the diner, Aven curled his nose in distaste.

"Really, Kitten?"

"You told me not to make any drastic moves. He's been telling me to color my hair brown for Rome. Said he wants me to blend in."

"Right. As if changing your hair would do that."

"Did you order?" she asked, sitting across from him, listening to Paula sing a hymn in the kitchen.

"You forgot to color your brows."

Kitten huffed and jerked her purse from her shoulder, taking out her digital styler.

"Does that thing color the carpet to match the curtains?" Aven leaned his head down as if he were going to peek under her skirt.

Kitten kicked him in the shin before she pressed the styler to her head. She tinted her roots in a pastel pink, and the rest of her strands blue before smiling in a compact mirror and snapping it shut.

"There. Happy?" she asked.

"Very." Aven smiled. "Thank you, Barbie."

Kitten wasn't amused with the new nickname. "Barbie has degrees. She's been a vet, a doctor, a ballet dancer, a—"

"Professional singer?"

"Dreams don't come true, Aven. That's for pretend. If I ever want to have anything or be someone, I have to stop letting you take care of me. What if you're wrong about Nick? What if what your uncle put in those files is just some made-up blackmail to make the Circle look bad?"

"One. It's a truth you refuse to believe. Two. I'm always right. And three. I like taking care of you."

"You like telling me what to do, like when we were kids."

"So what?" Aven shrugged. "I'm bossy. But so are you."

"I'll take bossy, but I'm not some rebel without a cause. I just want to be normal."

"You have style, Katharine. You were made to stand out. That's what makes us a great couple. Two trendsetters out to travel the world before its impending doom."

Kitten rolled her eyes. "We're *not* a couple."

"Everyone else thinks we are." Aven gave a playful grin and wiggled his brows. "You're the one who won't admit you're in love with me."

"Because I won't say those words," Kitten said. "Ever. You know I haven't since—"

Since Mom passed away.

Nicknames. It was something Kitten and her mother had used instead of "I love you" after her father left. The words lost their meaning to Kitten during the arguments between her parents. So her mother made up a name to call her when she scolded Katharine.

Silly girl.

It was a way to say she was mad at Kitten, but that she loved her and wouldn't leave her no matter how upset she got with her.

But her mother *had* left her, dying at the young age of twenty-nine. The Creys adopted her, treated her like family. Kitten couldn't help but think their kindness had always been about the sacrifice, but she also didn't want to believe it. After staying up all night debating what she saw in the Memory Lapse, she decided that Jimmy's journal entries and evidence footage were dramatized hearsay.

"And I won't say them," she continued. "Not even to Nick."

"Stupid Boy," Aven said, leaning forward. "That's what you say instead of those three little words. You've been saying you loved me since we were five. It's all so clear now. Psycho Lover Boy doesn't have a nickname, does he?"

"He can give me something you can't."

Aven lifted that perfect brow of his. "Anything he can do, I can do better. Name something he can provide that I'm incapable of."

Kitten hesitated. "A family."

She was right. He couldn't provide that. Aven remembered distinctly how Kitten always loved to play house. When they were children, he would often find her in her room, setting up her dollhouse. She had designed the furniture herself, the clothes on the dolls, and had even styled their hair. It was a 1950s theme. The All American Dream, a dream Aven could never give her. Not with his curse.

Aven slapped a hand on his chest as if he'd been shot in the heart. "Ouch."

"Not that you would ever want kids," Kitten said, looking at the paper menu.

"Do you?"

"Of course I do. Everyone wants that."

Not Aven . . . or so he thought.

Studying Kitten's facial features, he wondered what their children would look like, what kind of parents they would be. But it couldn't happen. It was his fault all of this doomsday stuff had sped up Katharine's baby-making clock to full speed.

"Fine." He shrugged. "Adopt. I'll buy whatever you need to play mommy."

"I hate it when you act like this. Just because you don't want to have kids doesn't mean I can't."

"I never said I didn't want kids. Just not right now. Could you imagine the terror Nehia would put a helpless baby through?"

"Well, women don't have the luxury of copious amounts of sperm. We have a limited number of eggs to–"

"I know all too well the anatomy of a woman's body, Kitten. Even on *those* days."

"Say you're wrong about the end of the world. Say life goes on. In three years I'll be thirty. If I never choose to leave this 'job,'" she mocked, "I never will. I'll be stuck childless, wheeling you around when you're eighty."

"Hover chairs, my dear. You won't have to push, you can ride in my lap."

"I'm serious."

Aven sighed. "You really want kids with Ken's evil twin?"

"I like Nick and I wish you wouldn't give me grief for how I feel about him. We can't help who we fall for."

Claire. Point for Kitten.

Aven leaned back in his chair, defeated. "Do you love him?"

"I don't know," Kitten said, staring at the table. "I know I feel something for him."

"Take it from someone who knows all too well the excitement of an impulse buy. It never lasts."

"You don't know that."

"I do. You'll ooh and aah seeing Tuxedo Ken on the shelf. Pay whatever it takes to get him home to play house. But after a few years, the joy fades. You realize Ken's smile is painted on, and you're left with nothing but regrets and a lavish dollhouse void of laughter. Barbie doesn't need Ken, Kitten. That's why they're sold separately."

"Oh, my word! Look at you, sugah!" Paula squealed, coming out from the kitchen.

"Paula!" Kitten jumped from her chair and hugged her tight.

Paula rocked her from side to side like she had when she was a little girl. "My lil' Kit Kat. I haven't seen you in what?" She shot Aven a glance with raised brows. "Four years? What brings you to this side of town?"

"Employment," Aven informed her as he stood and buttoned his jacket. "You need someone to look after you when you get that hip surgery."

"Hip surgery? Whatcha talkin' bout, boy?"

"You know"—Aven gave her a pointed look—"the one you're getting in a few days?"

Aven had called Paula, explained his sneaky plan to keep Kitten away from Nick. Working for Paula was the best excuse. She was a good influence and protective. If anyone could keep Nick away, it was her. Not to mention Nick hated coming to this part of town. The pancake house was, after all, on Fremont Street. It was rundown, halfway abandoned, and overflowing with drug dealers. Aven had tried for years to get Paula to leave the dump so he could set her up on the Vegas strip. But she had always turned him down.

"Oh." Paula drew out the word. She then favored her hip, leaning to one side. "Oh, my surgery. That's right. I've been so nervous 'bout it."

Aven held back a grin at Paula's terrible acting. Paula had always had hip issues, but she refused to see a doctor.

"A job," Kitten said flatly. "I work for you. I mean I did." She looked at Paula. "I quit because he's acting like a five-year-old."

Paula gave a light chuckle. "Empty threats again?"

"Aren't they always?" Kitten joked.

Aven cleared his throat, demanding their attention. "Until I get back from the UK, Kitten will help you run the restaurant. After the surgery, she will see to it your prescriptions are filled, and that you're taken to your check-ups. Won't you, Katharine?"

Kitten withdrew her hateful gaze from Aven, bringing forth a sweet smile, and said, "I'd be delighted to."

UNBIRTHDAY

Sunday, 11:22 p.m.
Las Vegas, Nevada

"ARE you ready to talk about your feelings yet?" Aven asked, flipping over a card from the deck in front of him.

"Nope," Kitten replied flatly as she shot a glance at the three empty liquor bottles on the table. "You're buzzed."

"Hashtag Demigod problems." Aven grinned, turning up another bottle of bourbon.

The stakes were up to ten grand now, and Kitten was ready to take Aven for more. She was still mad that he tricked her into working at Paula's. She knew the hip surgery was a lie to keep Nick away from her. Nick loathed that side of town. Kitten didn't care for it much either, but she loved Paula. Paula had given Kitten her first job at the pancake house. Aven had always dropped by and ragged Kitten, ordering a slice of

Paula's famous coconut pancakes just because Kitten couldn't stand the smell of them.

"That's why you burn off alcohol so quickly." Kitten noted. "That's why when you get slashed by a demon, it heals within minutes. Why you're good at Persuading."

Aven gave a clever grin.

"Is there more?"

"There is," Aven said, leaning forward on his elbows. "If you ask nicely, I'll divulge my sinful secrets."

"Show me."

Aven seemed to hold back a grin. "I said nicely."

Kitten rolled her eyes. "Show me more of your powers, oh great one."

Aven leaned back in his chair, and a sly smile formed on his lips.

A moment of staring ensued.

"Well?" Kitten said, finally.

"Well, what?"

"Do your stuff."

"I did."

Kitten glanced at the poker table. "Nothing happened."

"That you could see in plain sight."

"So you *don't* have any other superpowers." Kitten scoffed and picked up her bottle of malt liquor.

Aven cupped his mouth, but she could still see a deviant smile dimple his cheeks.

"What?"

"Nothing,"

Kitten tilted back her drink and gagged.

Aven's laughter lit her face on fire as she rushed to the sink to wash out her mouth. "You know how much I detest coconut water!" she yelled and swished her mouth again.

Aven slapped a hand several times on the table, still giggling like a schoolboy.

"You're such an ass," Kitten gritted out through her teeth as she came back to the table. "Don't do that again." She popped the top of another wine cooler and sniffed it before guzzling down half the bottle.

"Cool, right?" Aven asked, clearly entertained.

"Annoying." Kitten drew a card. "It would be cool if you could get Nehia to take a hike."

"Now that would be some trick."

Kitten glanced at her phone on the table as it vibrated a notification. "Shit," she said, reading Nick's message.

"Killer Ken's fifteenth attempt, I believe."

"He's pissed about our delay to Rome. I should go."

"Nick, schmick. You say I can't let Claire go, but here you are still drooling over that sadist son of a bitch."

"What happened to 'watch that pretty mouth of yours'?"

"Screw the Circle and their rules. They're hypocrites. Especially Nick."

"I'm not having this conversation with you again. I told you he's changed. And whatever you read in those files—Aven, you have no proof."

That was a fact. There was no proof. Words, even in print, were hearsay. Pictures and video footage could be manipulated, edited. The gruesome things Kitten had seen were something she didn't want to believe. If it were true, that meant that everyone she knew had done terrible things, hiding behind a mask of charity. If what she had seen in the Memory Lapse was true, it meant she had been sipping champagne with killers.

"Kinda hurts my feelings you won't give us a chance but have entertained the idea of having kids with someone who murders them." Aven ridiculed.

A chill went down Kitten's spine. That part, the one about how the Inner Circle had murdered innocent children, used their untainted blood to do tests, that had bothered her more than anything she'd seen in the files. She still couldn't get their pale little faces and wide lifeless eyes out of her head.

In a way, she knew that playing poker and drinking would help take her mind off of it all. This was what she and Aven had done when he came to visit during college breaks. One of those times, he played bartender. She had pecked him on the lips before blowing chunks of apple martini and sushi all over his white-collared shirt. She wondered if he remembered that night. She had paid enough hotel cleaning bills after his one-night stands to figure as much.

"All I'm saying," Aven said, laying down four of a kind, "is that we basically treat one another like husband and wife, anyway. If it doesn't work, we can go back to being professional."

No matter how much Kitten wanted to try, no matter how much their kiss still lingered, she couldn't get her heart broken. Claire would call him eventually. The girls he broke up with always did. No matter what, they always wanted him back.

"Getting feelings involved would make things complicated," Kitten stated, folding her cards. "Especially watching you do what you have to do."

Aven raised a brow. "I don't think, I follow."

"You'll still be entertaining. It's better I stay closed off."

Aven shuffled, dealt, and laid down the flop. "You've always been jealous of my encounters?"

"That's usually what happens when you have feelings for someone. Raise."

"So you *do* love me." Aven bit his bottom lip and called her bet. "Why is it so hard for you to say the words?"

"Check," Kitten said and took another drink so she wouldn't have to answer.

Aven fingered his stack of chips. "Have you ever thought about us—you know—"

"You haven't."

"That's not entirely true." Aven grinned and raised his bet significantly.

Kitten's heart skipped a beat. "You're bluffing."

"Am I?"

She glared and matched his bet.

"After all, I did get you wet in the pool."

Kitten thought about smacking that sinister smirk off Aven's face until a bottle of water on the table flinched. The top unscrewed as his smile spread.

"Don't. You. Dare," she warned.

"Now who's bluffing?" Aven teased.

Kitten swallowed back the saliva pooling in her mouth and laid her cards face up. "Boat. You lose."

Aven flicked his tongue across his lower lip and leaned back in his chair.

Kitten shuffled, dealt, and laid down the flop.

Aven stared at his cards a long moment.

Kitten drummed her fingers on the poker table. "I'm waiting."

"I'm thinking," Aven said, slipping a cigarette between his lips. He cupped his hand around his butane lighter, paused, then looked up through his long lashes. The air purifier turned on without his vocal command, and that deviant smile of his widened.

He mirrored a scene from the Memory Lapse, the one where he was in the cab after the earthquake. This time he levitated the lighter above his palm with complete confidence. The lighter flipped back its metal top and scratched the starter, sparking a flame. Aven took a long drag off his cigarette, parted his perfect mouth, and let the plume of smoke kiss his lips.

"Aven, it's your turn," Kitten reminded him, ignoring her racing heart.

Aven's cheeks hollowed as he took another long draw, burning the end of his cigarette bright. When he closed his eyes and leaned his head back against the chair, he exhaled with a soft throaty groan.

Kitten had heard Aven make that sound before. It had always been accompanied by a rhythmic pounding against a wall, and wail after wail of pleasure from his encounters.

What do you do to make them breathlessly cry out your name, Crey?

"And now you're thinking about it too." Aven sat up and leaned into the fog, slitting those hooded blue eyes. "Aren't you?"

"Are you going to bet or think?" Kitten snapped.

"Let's raise the stakes, shall we?"

"Fine. Thirty grand."

"As you wish." Aven tossed his chips into the pile. "But if I win, you have to Mind Walk so I can show you."

"Show me what?"

Aven leaned forward, "What I do to make them breathlessly cry out my name." He splayed his hand, biting back a seductive smile.

Kitten sat stunned.

It was a royal flush. All hearts.

Her poker face replaced her initial shock, but she couldn't ignore the drumming in her chest as she scooped up the cards to shuffle. She didn't know if Aven had read her mind, so she tried to think of anything other than every fantasy that had zipped through her mind only seconds ago.

"I haven't had an encounter in a few weeks," Aven said. "I wonder how long I can fight Nehia off before she makes me cut myself into little pieces."

Kitten froze, took one look at Aven, and chucked the cards at his chest.

They thudded against his breastbone and tumbled to the floor.

"I thought you hated fifty-two pick up," he teased.

"What the hell, Aven? A guilt trip? Are you really that desperate to get off so you can get some sleep?"

A ding came from Kitten's phone, and she read the harsh message. "Great. Now Nick thinks there's something going on between us."

"Good. Because there is."

"Aven! Enough! Go find an encounter!"

Aven crossed his arms like a pouting toddler. "No."

"Cheater," Kitten growled and shoved her chair back.

"Sore loser! You could have at least finished the game."

"Oh, you mean while you distract me and slip cards from your sleeves?"

Aven's mouth dropped dramatically before he said, "You think I—"

"Asshole. I was letting you win until—you know what? Forget it. I'm going to Nick's." Kitten retrieved her white-studded leather jacket from the coat hanger.

"Katharine, wait."

"When Nehia shows up again, I won't be by the phone to run to your rescue. If I were you, I'd go by the whore house."

"Fine!" Aven shouted, smashing his cigarette into the ashtray. "Walk out on me on my unbirthday."

The unbirthday trick. It was Aven's Hail Mary, a way of groveling without getting on his knees. Declaring it was an unbirthday meant Kitten was in charge and that Aven was at her mercy. Or at least, his wallet was. All Kitten had to do was play along with his stupid game. But it wasn't the idea of gifts that made her want to play along. It was the assurance that Aven would be safe from Nehia if they stayed up until dawn.

"I really hate you," she told him, throwing back her head.

Aven gave a playful grin. "Say it."

Kitten feigned surprise and swooped her hands to her chest. "Then that means it's my unbirthday too!" she said dramatically.

Aven slapped his hands together as he came to his feet and then pointed at her. "That means you get an unbirthday present."

Kitten laughed. "You're so stupid."

"You love it," Aven said, dancing his way to her. He twirled her in his arms and dipped her.

"To Finnegan's?"

"To Finnegan's!" Aven held up a triumphant fist. "For the best rum Coke floats the world has ever known!"

14

LEVI

MONDAY, 12:33 P.M.
OAHU, HAWAII

BEFORE leaving Georgia for her trip, Claire had stared at the amount left in her savings account. She knew it was crazy to spend the few thousand dollars to go to Waikiki, but she had transferred the money. She was here, walking up the steps, and into the lobby of the pink hotel.

After checking into the Royal Hawaiian resort, she took the elevator to the room number Serena had given her and knocked on the door. There was no answer, and after two more taps of her knuckles, Claire leaned against the wall, dragging a hand down her face.

"I'm such an idiot," she said under her breath and made her way back to the lobby.

Leaving her luggage with the check-in clerk, Claire pressed her canvas bag flush against her side. The illegal item inside had been the reason she had taken a private plane, the reason she lied to Laura about why she came to the island.

She had told Laura about reconciling with Serena, that Serena had informed her that her grandfather, Mr. Robinson, was in Hawaii. That had all been true, but the lie was that Claire said she had asked Serena if Mr. Robinson still had connections with anyone in the military. If he did, he could call one of his connections and find out anything about Claire's mother.

At the mention of Claire's mother, Laura hadn't asked any more questions and set her up with a private plane, paying the best pilot her dad could hire—with money or favors, Claire hadn't been sure.

Knowing somehow that Hawaii meant something special, Claire squeezed the book in her bag and walked to the shore. Seeing the tropical paradise, she strained to remember her visions and dreams that looked so much like this place. Pieces were connecting, faces were coming into view again, but they vanished as someone touched her shoulder.

Turning, Claire found an elderly man smiling as if he knew her. Age wrinkled the corners of his eyes. His short hair was white, as was the patch on his chin. Claire studied his eyes. They were still the same deep brown she remembered from her childhood. They seemed to brighten with joy as he opened his mouth to speak, but there was no voice that came with the movement of his lips.

"Hello, Mr. Robinson," Claire said sweetly, signing a greeting with her hand.

It was hard not to stare at the scar along Levi's throat, remembering how GG had left out the gory details about Levi's near-death encounter. GG had been the one who had nursed him back to health in the infirmary during World War III. That was how they became such good friends and stayed in touch after the war was over.

"Have you come to take me home?" Levi signed.

Claire's attention moved to his fingerless gloves that had voiced a semi-natural robotic reverb. The leather of the gloves was faded, as was the red InfiniCorp logo stamped upon them.

"Take you home?" Claire asked out loud, hoping he hadn't lost his hearing yet.

Levi dropped his hands as if disappointed and squinted at her. He appeared confused, as if he had expected a different answer.

"I'm Claire," she said, putting a hand to her chest. "Evelyn's granddaughter. Do you remember me?"

Mr. Robinson's eyes lit with recognition. **"Claire. You look just like her."**

Claire let out a small laugh and signed. "I hear that a lot."

"He had this all planned out, after all,"

"Who did?"

Levi smiled and pressed his ring finger to his leather palm. The lights on the gloves went dim as Mr. Robinson smoothly moved his hands in the air to sign, **"The Creator."**

Claire glanced at his neck again, now seeing a thin waxy cord tucked beneath his shirt.

Mr. Robinson lifted up the key charm attached to it and smiled.

"Have you had lunch yet?" Claire asked.

Surf Lanai was a beautiful outside restaurant adjacent to the hotel. It matched the pastel theme with white tables, pink umbrellas, and pink chairs. The table had an interactive screen that displayed the menu. Claire swiped her finger across it, looking at the lunch options, and gulped at the prices.

"Aloha," a waiter greeted as he approached Claire and Mr. Robinson's table. "Welcome to Surf Lanai. What can I get you to drink?"

"Water please," Claire told the waiter with a meek smile.

"Same, for now," Mr. Robinson's gloves said for him.

As the waiter left, Claire hugged her canvas bag, scooting her chair closer to the table. "Mr. Robinson—"

"Please, call me Levi."

"Levi. Can I ask why you thought I was my grandmother?"

Levi silenced his gloves again and signed with his fingers, "I always thought Evelyn would be the one to welcome me Beyond The Veil."

"What did you mean by the Creator planned this?" Claire signed. She knew better than to say "Creator" out loud. One religious word and the hidden recording devices would flag her and Levi.

Levi's eyes shifted to the bag Claire was holding tight. "You have questions about what's inside."

"How did you know?"

Levi took a wooden box from a worn leather bag and sat it on the table. He lifted its top an inch, letting Claire peek inside. Gold sparkled in her vision, but he quickly closed the box and looked around the dining area before putting it away again.

"Is it the same text you and GG were deciphering? You can read it?" Claire signed.

"Can you?"

"I think. I'm really not sure."

"Here you are," the waiter said, placing two waters between Claire and Levi. "Soup of the day is our Hawaiian Saimin, and our special is the marinated rancher's skewed beef with a local mix of fresh greens, crispy cassava, mint, and cilantro with a kaffir lime vinaigrette."

Levi pressed his ring finger to his palm. The leather gloves lit up and said, **"We're still waiting on one more."**

"We are?" Claire blurted out.

"Of course." The waiter nodded. "Can I get them something to drink?"

"Water, please."

"Yes, Sir," The waiter said and went into the restaurant.

Claire was curious about who would be meeting them, but decided to make pleasant conversation to distract herself from inquiring.

"I met your grandson, Little Levi," she said. "He's a sweet kid."

"Full of energy. He wants to be a fireman."

Claire's smile fell as she looked past Levi. A man was coming up the patio steps, a man that shouldn't be there.

"Did I say something wrong?" Levi's gloves asked without concern.

"No. I'm sorry. What were you saying?"

The words from Levi's gloves trailed off as Claire glanced at the man again. He was staring at her.

You can't be here.

She placed her suddenly frigid fingers on her hot cheek.

I'm dreaming...

"Can you excuse me for just a moment?" she asked Levi as she stood.

"Of course,"

Claire kept her gaze fixed on the man wearing a white T-shirt and jeans as she weaved her way through the chairs.

He ran his fingers through his blond hair as she stood before him and she wondered if it was a nervous habit.

"Claire, what are you doing here?" Will asked.

Her mind had made him appear just as surprised as she had been. She watched his eyes search hers. They seemed to ask for an explanation. But there was none. At least, not one that sounded remotely sane.

"I'm still on the plane," Claire managed to say finally.

"You're what?" He asked.

"No, I wouldn't have done that." She scoffed at herself. "I'm at home in Dad's chair, asleep. My brain is trying to cope, it's trying to make me feel something good again." She turned to look at the ocean, waiting for the sky to go dark, waiting for the tidal wave to build in the water.

"But it won't be good for long," she said. "It will only end the same sad way it always does. Soon you'll disappear into the white light. You always do."

Her heart thudded while she waited for the dream to shift into something haunting, but it didn't. There was only the cheerful chirp of the birds, the soothing sound of lapping waves, and the soft chatter of the tourists in conversation around her.

"You're shaking," Will said, taking her hands in his.

Claire relished his touch and his soothing warmth, but it wasn't real. She was dreaming and there was only one way to wake up.

In one swift motion, she stood on her tiptoes and wrapped her arms around Will's neck. She pressed her lips to his, melting into his strong arms. She savored the scent of his woodsy aftershave and the taste of his sweet minty tongue.

Will pulled her in closer and kissed her again.

Claire didn't stop him. It felt good to be in the warrior's embrace, to feel that rush between them, to feel safe.

Any moment you'll disappear.

Will didn't.

He pressed her closer to deepen the kiss.

Claire's chest lit to flames. Every nerve, every fiber of her being sparked like lightning with each movement of their mouths. She hoped this dream would last; now thinking the nightmare had changed into something wonderful, that it would finally have a happy ending.

When Will gently parted from her lips, he gazed down at her, seeming unsure, but at the same time, confident.

Still dizzy from their kiss, Claire managed to look into his eyes and whisper, "You're not supposed to be here."

Will's smile fell in an instant.

"You can't be," she said, taking a step back as stark alarm shot through her. A prickling heat crawled up her neck, and she pressed her fingers to her flaming lips, daring to gaze around the dining area.

She wasn't dreaming.

Horror widened her eyes. She took another step back, bumping into a man in a chair behind her.

Will reached out a hand to help her.

She couldn't breathe, couldn't speak. She clutched her arms to her chest and said, "Excuse me," to the stranger she had bumped into. She took one look at Will and spun on her toes to make a beeline for the bathrooms.

Will wanted to go after her, but he only watched Claire quicken her strides inside the hotel. The flashes from his dreams during their kiss were fading now, but there was one thought, one glowing face that still remained. He had never been sure before, but there was no denying who he had been sketching all these years.

Claire was the angel from his dreams.

Tracing his lips, he lifted his gaze and glanced around the dining area. Several tables away, an elderly man with short wool-white hair waved Will over.

He recognized Mr. Robinson from the photos Jeremiah sent and threaded his way through the tables and chairs. When he got to Mr. Robinson's table, he extended his hand for a proper introduction.

"William," Mr. Robinson signed before he shook Will's hand. "You're the spitting image of Charlie. If I didn't know better, I would think he had come back from Beyond the Veil."

Will glanced at the fingerless gloves that were turned off and noted the InfiniCorp logo. Sign Language. It was something Will had been required to learn in the military. In a way, it was like smoke signals. Most countries had forgotten the lost language. With technology these days, there was no use for it. It appeared Levi assumed Will had served.

Guess he knew I would take after Granddad Charlie.

"Mr. Robinson," Will smiled, "it's a pleasure to meet the man who served with him."

"Please, call me Levi,"

Will's gaze wandered to the ladies' restroom sign as he placed his shoulder bag over his chair. He tugged the flap, making sure it covered the illegal book inside.

"So. I see you know Claire."

Will shook his head, trying to ignore his flushing cheeks. "Not that intimately," he admitted and fixed his eyes on the menu screen, trying to read the lunch options.

It only took seconds before his gaze wandered back to the bathroom sign again. When Claire appeared beneath it after a few moments and headed back to the table, Will's shoulders fell in relief.

"Did you order yet?" she asked Levi as she sat at across from him.

"Not yet,"

The waiter came by, placing a glass of ice water in front of Will before he held out his tablet.

A *bing* sounded at the press of Will's thumb.

"Will you be having a coffee today, Mr. Stryde?" the waiter asked, tapping on his tablet.

"No thank you," Will told him, then looked back at Claire, who dragged a finger carefully down the table screen. He studied her, seeing her cheeks were still as pink as the potted flowers scattered throughout the dining area.

"I'll have the special,"

"Same." Will nodded.

"The salad, please," Claire said, glancing quickly over Will's head to look at the waiter. She then brought her attention to the rolled-up napkin by her plate. Will noticed a canvas bag in her lap as she placed her napkin over it. She put her eyes back on the screen and scrolled through a pamphlet about the hotel.

Will narrowed his eyes on her. "What are you doing here?"

"Did you know this place was built in the twentieth century?" She asked Levi. "It says here that in September 1974, Japanese businessmen—brothers Kenji Osano and Masakuni Osano—purchased the Royal Hawaiian Hotel from ITT Sheraton. They formed Kyo-ya Company Limited, a subsidiary of Kokusai Kogyo Company Limited, as the corporate entity to manage all their hotels."

Will didn't take his eyes off of her. "Claire?"

"Oh, wow. They have sailboat rentals." She glanced up at Levi. "Have you ever been on a sailboat?"

"Levi, do you have a pen and paper?" Will asked.

Levi patted his blue Hawaiian shirt. **"No, I don't believe I do,"**

"That's a shame," Will crossed his arms and tilted his head. "Seems Claire can't communicate with me unless it's scribbled in ink."

Claire scrunched her face as if she had suddenly become ill and brought her gaze to Will slowly. "I thought about texting you, but you were at the funeral and . . ."

Her eyes darted to Levi, but he looked away, covering a wide grin. It was clear that he thought this to be some kind of lover's spat, that Will and Claire had once been a thing.

"What-what are you doing in Hawaii?" she asked, fumbling over her words.

Will's eyes narrowed. "I asked you first,"

Claire clutched the bag in her lap and gave a pleading look to Levi.

"He came for the same reason you did,"

"You did?" Claire asked, her gaze darting to Will. "You came to ask him about the—"

Will placed a finger to his lips before he lifted his shoulder bag from the back of his chair and placed it on the table. At another nod from Mr. Robinson, Claire took her own bag from her lap and sat it next to Will's. Levi put his box on the table, turned off his gloves, and signed with a proud smile,

"We follow our destiny, unaware, for it is the Creator that set our path, leading us to a place of purpose."

THE BOOK OF

ARAMIS

Monday, 3:00 pm
Oahu, Hawaii

CLAIRE was glad she had eaten a light lunch. Her stomach was twisting into knots as she sat on the couch where Levi had settled.

During lunch, Levi, Will, and Claire had only made pleasant conversation about the island and after, Levi suggested they talk further in private.

Claire dared to glance at Will as he checked Levi's room for recording devices, but she averted her gaze to the floor as he looked at her and said,

"We're clear," and picked up a chair to sit in across from her and Levi.

"I'm curious," Levi looked at Claire. **"How did you two meet?"**

Remembering the thugs, how Will had swooped in and rescued her like a white knight, made Claire lift her head. She held a breath, losing herself in those bright blue eyes as she fixed her gaze on Will. That had been the first thing she had seen when Will had slid back his white hood in the car after rescuing her. They weren't soft like they had been after their kiss, but hard, a bit hurt even.

"In Vegas," Claire informed. "Will saved me from some bad guys,"

Will's eyes softened and Claire thought he may have held back a smile as she held his gaze for a few pounding heartbeats.

"As it was before, so it shall be again. The Guardian protecting the Truth Keeper,"

"Truth Keeper?" Claire asked with curiosity. She had only heard that title once before when her grandmother had read to her.

"To know who you are, you must start at the beginning."

Levi looked to Will and nodded once.

At the cue, Will took his book from his shoulder bag and placed it in his lap.

Claire followed suit, staring at Will's book. It was a bit more tattered and torn at the edges, but still bore the same gold emblem on the cover as hers. She traced the one on her book until Levi placed his own matching book in his lap, and took off his necklace.

Claire's eyes grew wide, seeing Levi's skeleton key charm gleam in the sunlight coming in from the window. When Levi nodded to her once, a cue for her to retrieve her own key, Claire unclasped her father's gift, watching Will slide his own key charm off his key ring.

"It is time to unlock the truth,"

When Levi placed his key in his lock, Will did the same, and Claire followed.

The locks clicked in unison.

Levi looked to Will and then to Claire with all seriousness, and motioned with smooth hand gestures. **"There is an ancient story that has been passed down from generation, to generation. Words of Old, or so they are called these days."**

Levi pulled back the cover of his book.

Claire and Will mirrored him, turning to the first page.

"Long ago, before the age of the flesh men, we, all of us, lived with the Creator, and the Seraphim in the Infinite Realm. We were lower angels, living peacefully. We went to and fro from a paradise, called Earth, until the day, Samria revolted against his maker. A war of truth and lies raged until Aramis assigned councilors, Truth Keepers, to remind the confused souls of his great love for them.

"On the day of Samria's demotion, numerous Truth Keepers turned and followed him. Aalok, no longer called Samria, gained numbers quickly during a few millennia. And one fateful night at one of the King's Grand Ball's, on the Ten Thousandth Millennia, a third of the souls rebelled against their maker.

"Knowing Aalok had an army of souls willing to fight to overthrow him, Aramis came up with a plan that deeply pained his heart.

"And so, the first aeon ended, and the souls, all of them, save the fallen Seraphim who refused to be placed in flesh, were given a new body with no memory of their life from before, to be given a second chance to reconcile."

The golden edge of the page sparkled in the sunlight as Levi turned it.

"The Creator. Chapter One. In the beginning, He made the heavens and the Earth. The stars sang with joy, but that joy was soon dimmed with darkness."

Claire glanced up, waiting for Levi to continue but he didn't. He only smiled at her, **"Can you read the next line?"**

Claire squinted at the text, but it didn't take long before it shifted into words. "And the spirit of Him moved upon the face of the waters. He said let there be light, and there was light. And He separated the light from the dark, and recreated the paradise that had once been without form, making it pleasing to his eyes once more."

"Good. Will?"

Will's throat bobbed as he set his eyes to the book and read, "And He again made his creations, the beasts of the fields, the birds of the air, every living thing was made by Him. And it was good."

Levi grinned wide, and he continued motioning with his hands. **"And then He said to the Seraph as they watched his creation come to fruition, 'let us make man in our image, in our likeness, and He** made them, male and female, and told them to go forth and multiply.'

"And they were spread throughout the lush earthly paradise.' This was the completion of His work, until the eighth day, where He made a man after his own likeness. His likeness became a multitude, and that multitude scattered all over the earth, bringing forth many councilors. But over the centuries, the chosen, the Truth Keepers, were martyred, as was Aramis himself, who was born, only to die at the hands of his own creation."

"They betrayed him?" Claire asked. "The Creator came in human form and they killed him?"

"Not the Truth Keepers, the ones who followed Aalok from before. Even to this day, they do his bidding."

"The name 'Aramis' is in gold," Will noted of the Creator's name as it glittered in the text.

"Flip through the book. See if any other names are in gold."

Claire flipped the pages to the middle of her book until she saw a name. It called to her as if she knew it well, as if it was so familiar that it could be her own.

"Did you find one?"

"Sophie," Claire replied.

Levi scooted over to Claire, signaling Will to come too. Levi flipped through his book to Claire's page, dragged a finger down it, and then pointed to another name in gold. "Zeruiah,"

Will's eyes darted across the books and held his own up beside Claire and Levi's.

Levi looked at Will. "And you?"

"Alexander," Will pointed.

Levi let the edges of his tome, flit across his thumb. **"Now you have eyes to see,"**

Will and Claire flipped through their books, finding every page, every word, now finally revealed.

"How is this possible?" Claire asked, not having to squint to read the words.

"It is said, that when two or more Truth Keepers gather, Aramis is with them, unveiling what had once been hidden. Both of you have known deep down, ever since you were children, that your souls had been calling you to remember, to search for something more than this life could offer. That you had a purpose, a destiny."

"So we can only read the book when we are together?"

"Claire, when your grandmother and I began reading, we stumbled upon something else extraordinary."

"What?" Claire asked.

"The gift, to see who we once were," Levi gestured for her hand.

On instinct, Claire grasped Levi's forearm.

When Levi squeezed her arm gently, a bright light blinded Claire for only seconds. When it dimmed, Levi's face came back into view, but he wasn't an old man any longer. His wrinkles had smoothed, his smile had brightened, and a halo of white glowed a soft silhouette around his body.

"Zeruiah," Claire said under her breath.

"It was His will that we meet again after all," Levi said in a clear voice.

When Levi drew back his hand slowly the surrounding light dimmed and he was an old man with a thick scar on his neck.

"I was speechless too when I first saw,"

As Claire's mind swirled with visions of Levi as a young man, on a star sailing ship, Levi reached out for Will to take his forearm.

Will wiped his sweaty palms on his jeans, lifted his hand, but then glanced at his watch. "You know what? I just realized what time it was." He drew back his hand and rushed over to the chair, snatching up his bag. "I haven't checked into my room yet."

"There's an app for that," Claire noted.

"And the flight. I fly a plane," he informed Levi. "I'm pretty tired."

"Have you ever had visions of Hawaii, Will? Meeting Claire here? Meeting me?"

"How did you know?" Will asked, pausing from hastily putting his book in his bag.

"This very hotel room. This very moment."

Will nodded.

Levi appeared calm. **"But never of me before this day."**

"No," Will shook his head and then frowned. "Is that bad?"

"Sometimes frustrating. But no. We are only given remembrance of the people we are supposed to help or those who are to help us. Will crossed your path, Claire, as I have crossed yours, but Will and I . . . well, I can only assume my time in his life is short."

"I don't understand," Claire said.

"Remember I had thought you were your grandmother?" Levi's gloves asked without the emotion that was clearly on Levi's face. **"That I saw her young?"**

Claire nodded.

"But I met her much later in life when you were little. You had only visited my home a few times before your grandmother was-" Levi's fingers stopped signing abruptly and Levi's throat bobbed. **"All that matters now is that everything happened the way it was supposed to."**

Claire didn't understand what Levi was saying, not fully, but she had the inclination that soon, one of them would be sent to an institution, or worse, euthanized to free them of their 'insane misery'.

She glanced at the urn on the coffee table. "Did you see your wife before you met her?"

Levi patted his chest. **"My heart was searching for her long before I ever laid eyes on her. The soul never forgets."**

Claire's shoulder's slumped. "You only came because she passed. I'm sorry, I-"

"Don't be. It was her time. She's waiting for me Beyond the Veil and I'll be able to join her after I have finished my mission."

"What mission?" Will asked.

"The one that involves me teaching you everything you need to know about how to survive the end of this aeon."

COINCIDENCE

"WONDERING if you're going to wake up?" Will asked Claire as they waited for the elevator in the hotel lobby.

Claire rocked on her heels. "Yep."

"It's a lot to take in," Will said, feeling that it was.

Part of him was overwhelmed, but he was also relieved that he wasn't losing his mind. He hadn't left Levi's room as he had intended to. Exhausted or not, he had stayed, taking turns reading ten chapters of the book. That was until Levi yawned, and Claire offered to accompany him to release his wife's ashes that evening. Will agreed to join them at sunset and escorted Claire to the lobby.

When the elevator doors whispered open, Will gestured Claire to go in first. He pressed the number five on the screen and then asked Claire for her floor. When she told him "the same," Will stepped back. He crossed his arms and leaned against the cold steel wall, trying to mentally shrug off the coincidence. But it was becoming apparent that nothing was coincidental. At least, not when it concerned Claire.

Claire mirrored Will, staring at the screen as floors two and three lit up, before she asked, "Is that how this works? That everything seems like some sort of coincidence?"

"Seems that way, doesn't it?" Will answered.

At floor five, Will gestured for Claire to go ahead of him. She glanced over her shoulder as he walked behind her, then paused at room 505. Her mouth parted as she watched Will press his finger to the door next to hers. When his door lock lit green, she pressed her thumb to her own door lock. It lit green as well.

Claire tilted her head, wrinkling her face in what looked like suspicion. "Did you ask what room I was staying in?"

"No," Will admitted. "My friend booked it for me."

Claire's face smoothed. "Of course," she said with a light laugh before she drew an invisible line in the air as if it were a tally. "Another point for destiny."

Will let a smile form on his lips and entered his room as Claire's door shut.

Laying his shoulder bag on the dresser, Will fell onto the neatly made bed and let out a groan. He hadn't lied about being tired. The flight had been hard on him, not to mention all that had happened that day. He lay there, mentally and physically exhausted with his eyes closed, still trying to process all that he, Claire, and Levi had read.

According to *The Book of Aramis*, he, Alexander, had been a great warrior, a Guardian for the king. Claire, or Sophie, had been a Truth Keeper. Alexander had been sent to protect her from a fallen Seraph named Aalok. They had been caught between a war of truth and lies, and despite the impending apocalypse of the first aeon, Alexander and Sophie had fallen in love. And when they had stood on the shore as the wave came, they made their vows, praying that their souls would lead them back to one another again.

Soulmates. Did our souls lead us back together?

When Will's mind went through a replay of his life, he studied every major detail. He realized enlisting into the army had never been a choice, nor was coming back to his sick mother, or searching for Aven, or saving Claire.

Every choice, every path I took has led me here. Why? Why me?

Will didn't see himself as anyone special. If anything, he was someone with more flaws than he could count. More blood on his hands than he could stomach. In a way, he wondered if the path that had been laid out for him was a path to forgiveness.

Hours had passed before Will woke to a knocking at his door. When he opened it, he found no one standing in the hallway.

Another knock soon sounded on the door adjoining his to another room.

Will bit his lip, knowing who had been knocking on the other side of the door, but when he opened it, his heart stopped at the sight of the girl in the doorway.

"Hi," Claire said sheepishly.

Will's eyes roamed her off-the-shoulder dress. His fingers itched to touch her glowing tan skin, to trace the perfect lines in her collarbone leading up to the slender neck he wanted so badly to trail with soft kisses.

He met her eyes and whispered in his mind, *"You're a perfect portrait of delicate."*

"You look nice." Will smiled, remembering she had told him that in Vegas before the gala. "Really nice."

Claire patted the back of her braided bun as her cheeks became rosy.

"Thanks," she said and shied away, glancing at the clock on the nightstand behind her.

"Levi said at sunset," she reminded him, meeting Will's gaze again. "I know it's a bit early, but I wanted to see if you wanted to walk the beach before it gets crowded."

Will glanced at his watch, seeing the time. "I still have to change. I fell asleep when I got in the room. See you down there?"

"Sure," Claire nodded with a meek smile. "See you soon."

With a palm to her fluttering stomach, Claire gently shut her door and pressed her back against it. The cool metal felt good against her burning skin. It was Will's eyes that had this feverish effect on her. She had lost herself in them before their kiss. She couldn't get that moment out of her mind. She had thought about it when taking a shower, when picking out her dress, and even when putting on the makeup she hadn't intended to wear. She was disappointed they weren't walking down together. Will was always so closed off, so distant. Which reminded her of how Alexander was described in the book they had read only hours ago.

Is he the Guardian? Am I the Truth Keeper? Are we soulmates?

Claire wasn't sure. All she knew was that Will had rescued her in Vegas, and by some twist of fate, had come to Hawaii to find Levi too.

Maybe it wasn't a dream, after all. Maybe I've been having visions of this paradise. Maybe my soul led me here. And Levi...

When Claire grasped Levi's arm, it had been on instinct. Something deep within her gut had moved her, whispered in her heart to grasp his arm and not his hand. It had been real, all of it, but she still couldn't believe it. Not fully. Even with the vision of Levi and a foggy painted depiction of a crystal castle, Claire couldn't align her dreams with the plot points of the book. But there was still one face, one warrior in white that had always seemed to be in every single glimpse of her supposed past.

Even if the book was a work of fiction, even if she couldn't believe it completely, Claire could finally believe that everything did, in fact, happen for a reason.

SKY LANTERNS

MONDAY, 6:45 P.M.
OAHU, HAWAII

"ALOHA, Aunty!" a tan young man with dimples greeted. He offered Claire a pink plumeria.

"Mahalo," she said before sniffing its sweet fragrance and tucking the flower behind her ear.

The aromas of jasmine and gardenia lured Claire toward the shore and the people gathered there. They were writing on lanterns, scribbling their messages to loved ones who had gone Beyond the Veil. Claire wished she had bought one of the prayer boxes. There were so many loved ones she wanted to send a message to, so many apologies and thanks she had yet to offer.

She found Levi by the ocean's edge, hugging his wife's urn.

"Where's Will?" Claire asked.

Levi met her gaze with damp eyes, and Claire wondered if he had been crying. **"THERE,"**

Claire set her eyes on the setting sun, finding Will at the helm of a boat with royal blue sails coming to shore.

His hair was combed neatly; clearly damp from a fresh shower. His face was smooth, and she could smell his aftershave in the breeze as he got off the boat and greeted them.

"ALL ABOARD?" Levi's gloves asked.

"All aboard." Will smiled and helped Levi on deck.

A flush of heat flowed through Claire's body as Will took her hand and helped her on deck too. Nothing was said between them, at least not with words.

Claire watched Will turn the helm with ease. It was clear he knew how to sail, and she could only assume he had rented this boat for Levi to make the occasion special.

He's always so thoughtful. Mysterious but so beautiful and kind, and . . .

He was staring at her.

Claire's face flushed. She glanced over her shoulder to the crowd of people wading in the shallows near the shore. They had come from all over the world to gather, to send up their prayers to their gods. She wondered how many of them believed their loved ones were Beyond the Veil, if the prayers would rise from the smoke of the incense and whisper into the ears of unforgotten family and friends. As they lit their incense cones and placed them in boat lanterns, hope filled Claire's chest.

Someone tapped her shoulder.

"When Serena called me and said you were coming, she told me about your family," Levi's gloves said. **"I'm sorry. I know the grief of loss, for it is still very fresh in my mind."**

Claire wiped her tears and took Levi's offering. Turning the little box, she studied the paper-like windows, wondering what sort of textile was used for them. She forced a smile and placed her fingers, damp with tears, to her chin with a sign of thanks.

Sitting at the bow of the ship, Claire wrote her prayers. She scribbled an apology to her mother about the mortgage, thanked her for the best peach cobbler on earth, and for teaching her how to be a young woman of grace. In another window, she wrote a prayer to her brother, reminding him she would get him back for all the pranks he pulled when they were kids. She also wrote to her nephew, telling him she couldn't wait to see his sweet little face.

How old will you be when I see you again? You never had a full life. Would it have been good or one filled with pain? Maybe it was best you never got the chance to grow up on Earth. It's a horrible place right now. Well, Hawaii isn't, not with Will and Levi.

Tears poured down her cheeks as she wrote a note to her father, telling him she had made peace with Serena, that she would give him the biggest bear hug when they were reunited again. She then wrote a note to her GG, thanking her for the stories and telling her that she now knew why they were read to her.

When all four sides of the lantern were covered in biodegradable ink, Claire sniffled and set her gaze to the sunset—until she heard the squeak of a marker.

She looked behind her, seeing Will's bowed head and furrowed brows. When he glanced up, she thought he would shield the paper-like pane with his hand, but he didn't. He only wrote "Love, Big Brother," and then glanced up again with a small smile, snapping the cap onto his marker.

"Ready?" he asked Levi.

When a distant instrumental of guitars and ukuleles signaled the release of the lanterns, Levi nodded. He took the tiny incense cone Claire had lit for him, buried it an inch into his wife's ashes, and offered the lantern to Will, who placed it gently in the water along with the others.

When a choir of voices from the shore sang along to "Aloha Oe" in a slow and sad tempo, Claire couldn't help but let more tears fall and looked up to the sky.

More paper lanterns soared beneath the dark blue atmosphere. Claire let out a faint laugh watching the breathtaking sight. Between the orange glow on the water from the boat lanterns and the yellow dots floating to the heavens above, the ocean looked like a sea of stars.

A passage from *The Book of Aramis* about the ending of the first aeon came to her mind then, and she silently quoted a few lines as best she could.

He eyed the destruction of the earth below, and the void before him. He was the only light in existence, all but the stars of his slumbering children floating toward him.

Claire wondered for a split second which side of Paradise her family was on, if they were together. But she put her doubts aside and pictured them smiling down on her through the golden lamplight of offered prayers.

Will watched Claire admiring the lanterns. He too was letting himself feel pain and joy and reminded himself that one day he would be with his family again Beyond the Veil.

He'd been there several years ago, but only for a moment. He wouldn't fight death the next time it called him home. He would welcome it and hope that the second time he walked upon the sands of the Infinite Realm the Creator would allow him to stay.

Leaning against the helm with his arms crossed, Will eyed the buttercup hue against Claire's skin and her soft brown hair curling against her bare shoulder. He vowed to paint this moment when he returned home. When his artwork was finished, he would ask Claire over for dinner before presenting her with the depiction of this fond memory.

Claire looked over her shoulder and met his gaze with sparkling jade eyes. Even during this time of grief, she seemed at peace. When she smiled sweetly and mouthed "thank you," Will returned a "you're welcome," realizing in that instant that it wasn't him who saved her. Claire was the one who saved him. He hadn't been sent back because it wasn't his time to be with his family; he had been sent back to keep a promise to a Truth Keeper.

SAME SOULS

"SNEAKING away from your birthday party, I see," Kitten teased.

Aven looked over his shoulder and noted to himself how beautiful she looked in the unbirthday present he bought her last night.

He flicked the ashy nub of a cigarette over the balcony. "Something like that."

"You look bored," Kitten said as fireworks razzed into the sky.

"Just reminiscing."

"About?"

A smile tugged at Aven's lips. "Jumping off a balcony."

"The Memory Lapse."

"You know," Aven said, feigning curiosity, "I can't help but think that if Serus had heard Aerith say the words, everything could have been different."

"She was pouring her heart out and Serus still didn't get it. But you're right. Maybe if he had, she wouldn't have run into the hall and bumped into that bitch Jazrael before she died."

Aven's eyes narrowed with suspicion. "How do you know that name?"

"I had some weird dreams last night. Must have been those cookies."

"I took away your dreams," Aven reminded her.

"Maybe you unlocked them again. Which doesn't make sense. I was in your subconscious. Not mine."

"Maybe you'll dream about you and I—"

"I'm not Aerith, Aven. You're not Serus. Whoever we may have been—" Kitten put a hand to her forehead. "What am I even saying? This is us. Now. Not then."

"Different names. Same souls."

"Whoever we *might* have been, whatever we did, it's in the past. It doesn't matter."

Aven brushed back the waving strands of Kitten's long purple ombre hair. The color matched her mermaid gown perfectly. He smiled, pleased she was being herself no matter what Nick had asked her to do.

"It matters," Aven said softly. "We're soulmates."

"You don't know that."

"Why else would we be brought together? You're the only girl who's never been afraid of my demons."

"Only because you built a wall in my mind."

"Even the times before they haunted you, you stood by my side, fighting. You've carried the burden with me. You counter every weakness and vice versa. That's why we're so great together. That's why it's so easy."

"It's not even close to easy." Kitten huffed. "Which is why we need to talk about last night."

Last night. It had been one of the best unbirthdays yet. They had ridden around town, spending thousands of dollars on whatever their hearts desired. They ate a custom-made cake until they were sick and stopped at a dispensary for some very potent cookies labeled "Eat Me" to settle their stomachs. They had stayed up for hours until Kitten had fallen asleep in Aven's arms. It had been the perfect night.

"You mean about how you were cuddling me?" Aven said, wiggling his brows mischievously.

"I was restraining you," Kitten said with agitation. "You woke up screaming in some strange language. You reached for your gun, and when I saw your face—"

"What? What was wrong with my face?"

"Your eyes were black, Aven. I've never seen them black before."

"Nehia. She must have—"

"Possessed you? Yeah. I figured as much when you started counting, and I knew I had less than ten seconds to hide."

Hide and seek. Nehia's favorite game.

"I broke three nails fighting you off before your alarm sounded."

"Katharine," Aven said softly, cupping her face. "I would never hurt you. You know that."

"But Nehia would," Kitten drew back. "She's getting impatient, Aven, and so am I. You're not going to be happy. You may even hate me for a while, but–"

Aven tilted his head, studying Kitten's expression. She looked like a little girl afraid of getting scolded for a lie.

"What did you do?"

"Nick knew I was upset when he came to pick me up."

"Please," Aven said through his teeth, "tell me you didn't say anything to him."

"He showed me how to do the spell. I wanted to do it tonight, for you. For your birthday."

Aven's stomach plummeted. Kitten had been the one he confided in, and she had betrayed his trust. She conversed with his enemy, had plotted an attack.

"Why are you doing this to me?"

"Because I–"

"Because you love me?" Aven snapped. "Then say it. Say the words, and I'll let you do the spell."

"You know I can't say them."

"Because of your mother?"

"It's not that,"

"Because of my encounters?"

"Aven."

"My drinking problem?"

"Aven, stop."

"Tell me."

"I can't!" she shouted.

"And why not?" he shouted back.

"Because you're still in love with her!"

Aven took a step back. "Her who? There's no one else."

"Sophie. You were calling out her name last night between all the gibberish."

Aven wiped the corners of his mouth and put a hand on his hip. He nodded, knowing what it had been to push Kitten over the edge and into Nick's arms. "Claire. That's what this is about."

"Were things better when she was around?"

Aven let out a ragged breath. "I would be lying if I said no."

"You said she kept the demon away. Maybe she can still help you."

"The demon was toying with me. She wants to corrupt Claire, or worse, use my body to kill her."

"I have a feeling I'll be first."

"Kat."

Kitten's phone binged a notification. "Nick's looking for me."

"Of course he is,"

"I'll save you a dance. It is your birthday, after all."

As Kitten kissed him on the cheek, Aven kept a cold stare on the skyline. When the tapping of her heels faded, he hung his head. He was damned, cursed. He had chosen this in his past life. He had been too selfish, too full of pride to change. No one could save him. Not Kitten, not even Claire.

He hated the way Claire looked at him after his mother had died. Her eyes had been full of pity. That's how Kitten had looked at him before she walked away just now. The sympathetic stare had made him feel like he was a lost little boy again. But he wasn't a boy. He was a man housing a monster.

The devil in me. Always hungry. Always waiting.

He couldn't rid himself of Nehia. Ever. She was his curse, a demon *he* had conjured. He would spend his life alone until the last days, Persuading his way through his meaningless existence until death came for him. And that death, from what he saw in his dreams, wouldn't be too far off from today.

Broken glass. A pool of blood. Dim eyes staring.

A chill ran down his spine as he remembered the blood on his hands, the lifeless body, the pale face with dull eyes staring back at him.

Alex.

There was no getting rid of the images of the girl. They were forever burned in his memory. He let Claire go to save himself from seeing her like that. Maybe he would have to let Kitten go too. He wouldn't give Nehia the satisfaction of possessing another single soul. If she wanted true pleasure from his pain, she would have to kill him before he joined her in hell.

Watching the fireworks, Aven thought of that night in the garden with Claire, but the peaceful images fled at a pang of guilt. He wanted to tell her the truth. He wanted to explain he didn't hate her, that he hated himself. Gulping down his fear of rejection, he withdrew his phone from his pocket and stared at Claire's name.

A PRESENT

"HAPPY birthday,"

Aven clenched his teeth as Bree's voice slithered into his ear. He turned, finding a pillow of full perky breasts peeking out from the tight corset of her black evening gown. An animalistic desire swam through his veins as she dragged her nails across his five o' clock shadow. His body may have betrayed him, but his mind still stood firm. It didn't matter if she was the best lay he'd ever had. She repulsed him. Seven years ago he had made a deal with the devil, and here she was, standing before him, reminding him of his fuck up.

A plethora of dicks to choose from, yet she begs for mine with those lustful wandering eyes.

"It was until you showed up," Aven sneered.

"And to think I brought you a present," Bree cooed.

"I don't want any more gifts from you. The last one was enough." He turned his back on Bree and typed a message to Claire, only to delete it and type another.

"I doubt she'll get service where she's at."

"Who?"

"Why, your little saint of course." Bree closed her eyes and drew in a breath through her flaring nostrils. "Warm beaches, blue sails, orbs of light."

"Your minions are watching her?"

Bree opened her lazy eyes and gave a slow seductive nod.

"If that's so, then where is she?"

"Soul searching."

"For?"

"Answers."

Aven glared. "You should call them home to watch your back."

"Someone's tense," Bree teased. "Trouble sleeping?"

Aven took his glass of bourbon on the balcony ledge and threw back the drink. "No thanks to the last birthday gift you gave me."

"You're blaming your insomnia on me?"

"Is that what we call pillow talk with demons now?"

"Nehia wouldn't be so forceful if you would just give her what she wants. And what she wants is to give you all that you desire, all you seek to know."

"What is it that you want, Bree?" Aven asked, although he already knew the answer. Nehia had divulged such information to him years before he denied her possession. The truth was Bree had seen her future during Aven's initiation. That had never happened to an Oracle before. They could foresee possible futures for others but were never able to glimpse their own. Consummating Aven into the Circle had given her a preview of her demise. What had scared her most, what had made her so desperate to be in Aven's good graces, was that she saw her death would happen by his own hands.

"The question is what do you want?" Bree taunted.

Aven scrunched his brows, remembering her saying those exact words before. Not only the night he was "gifted" the succubus, but in another life, when his name was Serus. He raked his teeth across his tongue, trying to get the taste of ash out his mouth from the vivid vision before he said, "What I want is for you to take the whore back."

"Sorry." Bree shrugged. "There are no refunds on spirit guides."

"Surely there's some other miserable soul who would be delighted to have her. Someone more than willing to do all the vile things she takes pleasure in. "

"She has waited thousands upon thousands of years for you to arrive on Earth, Serus. There is no other soul she would rather be with."

"So what? Should I have some life-changing revelation then? Hm? Realize what a dick I was before? I know I deserve to be damned for my previous transgressions, but it seems a bit much to be tortured on my way to hell."

Bree licked her red-painted lips. "You look thirsty. Perhaps we should have another drink."

"You're right. I'm parched. Must be the dry conversation," Aven said and brushed past her.

"So then you don't want to see how she dies?"

Aven froze at the stab in his chest before he spun around. "I swear if you do anything to Katharine, I'll—"

"Not her."

"Claire?"

"She drowns tomorrow," Bree said as if it were nothing. "I thought, what better gift to give you for your birthday than the opportunity to save her."

"How generous of you," Aven mocked. "What's the catch?"

Bree closed the space between them and drew a fingernail from his lips down his throat. "I want you to make love to me like you did to your precious angel."

"I'd rather burn in hell."

"Oh, you will, but why not save the Truth Keeper first with your gifts, shall we say?"

"So Vincent told you."

"If she reads the book, you can save your precious Meager as well. Win, win."

"You've known about our heritage for quite some time now, haven't you? That's why you were chosen as the Oracle. A descendant of Zarak, is it? He's an interesting fellow."

"The truth of what I was destined to become was revealed to me as a child. And now, that knowledge has been revealed to you."

"And why did it take so long for this information to be disclosed?"

"Half-breeds don't get a free pass. Your loyalty had to be tested. Thanks to my and Vincent's and intervention, the Inner Circle approved of your joining."

"How gracious of you both to speak on my behalf."

"I believe a proper thank you is in order," Bree murmured, slipping her hands under Aven's suit jacket.

Aven took a step back. "You know the rules, Bree. No one touches the Circle's whore unless it's in approval for a séance or initiation. If one was to proceed in such an act, off with their head."

"No one has to know."

Aven rolled around the idea of sleeping with Bree.

An act. That's all it would be. It would mean nothing.

"If I give you what you want," Aven offered, "will you take back Nehia and the hellhounds?"

"If I'm convinced."

"Of what?"

"That you're still in love with her."

Aven wasn't sure if he was still in love with Claire. Not with these new feelings for Kitten, not with knowing she, as Aerith, had been true to him and him alone.

Aven had known so many different types of love. Friendship, unfamiliar, romantic, and with Claire, a love so deep, so filled with hope, that it had lasted through several millennia. But being away from her, Aven was unsure if he had been infatuated with her goodness, or if his past self couldn't let go of what had once been. What took only seconds felt like hours of debating in his mind, but it was made up.

Sleeping with Bree was his only chance of getting rid of Nehia. No matter how much he detested the spiteful wretch, he had to be free of the devils. After it was all over, after he was finally free, maybe then and then alone, could he have a life. A real life. He could give Kitten the future she deserved, the happily ever she had always wanted.

"Deal," Aven agreed.

Aven had been gentle with Bree when he first laid her in her bed. He trailed light kisses down her neck, forced his hands to sweep over every curve of her perfect body. But his lips never met her mouth, not like they had Claire's. He glanced at his watch when Bree closed her eyes and arched her back with each sweep of his circling tongue. It was almost time, and he was almost free. The foreplay had simply stalled the inevitable.

When he slipped inside Bree, he moved on her slow, gently, just as he had with Claire. But the moment Bree moaned, clawing at his flesh, Aven couldn't hold back his resentment any longer. He flipped Bree over, letting his fury pound against her backside, bruising her hips as his hands gripped them tight. He was ready for the act to be over, ready to be free of his own disgust.

He clenched his teeth, driving each stab deeper, harder, until he could feel her on the edge of blooming. She was there, seconds away from a dizzying fall, but he wasn't about to let her off that easy. He ignored his throbbing need to finish, jerking back a clump of her hair and saying into her ear with a heavy breath, "I'm done with you." Then he shoved her onto the bed as his watch chimed the early hour of dawn.

Bree stared at him for a moment with pitted black eyes. A clever grin replaced her irritation as Nehia skittered from her body into a plume of smoke. The demon lingered a moment, glaring at him with those same dead black eyes. But at a few words from Bree's lips, the succubus vanished like a vapor caught in the wind.

Immediate relief came as Aven exhaled. The weight of Nehia's presence was now gone. Somehow the world seemed a bit brighter, clearer, but accompanying that clarity was a smothering guilt.

"Do the spell," Aven demanded as he snatched up his clothes from the floor, along with a bottle of lighter fluid on Bree's nightstand.

"You're not going to hold me?" Bree asked.

"I gave you yours, now I want mine."

Before Bree could instruct him, Aven bent down on one knee, drawing the sacred circle. Bree, still without a stitch of clothing, stepped inside to join him. After several chants of an ancient mantra and a slash at her palm, the circle lit to flames.

Aven watched the fire rise until Bree clutched his skull and dug her nails into his temples.

A flash came and went all too quickly, but Aven knew he had seen it all before. He thought the dream he had several nights ago was just one of Nehia's many mind games. Now, he knew she had in fact been showing him the future, giving him a glimpse of what was to come.

In the dream, he saw Will holding Claire underwater. Bubbles blurred her face as her eyes shot open, and she gripped his arm, struggling to surface.

Aven gasped, breaking from the vision with wide eyes.

"You've seen this before," Bree said. "Just as you saw your death."

"Where is she?"

"You know where."

Aven blinked. He didn't ask how it was possible that he could see Claire's presence pinned in the form of a red thumbtack on a map. Knowing her location, he snatched his phone from Bree's nightstand and booked the first flight he could get to Oahu, Hawaii.

"If I find out you've sent any devils to haunt her," Aven said, swinging Bree's bedroom door open. "I won't be coming back to strike a deal. I'll be coming for blood."

"You really are in love with her."

"What's not to love?" Aven said. "She's everything you're not."

FIST FIGHT

HAVING the ability to see four times better than the average human had its advantages—especially from this distance. When Will found Claire several miles down the beach, he took off. Maybe he was showing off, maybe he wanted to see if he still had his super agility. He wasn't sure, but it felt good to pump his legs.

When he came up beside Claire, she slowed to a stop and took out her earbuds.

"Will," she panted.

"Hey," Will said with a steady breath. "You always go for a morning run?"

"Um, yeah." Claire shrugged, avoiding his gaze. "It clears my mind. You?"

"Levi knocked on my door at six forty-five. Apparently, there's a lot he wants to go over today."

"Okay. Sure. I just need to shower and change. Are you going to walk him down?"

"No. The staff assured me they would help him to breakfast."

"Oh," Claire said. "Okay. Good."

Will watched her mouth part, shut, and then her gaze travel to the ocean. "Do you dream about me?"

Will raised a brow at her inquisition.

"I mean did you used to? Have you ever—because I dreamed about you long before we met," Claire said all too quickly. "I mean, not you. Alexander, at least I think."

She's been dreaming about our past?

"I mean, did you ever dream about Sophie before reading the book?" Claire restated.

Will crossed his arms. He couldn't say it outright. Not yet. "You saw my sketches," he said.

"I'm sorry." Claire scrunched her nose. "I couldn't help but look. But that's why I'm asking. I'm just trying to understand how this works."

Will licked his lips and looked over Claire's shoulder. "When I was in the war, I often dreamed of an angel. The dreams stuck with me after I got home. I still sketch her out of habit when I can't sleep. As crazy as it sounds, yeah. I'm starting to think I was dreaming about Sophie."

"That's why I kissed you. I mean—" Claire put a hand to her forehead. "I thought I was kissing Alexander. Jeez. This is *not* coming out right." Claire took a breath and slowed her words. "On my birthday, every year, I have this dream that I'm kissing this warrior in white; everything goes dark, and there's this enormous wave coming to swallow us. I'm always so afraid, but he's holding me, telling me to be strong. I'm staring into his gorgeous blue eyes and then this light comes, and it keeps getting brighter and brighter as the wave towers over us. And then, nothing. I wake up."

"That's why you pulled away," Will said, not a question but a statement.

"It's not that you weren't a good kisser. It wasn't you, it's—"

"It's not you, it's me?" Will chuckled.

"Yes. I mean, no." Claire placed a hand over her eyes. "I'm sorry. You're in a relationship."

"I'm not."

Claire's hand dropped. "But I thought—so the girl at 1919 isn't your girlfriend?"

"She hasn't been for a while now," Will said. "I broke up with Hannah before I went into the war. She's married."

"That's a relief. Not that you broke up with her and that she's married, but that I didn't cross a line. Not that I did."

"Claire." Will held back a smile. "You don't have to explain yourself."

"I know. It's just strange. Being here with you, in this place. It's almost like, I'm two different people now. If I *were* Sophie, and you *were* Alexander, and they were in—" She cut her words short and dared to look at Will.

"Love?" he said, finishing her sentence.

"Then," Claire said drawing out the word, "that would mean I have her past-life emotions or something, right?" Claire shook her head, staring off at the ocean. "It's like I'm living in some alternate reality."

It did sound crazy, but to Will, it also made perfect sense. He crossed his arms and glanced up. "If I told you the sky wasn't blue, would you believe me?"

"What does this have to do with anything?"

"Physics,"

Claire groaned. "I failed physics. I don't know. Something to do with sunlight?"

"The sky is a stage upon which all the colors dance," Will explained. "Light from the sun enters into Earth's atmosphere. The different colored wavelengths making up that light start bumping up against the air and"–Will wiggled his fingers–"'dance' differently. We see it blue most of the time because that color scatters the most and in smaller waves."

"Someone's a science geek," Claire teased playfully.

Will smiled brightly. "I wanted to be an astronaut."

"Like, go help colonize Mars and all that?"

"Yep."

"Why didn't you go to college?"

Will grimaced and looked down at the sand.

"Right. The draft," Claire cleared her throat. "The sky isn't blue. Got it. Next question," she said, bringing back their previous conversation.

"Why do you think we see it blue?" Will asked.

Claire lifted her shoulders. "Optical illusion?"

"You took art."

"I wasn't very good, but passed with flying colors,"

"Nice pun."

"Thank you,"

"So then you know that it's possible to sketch a picture that looks three dimensional."

"Sure,"

"So that means, reality is all about one's perception. The one who knows how to sketch the lines sees it for what it is, but someone else looking at it that knows nothing about drawing would see otherwise."

Claire stared at Will a long moment. "You make it sound so simple."

"That's because it is."

Claire shook her head and smiled, but that smile fell the instant she looked at the hotel.

Will watched the color drain from her face. "Claire?"

"This is going to sound crazy," she said, "but I think I see an optical illusion of Aven sitting on one of the hotel beach chairs."

"Hello, gorgeous," Aven greeted with his charming voice. "Sorry to break up this little moment you two seem to be having."

Anger and jealousy swarmed like yellow jackets in Will's chest.

"Did you tell him we were here?" he asked, trying to keep his composure.

"She didn't," Aven answered, slipping off his sunglasses and walking toward them. "Wouldn't answer my calls, actually."

"What are you doing here?" Claire demanded.

"I need to talk to you." His eyes darted to Will and then back to Claire. "In private."

"You owe Will an apology," Claire snapped.

"I owe you one first," Aven said softly, taking her hand.

"Don't." Claire curled into herself. "I don't want to hear it. I just want you to leave."

Will stepped between Aven and Claire. "Go tell Levi I'm going to be a little late to breakfast," he said, never taking his eyes off Aven.

Aven let out a long sigh. "Must you always be in the way?"

"Go," Will insisted.

"I didn't want to have to do this," Aven warned.

"Do what?" Will asked with suspicion.

Aven's lips quirked. "I promise I mean no harm."

Claire fell like a rag doll onto the wet sand of the shore.

"Claire." Will fell to his knees and cradled her in his arms, checking her over. "Claire?"

She has a pulse. She's breathing.

"She won't wake," Aven said.

"What the hell did you do to her?" Will bit out.

Aven lifted his chin. "I didn't come here for a fight, brother."

"No. You just came to toy with Claire." Will slipped her out from his arms and jumped to his feet, getting in Aven's face. "Undo whatever you did, you son of a bitch."

"Dear little brother." Aven tsked. "Is that any way to talk about our deceased mother?"

Will shot out a fist, but Aven caught his white knuckles like a wicked curveball.

Aven gave a smug smile and unfolded his fingers, one by one. "I went easy on you the last time," he teased.

"So did I," Will said and swung another fist. It missed, but his other made direct contact with Aven's jaw.

Aven stumbled onto his back.

Will straddled over him, aiming to crook Aven's perfect nose.

Aven jerked his head to the side.

Will's knuckles cracked in the sand by his ear.

Aven slapped Will's cheek. "Missed!" he taunted.

Will growled and grabbed a fistful of Aven's suit. He drew back his elbow, ready to knock the joker out cold.

A cool smack met Claire's face. She blinked the saltwater from her eyes and looked up to see a little boy standing over her and holding a pail. While the little boy ran off giggling, Claire rubbed her eyes with the back of her hand, trying not to get sand in them. She was woozy, drunk, but she could see Will sitting on Aven, and she knew they weren't horsing around.

"Will! Stop!" she shouted.

Will shoved himself off of Aven and came to her side.

"Are you okay?" he asked, looking her over.

"I'm fine," Claire said, combing back loose wet strands of her hair. She brushed past Will, but he grabbed her arm. He seemed hurt by the way he winced, but the longer she held his gaze, the more she wondered if it was his heart aching and not his face.

"Let me deal with Aven," she said softly.

Will lingered a moment, glaring at Aven over her shoulder before he headed toward the hotel without further objection.

Claire didn't know what had happened while she was out but could only assume Aven had poked the animal in Will. It never ventured out around Claire but often bared its teeth at Aven's ego.

"I just bought this yesterday," Aven whined, brushing off the sand from his suit.

"Why are you here?" Claire demanded.

"Oh you know, enjoying the scenery." Aven smirked, slipping his hands into his pockets. His eyes roamed her body, and Claire couldn't deny how her heart fluttered at his playful smile. He appeared more handsome than she remembered, and she halfway wondered if this had all been a dream after all.

"I'm serious," she said, crossing her arms.

"I have an estate here."

"In Oahu."

Aven nodded. "About two miles from here. You ran past my house this morning."

"I don't believe you."

"I didn't believe me either. I thought I was losing my head."

"So what? You saw me on the beach. It doesn't explain how you found me. Here. In this *exact* location."

"You tagged this hotel when you posted photos online yesterday."

"You're stalking my social media?"

"It's hardly stalking when it's public information, Princess," Aven declared.

Claire didn't understand why he was so undeniably amused. It irritated her. Immensely. "Why are you acting like this?"

Aven tilted his head. "Like what?"

"Like you weren't a complete jerk the last time I saw you."

"Well, I can't be a jerk if I'm about to apologize, now can I?" He bared his charming smile.

"Well, I don't need your apology," Claire spat. "Because I'm over you and all of your manipulating narcissism."

A clever smile curled Aven's lips. "You don't mean that."

"I do. And to prove it, when I get home, I'm filing a restraining order."

"Well"—the smile on Aven's face widened as he slipped on his sunglasses—"you're not home yet. Are you, gorgeous?"

Now Claire knew why Will had been on top of Aven. The man was infuriating with his witty remarks and perfect face she wanted to punch. But she couldn't, because Aven was already halfway to the boardwalk before she realized he had walked off.

THE PROPHECY

'SORRY,' Claire mouthed to Levi, circling a palm over her chest. She shot a glance at Will as she sat at their table.

He scowled at the table screen, swiping his fingers across it. Seeing the game of checkers displayed, Claire assumed Levi and Will had been playing to occupy their time waiting on her.

"I'm sorry about Aven," Claire said to Will.

Will didn't glance up. "How'd he find you?"

Claire swallowed the knot in her throat. "He saw the pictures I posted yesterday." She turned off the location option on her phone. "He saw me running this morning. Said he has a place a few miles down the beach."

"How did he make you faint?" Will asked, still glaring at the table screen.

"Faint? I didn't. He–"

"Put you under a spell?" Will asked, narrowing his gaze on the screen.

Claire glanced at Levi, knowing he didn't have a clue what they were talking about.

"When I was in Vegas," Claire began, "he offered to cure me of my fear of heights. I let him do hypnosis on me. I gave him my permission to use a keyword to put me under. 'I promise.' It's the keyword."

"So now he can render you unconscious whenever he wants?" Will asked. His tone was more of a reprimand than a question.

"I never thought he would use it like that," she admitted.

Will's hard eyes met hers. "But he did."

Defense washed over Claire. "Are you mad at me?"

Will let out a sigh as the table screen blinked "You Lose." "No." He leaned back in his chair with his arms crossed. "Not at you."

Claire glanced at Levi again. "Ex-boyfriend", she explained with her fingers.

Levi lifted his brows. "I see,"

Just in time to break the uncomfortable silence, the waiter came by. He took their orders and informed them of a luau dinner event. Claire and Will agreed to accompany Levi, ate their breakfast, and after, headed to Levi's room to study more of *The Book of Aramis* with no more talk about Aven Crey.

"And you shall be brought before governors and kings for my sake," Levi's gloves said as he read, "for a testimony against the workers of darkness, so that you shall stand before their master and allow me to give you the words that you shall speak to the nations. Only after these things will I return."

Claire carefully re-read the last line Levi stopped at, noting all of these words were in blue, making it known they were Aramis'. This had been a warning from His own mouth.

"So Aalok," Claire said shifting on the couch, "he's coming before Aramis?"

Levi nodded his fist and his glove replied, **"yes"** in its monotone robotic reverb.

"How will we know he's here?" Will asked, leaning on his elbows in the chair across from them.

"There will be no question. It will be broadcast throughout the world."

"Will there be any warnings? Besides the earthquakes and rumors of wars?" Claire asked.

"Many. I call them benchmarks. They are much like markers on a timeline. You get a preview or glimpse of them from your dreams or personal visions. Some may have already come to pass."

"How do we know when we see them?" Will asked.

"They stick with you. You can see them so very clearly, so vividly," Levi signed with emphasis. **"Scientists call it déjà vu. But no one can understand the way Aramis works. He is, after all, the Creator. So the world makes up reasons, explanations of these supernatural anomalies to make them feel more comfortable. To make them believe they have all the answers to the workings of our complex minds."**

Claire and Will remained silent trying to process everything they had gone over the past few days.

"Any more questions? This is the last opportunity to ask."

Claire pointed to a word in her book. "What's the millennium?"

"The thousand-year reign of Aramis on Earth before the final judgment. It's a time for teaching souls. The Creator is making sure all have a chance to choose a side without Aalok's lies and confusion. The Truth Keepers will have the opportunity to counsel during that time."

Will asked, "How will we know when Aramis has returned?

"If you feel yourself being convinced, pinch yourself," Levi motioned to his arm.

"Like literally?" Claire asked.

"We shed this skin and get our immortal bodies back when Aramis breaks the dimensional veil."

"What about our friends?" Will asked. "Can we warn them?"

"You can counter any attack, any lies with the Word of Aramis, but you cannot counter Aalok himself." Levi's fingers moved furiously. "If your friends are already convinced of his lies, no one can change their minds. As it is written, the world will beg for you to repent, to worship Aalok as the Creator. They won't know what they are doing. They will be blinded with wool over their eyes."

"How do you know it's us?" Claire questioned. "That we're the ones to do this?"

"I don't. Only your souls do. Your destiny calls from deep within you. You have felt it, ever since you were a child, and even more so during those close calls you've encountered."

"You've had some close calls, then?" Will asked.

Levi touched the scar on his throat and looked at Will. **"You know what war is like."** He then looked at Claire. **"And you almost died in a fire. Beating those kinds of odds has nothing to do with luck. But it has everything to do with purpose."**

Claire pressed her lips and then asked, "Will you be in line with us when we're brought to Aalok?"

Levi grimaced. **"I don't believe it is Aramis' will that I stand against him."**

Claire frowned. "Why not?"

"Just a hunch. But I'm grateful to be the captain of a ship, sailing you two toward your first destination. Soon, it will be time for you to take the helm."

When Levi gave an exaggerated yawn, Claire took it as a sign that he was done for the day. She and Will had learned so much, probed Levi again and again about the end and their part in it. The rest of her questions could be answered tonight at the luau.

"We'll let you rest," she said.

"You two should go check out the island. Perhaps the sight will spark memories that have yet to surface."

Will and Claire walked out of the hotel lobby into the breezeway. The tension from breakfast had dissolved completely. Everything in their life seemed so insignificant compared to what they had read, what they were destined to do. Nothing else mattered to them, nothing but the future and this time together—right here, right now.

"So," Will said, crossing his arms. He leaned against a column and stared at the ocean view.

"So," Claire said back.

"Have you ever steered a boat?"

A grin formed on Claire's lips. "Nope."

"Would you like to?"

"And where will we sail?"

When a breeze ruffled his hair, Will looked up to the sky, taking it as a sign from Aramis himself. "Wherever the wind takes us."

THE LEAP

TUESDAY, 2:00 P.M.
OAHU, HAWAII

CLAIRE tried to ignore the ache in her calves as she pointed her toes, keeping her legs together to steady her sketchbook. She and Will had hiked up and down the Hawaiian mountain trails for hours in search of a waterfall. They never found one. They knew from the book that there had been a secret spring. But even using an app with the map of Hawaii's most famous tourist spots, they couldn't access any of these places without a tour guide.

They settled back down on the sailboat to rest for lunch. After they finished eating, Will handed Claire a sketchbook from his bag. He asked her to draw what she thought Alexander might have looked like and told her he would sketch Sophie.

Drawing had never been one of Claire's strong suits. She knew by seeing Will's paintings in the attic studio that he was going to make a detailed drawing. With time ticking away she scribbled the warrior as best as she could.

"Time," Will called as a notification sounded on his phone.

Claire wrinkled her nose at her depiction. Alexander's face was all wrong; his strong jaw, his hooded eyes didn't resemble her memory. Even with Will sitting next to her, she hadn't been able to get the warrior's features right.

"You go first," she offered.

Will cracked a smile and gave a curt nod. "On three."

"One . . . two . . .," Claire and Will said in unison and both flipped their spiral sketchbooks. "Three."

Claire's mouth parted the moment she set her eyes on Will's drawing. Waving strands of the girl's hair caressed her soft features. They brushed across her lips, circling along the bare shoulder she was looking over. It wasn't the detail in the girl's glittering gown or how Will had captured the misty waterfall backdrop. It was the girl's eyes. They were so sad, so unbelievably real.

Will chuckled. "Is that a banana?"

Claire covered the scribbled sword with her hand. "I told you I'm terrible at this." She glanced at the smudges of pencil dust on his fingers. "But you."

She wondered if Will had fallen in love with Sophie because of the way he'd drawn her. It was the way he held the pencil, how he had let the pressure of his fingers press softly, shading the graphite of her delicate skin as if he had once touched it before.

"It's beautiful," Claire said, then pointed to the glow around the girl. "You drew her aura as well. What color was it?"

"It changed with each dream," Will said. "Sometimes it was white, but in one—" he paused.

Claire thought about Sophie and Alexander's moment in the starlit cave with the luminescent glowworms. Sophie's light had been dim because of her sadness, but she soon glowed with Alexander's kiss.

"It was blue?" she asked, somehow knowing that's what he was going to say.

Will nodded to confirm her assumption.

"I wish we could still see them," Claire admitted.

"Auras?"

Claire gave a slow nod.

According to the book, auras had once been a tell-all of emotions. Not only could one see them, but they could also feel them. They weren't like facial expressions and gestures. Even those were not so telling. At least, that's what Claire thought when she looked at Will. She could never tell if he was in deep thought or bored with irritation. But if it were true, if Will was Alexander incarnate, it made sense why he was always brooding and why she felt the way she did about him.

She thought about the chapter of *The Book of Aramis* that spoke of the cave of starlight. Claire had never dreamed of it, but reading about the scene, the moment of Alexander and Sophie's kiss, Claire's chest warmed. Alexander had held back from telling Sophie how much he loved her. He had been so selfless, so righteous, and Claire could see those same qualities reflect in the light of Will's blue eyes. Yes. It was hard to tell by his mixed facial expressions what he felt, but somewhere hidden in that hard stare was the truth, and Claire was dying for Will to speak it.

"Will," she began, tucking the hair behind her ear as he stood. "About our ki–"

Claire stopped her sentence abruptly as Will peeled his white T-shirt from his toned torso.

"Going for a swim?" she asked, feigning nonchalance.

Will glanced over his shoulder. "Take off your clothes."

Heat flushed Claire's cheeks, setting them on fire. Her stomach fluttered. Her heart sped up to an alarming rate. "Everything?" she asked.

Will let out a laugh. "Not unless you want to get a fine for skinny dipping. It's up to you, but I'd rather you not get a sunburn, you know"–he glanced at her chest–"there."

It was a reaction to cover her chest, but she knew Will hadn't been serious. She followed his gaze to the black cliff in the Waimea Bay. She had seen the diving attraction while researching "things to do in Oahu" on her phone during her flight.

Sophie and Alexander had jumped from the cliff of a waterfall. Since she and Will had never found a waterfall, Claire could only assume Will thought it was the perfect opportunity to relive that moment. As he dove into the water, the air rushed from Claire's lungs. She watched the way his shoulders and back muscles tightened and couldn't help but wonder what it would be like to smooth her hands over his hard body.

She then thought about her reason for running this morning. It hadn't only been because of Aven's text messages. It had also been because of an erotic dream, and Aven hadn't been in it. Will had. He'd been on top of her, kissing her with that deep urgency like he had when she'd thought he was a dream.

Claire blinked from her thoughts and found that Will was halfway to the black rock. Remembering Alexander had told Sophie she was slow at swimming, Claire hurried to take off her shirt and shorts, stepped up on the boat, and jumped, exerting herself to catch up to Will.

When she tagged the rock, Will helped her onto its base before they climbed to the plateau. They stood at the edge, setting their gazes on the sunset and the bay, empty of any tourists. Claire peered over the edge, recalling a yellow sign on the shore and glaring a warning that diving or jumping off this cliff could cause "SERIOUS BODILY INJURY OR DEATH," and for their own safety that they should "STAY OFF THE ROCK."

Claire's breaths came short with panic.

We're breaking the rules. What if one of us gets hurt? I don't have a phone on me. What if—

"They were much higher up than this," Will said, "about two hundred feet."

Claire tried not to look at his rippling torso. She feared another dizzying rush would return, and she'd tip over the ledge. "You remember?" she asked, keeping her voice steady.

Will gave a playful grin. "This is only about thirty."

"You go first," Claire told him and took a step back.

Will aligned his heels with the edge of the cliff. "See you at the bottom,"

The echo of Alexander's words replayed in Claire's mind, and she watched Will copy the exact way Alexander had bent his knees, winked, and jumped backward.

It seemed so effortless how he flipped in the air, how he pointed his toes and punctured the water like a spear.

"Claire," he called after he surfaced, flicking his hair against his forehead. He gestured with a hand for her to join him.

"Did you see anything?" she shouted.

"Jump."

"I don't think I can."

Will swam with ease around the cliff, and Claire waited for him to climb the rock again and come to a stand, dripping wet, in front of her.

She stared at the droplets glistening in the sunlight as they trickled down his defined chest; how his stomach muscles tightened against his ribs with each breath.

"Your turn," he said.

"What if I hit the rocks?"

"You won't."

"How can you be sure?"

"Deep breath," Will instructed, placing his hands around her hips.

Claire gulped as he nudged her to the edge. Every time he touched her, every time he was this close her heart felt like it was going to burst. When he slipped his fingers away, she forced herself not to lean back to feel his chest against her back. She drew in a ragged breath and closed her eyes until she felt a tickle of warmth by her ear.

"Faith, Claire. Take the leap," Will whispered.

"You did see something," she said, whipping around. She wobbled, flailing her arms to regain her balance.

Will wrapped an arm around her waist and laughed. "Maybe," he said and laced their fingers. "Together. On three. One."

At his gentle squeeze, Claire's heart raced faster.

"Two."

He gripped her hand tighter, making it known he wasn't letting go.

"Three!"

Claire's pounding heart leaped into her throat as Will tugged. She stifled a squeal by holding her breath and focused on the wind rushing over her body. Her feet hitting the water had been the trigger; the whoosh of the ocean in her ears had been the catalyst. Every chapter, every verse spoken in *The Book of Aramis* rang clear. It wasn't just a flash of blurry images she had seen these past twenty-three years, but a total recall of a Truth Keeper, a princess, and daughter of the one true king.

CUTTING IN

IT was strange to see the details from a story come to life in Claire's mind. They didn't seem like some story from a book anymore, but memories, her memories. They were vibrant, filled with intense emotions. They were Sophie's emotions, but now Claire knew for sure they had been her emotions too.

The cliff diving had done that. Somehow, it had washed away the fog that had once been a black splotch of doubt covering the pages of her mind. Her heart was now filled with purpose, a calling. Her calling.

When dusk set in, Will sailed them back to the hotel. Claire showered, slipped into her favorite spaghetti-strap dress, and decorated her braided hair in fresh fragrant flowers. It was the last night before her flight home, the last chance to ask Levi her questions, and the last chance to tell Will how she felt about him before they said their goodbyes.

Not goodbye. It's only farewell for a little while.

She would see Will and visit Snow when she returned home. Levi didn't live far. She could drive to see him anytime she wanted. They could continue their lessons. They could keep reading the book, preparing for Aalok's arrival. Together.

Claire had taken comfort in that while she walked past the white linen-covered tables and chairs of the hotel lawn. But the moment she met Levi's tired eyes, she realized he had been saying his goodbyes all along. His time was short in Will's life and perhaps hers as well.

"Excuse me, miss?"

Claire glanced up at the man beside her and almost gasped. At first, she thought it was Aven, but this man who looked like his twin was somehow much more handsome.

His hair was jet black like Aven's, but longer. It kissed his broad shoulders, and curling beneath that perfect jaw were tips of it in white. Claire would have thought it strange, but then again, everyone dyed their hair in an array of stylish colors. She stared into his deep brown eyes. Somehow, they seemed more of a deep red, crimson even. They almost didn't seem real. Nothing about him seemed real, and for a moment she thought she was imagining him.

"I'm sorry to bother you," he said in a deep and mesmerizing voice. "But have you seen my grandson? He's about your age, perhaps a few years older."

Grandson? This man didn't look a day over thirty.

"He's lost," the man continued. "Perhaps you can help me find him?"

"I'm sorry," Claire stuttered. "How old did you say he was?"

"Claire?"

Claire turned to her other side, finding Will glaring a warning at the stranger.

The handsome man's lips molded into a crooked smile, and he held Will's stare for a few heartbeats before he bowed his head. "I apologize. You were about to join the festivities." He then fixed his gaze on Claire. "I'm sure he's nearby. Thank you for your time, my lady."

Claire watched the stranger slip his hands into his pockets, and in an Aven-like fashion, sashay confidently to the bar.

"That guy lost?" Will asked, crossing his arms.

"No," Claire answered with a heavy heart. "But I think his grandson is."

Claire didn't say much during dinner. No one did. They were all too busy watching the hula girls bounce their hips while the bare-chested fire jugglers flipped their flaming sticks. When coffee arrived after dessert, Claire leaned an elbow on the table and gazed across the lawn at the ocean. She watched the waves and the neon blue lights trailing across thinking of the starlit cave.

Pulsating lights. Soft lips. A warm embrace.

"You've been quiet,"

Claire blinked free of her daydream and forced a smile for Levi. "A first right? I'm processing every thing we went over today,"

"On the way down here, Will and I talked about one of his visions. It aligns with the end of the book."

Claire leaned in.

Will whispered, "I've had them before, but they were scattered. It wasn't until this afternoon that they came in clear."

"What was it of?"

"Two suns that brought nothing but darkness," Will said and then signed, "Somehow I knew Aalok came after that."

Claire looked at Levi. "How is he able to see the future?"

"The possible outcome of our lives was recorded by Aramis," Levi answered. "When we were placed in the flesh, he downloaded each possible outcome and locked it away. It's a bit like TV shows today. The fate of the characters is decided at the click of the button. Each choice takes you to a different scenario. As viewers, we know which path the storyteller wants us to take, how to get the best ending, but not all of us choose what the storyteller wants. We wish to have our own unexpected ending."

"And if we choose wrong?" Will asked out loud.

"You haven't yet," Levi signed. "On instinct, you follow his lead. Us Truth Keepers can't seem to help but let Aramis decide for us. For everyone else in the world, it's a guessing game."

"You said we could refuse Aramis to speak through us," Claire signed. "What happens if we do?"

Levi shook his head. "You won't. After the verbal beating you'll endure, you'll be more than willing to have him take over."

"Ladies and Gentlemen!" a man on stage said into a microphone. "If you will please gather near the breezeway, we will move the tables to the side and put down the dance floor. Please enjoy the open bar as you wait."

As Claire helped Levi stand to the side, Will went to the open bar. Seeing him grab a bottle of beer, she thought back to that rainy night they had gone to retrieve the Mustang, the bet of darts, and Aven's jab at Will about Alcoholics Anonymous.

"Mahalo for your patience," the announcer said. "You may return to your numbered table, unless that is, you care to dance."

"Joshua," Claire said, watching the staff work.

Levi met her eyes at the name.

"It was His name when He was human."

"Yes,"

"Why didn't He tell his friends to call him by his true name?"

Levi pressed his ring finger to his gloved palm and signed. "He has many names."

Claire chewed on her bottom lip. "But if he has so many names, how do I know I'm using the right one when I pray—"

"Prayer is about intent."

Claire remembered Aven saying something very similar in the bakery the night they were together.

"You don't have to say the name out loud," Levi continued. "He knows what's in your heart, what you're thinking."

"Does Aalok? Can he read my mind?"

Levi shook his head no with a comforting smile.

When the tables were moved, a slow song came on. Couples put their drinks on their tables and went arm in arm to the dance floor.

Claire watched them for a moment before she peered up at Levi. His lashes were damp, and his lip quivered slightly.

When his throat bobbed, Claire gently put a hand on his arm and signed with her other. "Are you alright?"

He sniffed, but that was the only sound he made. She knew if he had been able to talk, his voice would have cracked.

"This was my and Ann's song,"

"Maybe somehow she made sure they played it to let you know she's thinking of you."

Levi's shoulder bounced, but no sound came with the light laugh. "Not a coincidence?"

"I don't believe in coincidences." Claire smiled. " I believe in truth."

Levi gave a proud smile.

"Would you like to dance with me?" Claire asked, glancing at the dance floor. "I'll go slow."

Levi didn't bother getting his cane. Instead, he pointed to his chest, tapped his temple, and then put his thumbs together, moving them forward and back. "I think I can keep up."

Claire grinned wide at Levi's humor and let him escort her to the dance floor.

Levi and Claire swayed left to right a few times before she said, "I was reading last night about the TKs, the ones who wrote the words after He was—" She stabbed a finger in the air.

Levi nodded, showing Claire he clearly understood that TK stood for Truth Keepers and the jab in the air stood for murder.

"Let me know if I get this right," she went on. "So the ceremony is for one to dedicate themselves to the service of Him; it symbolizes how He was plunged under?"

Levi nodded.

Claire cringed at how it had been done. After Aramis had been arrested for his zealous teachings, he was sentenced to death. They had bound him in weights and slit his wrist before they dumped his body from a boat. Aramis sunk into a dark, bleeding out into an endless void of the sea.

A slow death. It must have been painful, terrifying.

Claire had never drowned before, but she had taken in water a few times at the pool as a kid. She had never forgotten the way her chest burned. She couldn't imagine looking up to the ocean's surface, knowing there was no way to reach it.

"During the ceremony," she said, "those gathered to recognize the TK's dedication would mask the light of the sun by huddling around the initiate. They were recreating the darkness, making it like the watery tomb He was sent to. They counted to three, symbolizing three days he was in the water.

"Then they would step back and raise the TK, who would open their eyes to the light shining on their face, a symbol of what they saw when He walked on the water to come and stand before them when he rose again."

Levi nodded.

"If I were to ask to dedicate my life to Him, would you witness it? Would you say the words?"

Levi took a step back as the song ended. "I'm not strong enough to dunk you or pull you up from the water, but if Will agrees to hold you down and raise you up, I'll say the words."

Claire glanced at Will.

He stood against a support beam at the breezeway with a bottle of water in his hand.

She smiled.

He smiled back.

"I'll ask him," she assured Levi.

"Sunrise. You can both meet me on the shore."

Claire hugged Levi's neck and helped him to the breezeway as an announcement came from the stage.

"Now if we can just have the couples on the dance floor. You newlyweds, you love birds."

"I'll get you a bottle of water," she offered, but Levi didn't let go of her arm.

"Will?"

"Sir?" Will lifted his brows, giving Levi his full attention.

"You should ask this beautiful young lady to dance. She's excellent on her feet."

"Someone needs to help you back to the table," Claire objected, a bit panicked at the thought of dancing with Will. She didn't know why she was anxious. It was only a dance.

"Mr. Robinson," one of the hula girls said sweetly, "would you like some assistance?"

Levi lifted his brows with a boyish grin plastered on his face. **"Yes, thank you,"**

As Levi was escorted to their table, Will tried to hide a shy smile as he offered his hand. He seemed nervous, timid even, as he placed his hand at the small of her back, keeping a proper distance on the dance floor.

"I'm a bit out of practice," he told her.

"Would you like me to lead?" Claire teased.

"If I start stepping on your toes, you can take over."

While dancing in a circle with Will, Claire gazed at the sea of people around them. She wondered if they were soulmates, if all of them had somehow found one another in this life by the hand of fate. It was the question she'd had about Will since reading the book, since finding out they had been destined to find one another. Not only that. It was the promise Alexander made to Sophie.

"I'll never stop looking,"

"This place," Claire began, "everything that's happened. It's all been so perfect. I'm afraid when I go home, I'll . . ."

Claire's voice trailed off. She didn't want to believe she was dreaming. She wanted this to be real, all of it, but doubt crept in again. It was the fear of going home to an empty house, realizing her family was gone and that she was alone. Somehow, she could tell Will knew what she was thinking. It was in the way his lips turned up, how his eyes went soft.

"The thing about taking that leap of faith, Claire," he said, "is you have to believe you'll make it to the other side."

Claire's heart fluttered as he pulled her in close, pressing his cheek to hers. He smelled wonderful, like a clean load of laundry hanging out to dry in a wood of pines.

"You believe wholeheartedly, don't you?" she asked.

"I have no reason not to. Everything has led me to where I need to be." He drew back and fixed his gaze on hers. "It led me to you."

He leaned in, and she wondered if he was going to kiss her, but to her disappointment, he didn't.

He pulled her in close and pressed his cheek to hers. "You should come by and see Snow. He's been looking for you."

"Has he been restless?"

"About as restless as I was when you left."

They danced for a few thudding heartbeats until Claire couldn't hold back her question about the beer any longer.

"Can I ask you something?"

"Anything."

"When we were at 1919, Aven mentioned you went to Alcoholics Anonymous. How long have you been sober? I mean, besides the bet for the keys to the Mustang."

Will pulled back. His face was hard as he stared at her.

"I'm sorry." Claire mumbled. "I didn't mean to overstep."

"Claire, there's a lot of things you don't know about me. Things I haven't told anyone."

"Does it have to do with the war?"

Will's throat bobbed.

"I won't judge you for your past. You did what you had to do."

"It wasn't a fair fight."

"What do you mean?"

"Did you notice the logo on Levi's gloves?"

Claire nodded.

Will's throat bobbed, and it seemed whatever he was about to say was going to be difficult. "InfiniCorp didn't just use robotics to help soldiers during World War E. They used other weapons, they used—"

"May I cut in?" someone said, drowning out Will's last word.

Heat prickled the back of Claire's neck at the familiar voice. She turned cautiously, finding Aven in a fitted black suit behind her. It was hard to breathe, hard to think with him so close. The scent of his cologne took her back to their night together.

The bike ride, playing piano, kissing those perfect lips, those same lips on her—

"I thought I told you to leave me alone," Claire managed to say.

Aven took a confident step forward. "I never got the chance to properly apologize."

"Will first," Claire stated.

"Sorry," Aven said to Will flatly and then offered his hand to Claire. "My lady?"

Claire's eyes fluttered, and she glanced around the lawn for his twin. The Aven doppelganger was nowhere in sight.

When she regained her senses, she glared at Aven. "Whatever you have to say, say it," she told him.

"I would really hate for you to *faint* in front of all these people, Princess, but since you insist on being stubborn, I pro—"

"It's okay, Claire," Will interrupted before Aven could say the key phrase. "I'll go talk to Levi. There was something I wanted to ask him anyway."

Claire's heart was heavy as she watched Will walk to their table. They had grown close, and now his past and hers had come back to push them apart.

"You look absolutely stunning," Aven snaked his arm around her waist.

"And you are absolutely the most selfish person I've ever met," Claire shot back. "You had no right to use the key phrase on me like that."

"Have I ever told you how beautiful you look when you get all flustered?"

"What do you want, Aven?"

"I made the wrong choice."

Claire met his eyes, finding something in them that looked like regret.

"I hurt you. I shouldn't have said what I didn't mean. I should have never left you. Not like that."

The clinking of silver brought Claire's attention to the birthday charm bracelet on her wrist.

"You said I needed it as a reminder," Aven continued. "But I never forgot. Seems it didn't take long before you did."

"You can't just show up here and pretend you didn't say what you did."

"What I said, I didn't mean. None of it."

"Then why were you so harsh?"

"I knew I didn't deserve you, so I wanted to make you hate me. I used everything about you that I fell in love with, everything that made you self-conscious. Used every single hurt you believed was a fault. It was you, Claire. You forgot our conversation in the elevator."

Claire's body went loose as Aven swayed them side to side, pulling her close. Everything he had said at the Luxor hotel, everything he told her that night about why he had been attracted to her flooded back into her mind.

"Good morals are nothing to be ashamed of, Ms. Grace."

Claire swallowed to soothe her dry throat. "You could have just told me you didn't want to be with me."

"You would have seen through that falsehood. You're like some human lie detector."

"Apparently not. I can't tell if you're telling the truth now."

"Try me."

Claire stared deeply into those beautiful eyes. They were bluer since the last time she had seen them, almost like the color when she met him at Lux.

"Was the demon I saw real?" she asked, keeping her gaze fixed.

"Yes."

"You told me we would face it together."

"If I hadn't walked away, it would have devoured you."

Claire was the one who paused in step this time. "You're not talking in a metaphor."

"No. This particular beast can't be slayed. I wanted to be with you, Claire. Because you're right. I'm selfish. I wanted you so badly it hurt worse than letting you go. But I knew if I could for once think of someone other than myself, you could find a good man that could make you happy. But as soon as I saw you on the beach with Will, seeing him look at you that way, it made me realize I want to be that good man. The only man."

"And now you want me back?"

Aven dipped her as the song ended and grinned. "If you'll have me, your majesty."

"And if I've moved on?"

Aven pulled her to her feet and stared at her a long moment. "Have you?"

BY BLOOD

"WILL?"

Will blinked from his fixed gaze on the dance floor and unclenched his teeth at the sound of a robotic voice. He'd been staring at the way Aven whispered in Claire's ear, how he let his hand rest a little too low on her backside.

"Sorry," Will said to Levi. "I was—what were you saying?"

Levi's eyes went to the dance floor. **"Is that the ex-boyfriend?"**

"Yep."

"Were they together long?"

"Long enough for him to put her under some kind of spell," Will said out loud before he signed, "So these gifts, these abilities. Do Truth Keepers have them?"

Levi silenced his glove and signed back, "Some. But there are others who are not Truth Keepers who also have gifts. They have learned by ways of visitors; the fallen Seraphim have taught them for many centuries how to improve upon their abilities. Those who have descended from the fallen are called Truth Seekers. And they stay in connection with the fallen through mediums and dark divinations."

"Evocation of evil spirits?"

Levi nodded.

"So they're bad guys."

"Not all. Some don't know the danger of what they do. They are being lied to. You see, the dead, those who wander on the wrong side, have nothing but time on their hands until Judgment. They enjoy toying with the living. The Truth Seekers use these wandering entities for information, and being the descendants of the fallen Seraphim, the Truth Seekers know all too well who it is that they conjure."

"Descendants? How is that possible? Aren't they spiritual beings?"

"In this dimension, yes."

Will's brows pinched together. "Then how?"

"The fallen Seraphim are now bound by laws, unable to pass through the veil in their true form. But there was a time they were able to freely roam the earth. You read of the first of the fallen that came and took wives and bore children. You also read how a great flood wiped out most of their tainted seed."

"The giants?" Will asked. Deformed cannibals?"

Levi nodded. "Many countries documented this truth in their history. But the first of the fallen that came were not the only ones. There was a second descent of the rebelling angels. They too planted their seed, and women bore their offspring. They don't look like monsters of their ancestors, but they are."

"Can one of these offspring put someone into a deep sleep by just a few words?"

"If they have been trained in the ways to do so. Hypnosis, which from what I can assume by the way you described Claire's fainting, has its roots in ancient cultural science. Long ago there were healing sanctuaries. They were called Sleep Dream Temples in which the afflicted would lay down and be put into trance-like states by a high priest or priestess. People claimed to be cured by a supernatural healing power of the divine realm. One must question, however, from whom such knowledge had been obtained in the first place."

"So my brother is—" Will blurted out and then signed, "part fallen angel?"

"Your brother?"

"Half brother." Will set his gaze on Aven. "It's like some cosmic joke."

"Nothing is done without a purpose. This was in the plan."

"He's the most selfish prick on the face of the earth, and I'm related to him. What's the purpose in that?"

"The relation means your brother has a chance."

"Of what? Getting his ass kicked?"

"Of being brought back from the wrong side in the afterlife."

Will furrowed his brows in confusion.

"Number 38462. 'We are judged according to our works, for our faith, but also for rejecting He who gave us life. They shall be put to the side, and at death an endless void awaits.'"

"An endless void." Will frowned. "Is that where he's going?"

"We are to be judged but are not to judge others. We can't assume to know how a person lives their life. It is only Aramis who knows the soul's true intentions. I've studied many near-death experiences. Most, about those who had a wonderful experience, but also about others, who said the afterlife was unpleasant."

"What was it like for those who experienced something unpleasant?"

"Most say it was a dark and endless void of nothing. Others, depending on how they lived their lives, faced an endless loop of their trespasses. What they had done to others was done to them. There was no escape. And then, there were those who were simply in a waiting place."

"Limbo?"

"Yes, but no. It seems in the afterlife we create our own heaven or hell as we await judgment. All of our good and bad deeds, no matter how small, are counted."

"You're saying sides. What separates them?"

"An impassable chasm, the gulf. Picture yourself standing at the edge of the Grand Canyon. You see a friend on the other side of the gap and wish so badly to be there with them, but you can't cross. Souls are separated from those they care about. Friends. Family. Everyone."

"What if those people are on the wrong side with them?"

Levi grimaced. "They wouldn't know."

"Why not?"

"Because we only have the knowing of our choices, our guilt, and our regret to torment us."

"Will anyone have a chance? Even if they are on the wrong side?"

"Yes." Levi smiled. "Because there are people all over the world who have never had the chance to hear the truth. They will hear that truth when the chosen speak, and thereafter during the millennium."

"What if they still choose to reject Him?"

"They will be blotted out on the Day of Judgment. It is the final death of the soul. There will be no second chances after that. Not only will the soul be gone, but the entity will be forgotten from the mind of every single soul they came into contact with. Every evil deed, every painful memory will be deleted. But again., we are not to place judgment. We are not to assume. Aramis knows all, and He alone gives the final judgment."

Will licked his lips, rolling around all the information in his head. "Can a Truth Keeper be sent to this place?"

Levi gave a slow nod. "If you and Claire are of the chosen few to stand before Aalok when he returns, you must not refuse Aramis' spirit to speak through you. It is unforgivable, for it is the only task he has asked of you. The chosen gave their word to fulfill their purpose. Number 5313: 'For it is those elect, the Truth Keepers, who are to be delivered before the fallen one, to be the mouthpiece, the vessel in which Aramis' words come forth. Everyone will hear, no matter their origin, for it will be spoken in their very own dialect, flowing like honey into their ears.'"

Will was quiet for a moment, watching Claire and Aven talk, picking apart their words as he read their lips. Aven was using his charm again, casting his spell of manipulation to try to convince her that he cared about her. It made Will furious, but then his heart went soft, worrying if Aven would be sent to the wrong side. He couldn't stand his brother, but he was still family, he was still blood, and Will didn't think Aven deserved to be tortured by an endless loop of regrets.

Levi tapped the table to get Will's attention and then signed, "Do you remember if you made a promise in your past?"

Will set his gaze on the flickering candle on the table. "Alexander promised Sophie he would find her."

"Anyone else?"

Will squinted his eyes. "I don't know."

"Think."

Will thought about Alexander's story, retraced every word.

Alexander's duel with Caius. Being knighted. His introduction to the Truth Keeper. The Outcast camp where she—

It hit him, like being slapped with a handful of stardust.

Serus.

"By blood and only by blood can one help retrieve another from the wrong side of the gulf before The Day of Judgment." Levi explained. "Only family can go to the other side and bring back their loved ones. Mother, father, sister, and brother. Only by relation."

"It's that simple?"

"No. Going to the other side is unpleasant. It's dark and confusing. When the two return, they must be cleansed, having been in a desolate land of sorrows."

"Away from those they love,"

"Everyone."

"Guess I should start packing my bags now. The selfish prick won't listen."

Levi looked at Claire and then back at Will. "There is someone else he has a connection with that can still counsel him before the end."

Will's chest caved in. Claire. She was Sophie, and she had made a promise to help Serus, to help Aven.

"As it is written, 'Put aside thyself or face the consequences when the time comes.'"

"Are you saying I should walk away?"

Levi's eyes went soft, and he signed slowly with emphasis. "I'm saying you should choose your path wisely."

DANCING ON
MY OWN

AVEN didn't need to be told Claire was looking at Will over his shoulder. It was more than apparent she had feelings for him. True feelings. Yes, Aven loved her too, in some form or fashion, but he didn't know what to call it. All he knew was that he couldn't stand the thought of being without her. It was childish, but Aven had never been good with sharing attention or affection. Sending Kitten to work for Paula had been proof of that.

The vision he'd had at Bree's touch came again. It still haunted him seeing Claire underwater, the air bubbles muddling her face as they rose to the surface. He couldn't let her die. No matter if he felt something for Kitten, he had to convince Claire to leave this place with him. If getting her to fall back in love with him would do the trick, so be it.

"You were right," Aven said. "I hid behind a facade, hid who I really am. I'm always running away, but I don't want to run anymore. I can face the music. I can be a better person. I can be what you need now."

"Aven, I'm glad I make you want to be a better person but—" She glanced at Will again.

Aven followed her gaze. "You two have grown close."

"We're just friends."

"Friends don't take trips to romantic places together."

"We didn't come together. He was already here."

"What a coincidence. Still. This place *is* romantic."

Claire huffed. "Why are you here? I thought I made myself clear."

Aven licked his lips. "I was worried about you."

"Why? Because I wouldn't answer your calls?"

"Because my brother is sick."

"Sick?"

"Mentally ill. He was enrolled in a secret military project with InfiniCorp. The tests they did on him messed with his mind. You're not safe with him."

Claire tensed. "He's not going to hurt me."

"He will."

Claire took a step back and searched his eyes. Her chest rose and fell with quick breaths, a clear sign of panic.

"You know I'm telling the truth. You have to trust me."

"You haven't given me a reason to."

"But Will has?"

Claire tried to slip away, but Aven held on.

"I'm trying to save your life," he scolded.

She looked up at him with her big doe eyes pooling with tears. Her lip quivered and her voice cracked. "You made your choice, Aven. Now I'm making mine."

Aven gnashed his teeth as Claire elbowed out of his grasp. She had said that line once before, long ago, as Sophie. He had seen that in a vision. It hurt just as much now as it did then. He watched her brush past the dancers and flee to the boardwalk before he dared to follow her.

"Like I said before, smothering."

Aven stopped at the steps of the planked wood and smirked at Will's voice. "Have you ever noticed how her eyes change color with her emotions?" he asked without turning around. "Fascinating how much they resemble a mood ring."

"Your wooing didn't go the way you thought it would, did it?"

"Well." Aven swiveled the tip of his shoes in the scattered sand. "Not when someone has filled her head with religious garbage."

"Speaking of religious garbage, does the Circle still do human sacrifices to conjure spirits or has that practice been done away with?"

Aven took a step forward. "I'd be careful if I were you, brother."

"Is that a threat?" Will glared, coming inches from his nose.

"It's a promise. Oh, wait, that only works on Claire."

Just as expected, Will snatched up a handful of Aven's suit jacket. "Your arrogance is really starting to piss me off."

Aven pried Will's fingers from his lapel with just a thought.

Will took a step back, looking at his hand as if it had betrayed him.

"A little lazy on the two-step," Aven teased, clapping a hand on Will's shoulder. "You should take some dancing lessons." With a smirk, he wiggled his brows and walked casually to the bar for a drink.

THE RAVEN

TUESDAY, 6:55 P.M.
OAHU, HAWAII

AFTER downing two bottles of bourbon in only thirty minutes, Aven thought about breaking into Claire's room with his abilities and waiting for her there–preferably naked. Sure he was rid of Nehia, but not his man parts, and it was hard to break the ritual of getting laid. But people were hard to Persuade. If sex didn't work, he'd have to tell her the truth–laced with little white lies.

He couldn't tell her about Vincent, that he had been instructed to bring her to his cousin so she could read the book. He'd already thought through his plan on his flight to Hawaii. It involved murdering his own blood to protect her.

How do you kill someone with superhuman abilities?

"Trouble in paradise?"

Aven looked up to find a man sitting next to him. He wore a suit much like his. His hair was the same blue-black, but an inch of it resting at his chin was as white as snow.

The man's eyes were a strange color, however: deep brown, almost crimson, something otherworldly.

"Do I know you?" Aven asked, tilting his head.

"Perhaps as a late visitor entreating at your chamber door or quietly rapping, tapping at thy window." The stranger offered his hand. "Mal."

Aven looked at the hand suspiciously as Mal's lips drew into an unnerving familiar smirk. "Aven Crey."

As soon as Aven clasped the stranger's hand, a vision flashed in his mind. It was of a balcony. His past life, the angel he made a deal with. His damnation.

"Malphas." Aven glared, drawing back.

"That hasn't been my name since the fall. I'm now known as Raum."

"'Raum is a great earl,'" Aven quoted. "He is seen as a crow, but when he putteth on human shape, at the commandment of the exorcist, he stealeth wonderfully out of the king's house, and carrieth it whether he is assigned, he destroieth cities, and hath great despite unto dignities, he knoweth things present, past, and to come, and reconcileth friends and foes, the one who hath governeth the thirty legions.' *Pseudomonarchia Daemonum*, Johann Weyer."

"The same." Mal grinned.

"I made a deal with you,"

"Do you remember why?"

"Yes, and it appears Raum the great god is a liar. You didn't keep your end of the deal."

"Is that so?"

"Quite so." Aven leaned in. "I found her on my own."

"Did you, now?"

At the raise of the angel's perfect brow, Aven wasn't so sure.

Mal grabbed Aven's bottle of bourbon and a glass from the bar. "Let's take a stroll, shall we?"

How did you orchestrate the meeting?" Aven asked as he and Mal walked into the garden area of the hotel grounds.

"With the Truth Keeper?" Mal questioned.

"Yes, and her name is Claire."

"Your fondness for the holy counselor is rather amusing."

"Tell me."

"I simply arranged the hotel and gave VIP access to your club. The spunky blonde was rather pleased. I was there, sitting at the bar when you came in."

Aven stared at the ground, trying to recall Mal's face among the ones José had been serving.

"Watching you puff your chest at your associate, Tony, I didn't have to guess how to get you to follow the Truth Keeper to her room."

"Tony wasn't stalking her?"

"No," Mal said. "He was too busy trying to have his way with the priestess. I'd be watching his punishment with the others right now, but I'm here helping you."

"It was you in the casino?"

Mal nodded. "I knew if I could make it appear as if Tony was preying on her, your protective instincts would kick in. You get that from your mother's side."

"The raven. You can shape shift."

"Unquenchable desire, however. You get that from me," Mal smirked, "grandson."

"You arranged it. So what? Everything else happened on its own."

"When I returned to the Coven, I found that Zarak had been summoned. Apparently, Nehia thought I was interfering with her playtime. I simply reminded her that our deal took precedence, that it was written in the stars long before this aeon."

"Are you expecting a thank you for sending her back to her little pit?"

"I don't have that power. I simply stated my right. She was there, watching just as she said. As the night progressed, she realized it would be to her advantage for you to seduce the Truth Keeper."

"Because she's chosen."

"Just as the angels rejoice when one of ours chooses the Creator, the demons squeal in wretched pleasure when a believer turns."

"Are you the one that made Claire wreck the Mustang?"

Mal gave a light chuckle. "Zarak was having a bit of fun."

The memory of Zarak flashed in Aven's mind.

Long white hair, red-tipped at the ends. The slaughter of innocence.

"Are all the Seraph here?" Aven asked.

"Yes. Perhaps you felt our arrival?"

"The earthquake?"

Mal grinned. "We are to spread the word of Aalok's soon return."

"And when will that be?"

Mal crossed his arms and looked to the sky. "When the red planet circles."

Aven stared at the stars with him. "I'm running out of time,"

"How much do you remember from before?"

"All of it." Aven sighed and stared at the bottom of his empty glass. "I see everything. That's my curse."

"You once said, 'the beauty of free will is that you have a choice.' What will your choice be, Serus?"

"I don't take sides. Didn't before. Won't now."

"There is no gray area in the matter. You are either with Him or against Him."

Aven bit his bottom lip and narrowed his gaze, wondering if he would be willing to change, if there was even time to repent for all he had done.

Mal fixed his gaze on Aven. "She's starting to remember,"

"Who I am?" Aven asked.

"Her promise. Her purpose. Her soulmate."

"And I gather I'm not him."

"No. But you already knew that, and yet you pursued her anyway."

Aven did know. Since Nehia's possession, since his Mind Walk with Kitten, he had been having flashes. He could only assume something had been unlocked when he'd been lying in a tub of his own blood. He had seen himself in Hawaii, but also, being in another place that looked like it. There was only one scene he saw clearly, however, one he knew that had been the breaking point for his past self.

A field. Sophie clinging to a warrior. Him, as Serus, in a fit of rage, chucking a telescope over his balcony. Bree, or Jazrael, taking pleasure in his pain.

"Is the Creator working to bring them back together?"

"The king watches as it plays out for all souls. He only intercedes against Aalok's oppression of the chosen when they call out his name."

"Then who helped them?"

A hint of pity was in Mal's eyes, but a clever smile tugged at his lips. "Why, you did of course."

The face of the warrior came in clear. He could feel that jealousy again, the heartbreak, watching the warrior hold Sophie and comfort her. "Will, he found her because he was looking for me."

"Fate has a sense of humor."

"Fate can go to hell." Aven turned his back on Mal to walk toward the beach, toward Claire. He would grovel, he would beg. Her fate and his could still be changed. She didn't have to die.

Mal appeared in front of him with a hand to his chest. "Time is running out, but I have the answer to how you can avoid your damnation."

"Go on."

"When two flesh become one, a single burning flame, not even destiny can intercede. You love her. You always have.

Even if it is not the love like that of her soulmate, it will suffice to keep you in Aramis' good graces. He can't break that sacred bond."

"Marriage," Aven said flatly.

"You know it's in her deepest nature to counsel, to fix what's broken. It takes precedence. She vowed to help you. She knows deep down that it is exactly what she was sent here to do."

"She's not going to marry me."

A sly smile pulled at Mal's lips. "I'm sure she can be Persuaded."

Aven turned his back on Mal again and tossed his glass into the bushes, thinking over his choices. Part of him hoped Claire still cared for him, hoped their love, whatever it was called, could atone for his sins. It would save her, and it would save him if they were together.

But marriage? What about Kitten?

"Why do you care so much about my soul? Hm?" Aven asked. "Do you earn back your wings if I'm somehow miraculously redeemed?"

There was no answer to Aven's question. Only the caw of a raven as it flew over his head and toward a starlit sky.

NEON LIGHTS

LUMINESCENT waves rolled over Claire's ankles. She studied the tiny glowing orbs in them, thinking of the cave of starlight from *The Book of Aramis*. She didn't look over her shoulder, listening to the footsteps in the sand as they approached. Somehow, she knew it wasn't Aven. She could always sense Will's comforting presence when he was nearby.

"Hey," he said.

"Hey," she answered, watching the waves crash with a flash of neon blue.

Will gave a nod to them. "Pretty amazing isn't it?"

"Yes. Whatever it is."

"Bioluminescence Plankton. They light up as a defense mechanism."

Claire swirled her hand in the water and it lit like sapphires at her touch.

"You okay?"

Claire shrugged and walked a few steps to sit on dry land. "Yeah, of course. I mean, it's not like my ex-boyfriend just showed up and acted like a complete jerk or anything. Not to mention he's apologized for being one and is trying to get me back."

Confliction stabbed at Claire's chest. All the feelings she had for Will hadn't changed when Aven had shown up, but it reminded her of how Aven had made her feel when they had been together. She couldn't deny their connection, but she also couldn't deny the need to be with Will either.

Will didn't say anything as he sat beside her. It reminded Claire of when Aven had stolen the mustang and drove away in the pouring rain. There was no pitter-patter of rain now, only the sound of the neon blue lapping waves, muffled music, and the tourist at the luau, laughing in conversations of things much less serious than the coming end of the world.

Chosen. It wasn't something Claire thought she would ever be. In her mind, she was nobody.

"Do you think Levi is crazy?" she asked Will finally.

"Do you?"

"Doesn't it seem just a little bizarre? I mean, we've been reading a book of numbers and symbols. We don't even know who wrote them."

"Those who wrote the book lived in different time periods, didn't know one another and yet, they wrote the same exact story from their own perspective. I can't call that a coincidence."

"But what if it's all made up? What if it was one person? What if they were mental?"

Will inclined his head and looked at the sky. "I thought you believed."

"I did, but after Aven said-"

"That you're crazy?" He looked at her, accusing with his eyes. "That I'm crazy?"

"It's not what he said, exactly. It's what I know about myself. I've always been unstable. I can never be sure of what's real. Not without a sign. Not without proof."

"Proof,"

The word was laced with disappointment.

Claire chewed on the inside of her cheek waiting for him to tell her something to convince her otherwise, but he didn't. He only stood and placed his hands on his hips.

"Hold out your hand and close your eyes." He instructed.

"Why?"

"I want to show you something that doesn't need to be seen."

Claire closed her eyes and waited several thudding heartbeats for something to happen, but nothing did.

"Will?"

There was no answer, only the sound of waves drawing back and trickling in. Soon, there was a warm tickle at her ear that felt like a whisper without words.

When Claire opened her eyes, she found a seashell in her hand. She didn't understand how it was there. She hadn't felt Will put it there.

"How did you do that?" she asked swiveling around.

"Do what?"

"This," She said, offering the shell

"How do you know it was me?" Will grinned. "You didn't see me put it in your hand."

"No, but-"

"You can only *believe* I did. Unless," Will crossed his arms and shrugged with a smirk, "you have proof."

Belief. That's what this was about. Another lesson.

Will laid the shell to the side and dusted the sand from her palms to hold her hands. "What do you feel when you read about Aramis?"

Claire was comforted by Will's touch, but a heavy sigh left her lips knowing he was trying to remind her of the chapter in *The Book of Aramis* when Alexander had asked Sophie that same question at the secret spring.

"Warmth, comfort," she said, "peace that I push away. I think subconsciously I would rather be angry with him then accept what happened to my family. To believe in him means believing it was for a purpose." She looked into his hopeful eyes. "I don't' know if I can accept that."

"What if it was out of his control? Aramis didn't want to end the first Aeon, but he had to make a choice."

Claire shook her head. "But this is different."

"No. It's not. We had free will back then, and we do now. Your mother made a choice to go to New York. You made a choice to go to Vegas. Whatever happened, happened. It doesn't mean Aramis is the one to blame. "

"But all of these terrible things have to happen before he comes back. He's the reason the world is ending."

"Is he?"

Claire let out a lengthy sigh. Will was right. It hadn't been Aramis' fault in the first Aeon that it should be destroyed, and it wasn't his fault the second had to end either. It was Aalok's. He was the reason they had died before. He was the reason she would have to die again.

"You're afraid to die." Will said as if he had read her mind.

"Aren't you?"

Will rested his arms on his knees and shook his head. "No. I've been Beyond The Veil."

"You've died?"

Will gave a slow nod.

"What was it like there?" Claire asked, watching him draw in the sand with his finger. It wasn't a picture, or words. She didn't think he was tracing anything with meaning. He appeared to be simply keeping his gaze on something other than hers.

"It's hard to describe," he said after a moment. "You still know who you are, remember your life, but all of that doesn't seem to matter anymore. Not really. There's no sense of time, no worries, no fear. There's nothing but an overwhelming relief and peace. It's like coming home from war."

"Did you see the friends you served with? Any loved ones who have passed away?"

"No." Will said sweeping what he had drawn to a blank slate. "I was sent back just as soon as I arrived."

"Do you know why?"

A small smile formed on Will's lips as he met her gaze. "You,"

Claire's stomach fluttered. "But see. You have proof of an afterlife," she stated.

"Do I, or was it just an illusion?"

Claire didn't know if she could accept Will's truth, that the place he had been was real. It did sound wonderful. It gave her hope, but it still wasn't enough. They could both be crazy. They could both be sick, as Aven had said Will was.

"There are endless trains of the faithless," Will said staring at the ocean, "of cities filled with the foolish, of myself forever reproaching myself, for who more foolish than I, and who more faithless? Eyes vainly crave the light, of the objects mean, of the struggle ever renewed, of poor results of all, of the plodding and sordid crowds I see around me; of the empty and useless years of the rest, with the rest me intertwined. What good amid these oh, me, of life? The answer," Will paused. "Is that we are here—that life exists. The powerful play goes on, and I may contribute a verse. What will your verse be?"

"That's beautiful. Did you come up with that just now?"

Will cracked a smile. "Walt Whitman, I ad-libbed."

"Who's he?"

"He was a famous poet at one time. My mother had a book of his on her shelf before the burnings. These days, you can't find any of his work online."

"Why not?"

"Have you ever seen anything without the FCC's stamp of approval?"

"I can't say I've ever paid attention," Claire admitted.

"If an artist has done any work, in any form, that offends, it never sees the light of day."

"You know this from experience?"

"You ought to see the paperwork for trying to sell an oil of horses in a meadow. It's more work than the art itself."

Claire let out a lite laugh to Will's joking tone. "These past few days are the most I've ever heard you talk."

"My words form better on a canvas. Brushstrokes can speak an artists mind with a single glance."

"Are eyes are not so telling?"

Will bit his bottom lip. "Sometimes,"

"Are mine?"

Will's fixed gaze was serious but his lips were still turned up playfully. "Very,"

"How so?"

"When you're hurt, or nervous, your eyes are dark green like a forest at dusk."

"And when I'm happy?"

Will reached up and tucked a rogue-twirling strand of her hair behind her ear and lingered. "They sparkle like a field of dewy clovers in the morning sunlight,"

Claire wanted to melt into his touch as Will looked at her lips. She didn't know if she could kiss him back if he made the gesture. Guilt was keeping them inches apart. She didn't know how she could let herself be with Will when she was sent to help Aven. A nagging pinch in the pit of her stomach made her draw back. She set her gaze to the sky, letting silence sit between her and Will.

"See those three together?" Will asked after a few moments.

Claire observed the night sky. "It's Orion's belt."

"Do you think it was some accident those stars aligned, or do you believe they were placed just right, so that when we look up, we could find the other constellations by this single one?"

Somehow, talking about stars was what made Claire understand. If she believed the story to be true and that she were Sophie, she was a star, a light. It was her destiny to shine bright. The Creator may have set her path in this vast universe, but she was at the helm of her own ship. It was up to her to steer toward the other stars and remind them of their maker. It was her choice to believe.

When they had sounded off every star in and near the constellation Orion, silence again fell between Claire and Will. He could feel her warmth, could tell she was back to believing, but there was something else holding her back. He couldn't tell her of disappointment when she had pulled away. He had wanted so badly to tell her how he felt, that he wanted her to choose him and not Aven.

He hadn't needed to read her mind to know Sophie's choice to stay with Alexander on the beach was weighing her down with guilt. Aven's soul was in danger because she had rejected him in the first Aeon, because she had fallen in love with her Guardian.

Will sent up a prayer to Aramis, telling him he trusted him, telling him he would choose his path wisely. He wasn't going to do anything to influence her choice. He had been sent here to see to it that she lived to stand against Aalok again. That was his mission then, and that was his only mission now. He would not fail Aramis again.

"I should get some rest for my flight tomorrow," Will informed as he dusted the sand from his palms and stood. "See you at breakfast?"

"Of course,"

Will forced a smile and headed for the hotel, but he had only a taken a few steps before Claire called out his name and jogged to him.

"I told Levi I wanted to dedicate my life." She said, "Will you do the honors of dipping me under?"

"What time?"

"Sunrise,"

"Then I'll see you at sunrise."

Claire looked down, and Will realized she was staring at his arm. He took her hand and grasped her forearm in the same farewell they had read about in *The Book of Aramis*. But there was no change in Claire's appearance and Will could tell by her frown, that she couldn't see anything different about him either.

"Thank you," Claire said, slipping away.

"Can't have Levi pulling out his back, now can I?" Will joked to break the tension. "The guy's pushing eighty."

"No. I mean for keeping your word." She traced the birthmark on her wrist as if it were a sentimental trinket. "Even if I doubt," She continued, meeting his gaze, "even if I lose my way, there's one thing I'll always remember."

"Aramis' words."

She gave a sweet smile. "And that my knight in shining armor will come to my rescue."

Will raised a brow. "And if he's late again?"

Claire gave a faint laugh, and Will knew she had caught the reference to Sophie's capture.

She set her gaze on Orion. "Then I'll gaze up at the stars and remind myself that he's on his way."

A BROKEN

LITTLE BOY

AVEN was trapped in his recurring nightmare. The room was always so black, always so cold when he was a little boy again. He felt his way down a dark hall, going toward the light. The floor creaked beneath his little feet as he tiptoed into his father's office.

He walked around the scattered broken glass and watched a pool of blood leak beneath his father's lifeless body. He met his father's aimless gaze before he glanced up at the man standing over his father's body.

"Aven," the man said.

Aven studied his eyes. They were filled with worry, with kindness. He then looked at the gun the man was holding. It was pointed at his uncle, Jimmy.

"Pick up the gun!" Jimmy shouted. "Kill him, Aven!"

"Aven," the man said again. His voice was soft, hardly a whisper. "I came to take you home. Your mom's waiting for you."

"He's lying!" Jimmy yelled. He favored his side. His fingers were covered in blood.

Aven picked up the gun by his father's hand.

It was always so heavy. Always so cold.

"This is your home," another voice said. It was one his age, one void of emotion at the scene before them.

Aven looked over his shoulder, finding Vincent and his boyish face scowling in disapproval.

"He killed him," Vincent hissed. "He deserves the same fate."

The blue-eyed man reached out his hand. "Your mom asked me to bring you home. I'm a friend. My name is Adam. Adam Carpenter."

Seeing his father's milky wide eyes still staring up at him, Aven's hands shook. The gun rose from his palm, hovered, and pointed.

"Please," Adam said softly. "She misses you. She asked me to come and save you."

The gun lowered.

"Save me?" Aven's little voice croaked.

"Kill him, cousin," Vincent ordered. "Blood for blood. A life for a life."

The gun rose again, and Aven knew he was not the only one controlling it now.

Was it hate or Vincent?

Aven never knew, no matter how many times he had this dream. He looked at Vincent, wincing at his cousin's hand on his shoulder as it squeezed. "Kill him."

"Pull the trigger," Jimmy pushed.

The gun shook hard in Aven's trembling hands, and he looked up at the blue-eyed man, this stranger, this killer, and this savior.

Should I go? Will he save me? From myself? From the shadows that haunt me?

"Do it!" Vincent bellowed in his ear.

Aven shuddered at his cousin's voice.

The *pop* of the gun rang in his ears.

With his mouth dropped open, Aven watched the blue-eyed man clutch his chest and fall back against the wall. Blood streaked behind him, pooling in his lap. His lip quivered as he spoke, but Aven couldn't hear what the man mumbled.

He wished he could have read the man's lips, wished Adam had told him where his mother's home was. But the stranger choked on the blood trickling from his mouth and then stilled.

Aven startled awake in a cold sweat and looked around his bedroom. Seeing the open wall of his villa and the glint of the moon on the lapping waves, he knew he was back in the present. He wasn't in his haunting past any longer, but he still felt small, like a ten-year-old boy all over again. He curled up into a ball and wept into his pillow.

Did I pull the trigger?

It wasn't a demon this time, but a darkness deep from within him that hissed a response. *Murderer.*

WAR STORY

A pounding at the door woke Will from a haunting dream. The blast from a gun still echoed in his ears. The horrific sight of Jeremiah, his best friend, lying in a pool of blood in dirty streets still lingered in his mind.

"Will?" Claire's muffled voice called. "Please open the door," she pleaded.

Will threw back his covers, damp with sweat, and unlocked the adjoining door. Behind it, Claire stood in a thin white cotton camisole and matching shorts. Her hands trembled, clasped at her chest.

"Are you alright?" he asked.

She slammed into him, body quaking, and wept.

"What's wrong?"

"It's my fault."

"What is?"

Her words came between gasps and blubbering. "I saw it. I saw the future. His face was ash. It was peeling away and then he was gone. He was gone forever."

"It was a dream," Will tried to assure her, but part of him wondered, part of him knew his visions and dreams had also shown him a possible outcome of the future. He prayed the one he'd just woken from could still be changed.

"No," Claire croaked. "It was the same dream Sophie had. It was The Day of Judgment. Serus was there in the flames. It's because of me. Because I didn't save him."

Will swept her sweat-dampened hair from her face and dared to look into her pleading eyes again. They were still so beautiful, still so hopeless and filled with fear.

A forest at dusk.

Will swallowed, but the knot in his throat wouldn't budge as his eyes set on his bed. He wanted so desperately to kiss her, to lay her down and caress her tears away. He glanced at her pouty lips once, and then fixed his gaze to the floor, putting want to the side. "You should try to get some sleep."

Claire's eyes wandered to his bare stomach and tensed as her delicate fingers smoothed over a scar at the elastic band of his boxer briefs.

"Appendix," he said.

Her gaze then went to a long scar wrapping around his ribs, then to the other circles of raised skin on his arms that had once been bullet wounds.

"And those?" she asked.

"Battle scars,"

Claire tilted her head, looking at the tan line on the underside of his bicep and tracing the faded ink. It was his only tattoo, one he kept hidden, one that had never seen the light of day until this trip.

"What do these numbers mean?"

Will swallowed hard, never taking his gaze off of hers. "The first three were for the number of my unit, the last two are just for me."

Claire looked up at him with eyes full of concern. "What happened to you?"

Will led her to the bed and sat down beside her. He raked his fingers through his hair, knowing that it was time to tell her about his past.

"I wasn't drafted into World War E," he began. "My little brother, Aaron, was. I signed up so that I could watch his back. After our training, and two years of being on the front lines, my unit was called in for special training. In the military, they give you drugs. They keep you focused, keep you calm, help you not dwell on the lives you took. But the contract I signed with InfiniCorp wasn't for that."

"InfiniCorp?"

Will nodded slowly. "They weren't always in the business of life; they were first in the business of death."

"What was the contract for?"

"Something that made me inhuman. Something that gave me abilities."

"Abilities?" She scrunched her brows. "Like what?"

"I've always been able to heal quickly, but the serum somehow boosted my body's capability to regenerate at a superhuman rate. My reflexes got a bit of a boost too, along with some other things."

"That's how you got to me so fast when I fell off Snow's saddle," Claire said. "That's how you put the sand in my hand without me knowing?"

Will's lips twitched, but he didn't smile. "We were taken into a white room, told to lie on a steel gurney. They stuck a needle in our hand, another in the other. One for the bag of fluids to keep us hydrated, the other for something that looked ink, like some kind of black goo flowing down the tubes."

"What was it?"

"I don't know. Whatever it was, it burned like hell."

Claire shifted. "Why were they using it? What was it for?"

"At first to put us into a deep sleep to condition us. They called it Mind Walking."

Claire's brows rose.

"Said it was the fastest way to download years of training within only hours. We were then instructed to take a pill every day during the next phase of our training. I never once got a cold, never had an ache or pain after that. That was until the torture. Six months we endured it, and the next six, we played games."

"Games?"

"War games. They would take each unit of five, put us in a room, and put us under, relocating ten units at a time. They would drop us in the same spot but spread us out enough to evaluate our new superpowers against the elements. All the countries participated. Sometimes we were in Asia, others times Africa, America, I've even been to the Arctic. It was every unit for themselves. Survival of the most inhumane. Murder or be murdered."

Claire drew up her knees. "What happened after six months?"

"The World-Wide Peace Treaty was signed, and we were told we could go home. While my unit and I waited to be shipped out, they had us disarming weapons and doing housework, as we called it. Three days before we were to be sent home, they took us out to Death Valley to disarm some land mines near the facility they had tested us in.

"We walked for hours but never detected any land mines. Then I heard this voice. It was like silk in my ear, a whisper so low I could hardly make out the words. But I heard them."

"What was the voice saying?"

Will stared hard at the floor. "Shoot to kill,"

Claire shifted next to him.

"It hissed in my COM, over and over. I told my unit to change our station, but the only thing I heard back was two pops of a pistol. I found Aaron standing over two of the guys in our unit, Duke and Blake."

"Where was the fifth guy?"

"Jeremiah was at the facility running our tech."

"When you said Aaron was standing over them, you mean . . ."

"Aaron had never killed anyone before. I had always done that for him. I went into the war because he was the type of guy that would cry after accidentally stepping on a bug. There wasn't a harmful bone in his body. But when he looked up, eyes pooling with black, I knew he wasn't himself. We fought. I got the gun away from him, but then he tried to choke me. He kept telling me he had to make the voices stop."

"He was trying to kill you?" Claire asked in a whisper.

"It wasn't him. He didn't have control. Once I figured that out, I yanked out his COM. He broke down, begging to go home. I swore to him that he would, but . . ."

Claire took Will's hand in hers. "I'm sorry."

Will licked his lips and swallowed to hold back the tears burning his eyes. "The ambush had been a setup, another game, another evaluation. I wanted to kill the other soldiers that had shot Aaron, but they were only following orders, just like I had, and Aaron was dying in my arms."

"Aaron couldn't heal?" Claire asked softly.

"No. But it wouldn't have mattered. They wanted us dead. I can only assume they were trying to dispose of their failed experiments and keep the ones they wanted without getting their hands dirty."

"What happened next?"

"I remember the sound of the helicopter, my stomach flipping as I fell before my face smacked the water, could taste the saltwater as I sank before going unconscious. And then there was nothing but black—until I opened my eyes again to the light."

"Beyond the Veil," Claire noted.

Will gave a halfhearted smile.

"So what happened after Aramis brought you back?"

"I woke up on a beach in Mexico. Found a way to call the only person I knew could help me. Caleb was my dad's best friend and used to work for the CIA. He helped me create a new alias, sent me to one of his bug-out cabins in Montana, and told me to stay out of sight, that I couldn't go home.

"The last time I talked to him was when he had called me to let me know my mom was sick, said it was risky to go to her, but that I should, that my dad would have wanted me to, and told me to never contact him again unless a life was at stake. I can only guess InfiniCorp was onto him and his involvement with my survival."

"So you were alone until you went to take care of your mom?" Claire asked in a sullen voice.

"Drinking had been my only friend. But we parted ways after my mom told me she couldn't lose another son."

"And now you're alone again."

Will set his gaze on Claire's and laced their fingers. He knew he told Aramis he wouldn't be selfish, that he would not intercede. But he couldn't help it. He couldn't fight the need to be with Claire any longer. "I hope not anymore," he whispered.

Claire looked down at their hands and furrowed her brows. He wished he could read her mind, hoped that she could accept him for who he was, *what* he was.

"Claire, I'm not Aven. I can't give you luxuries or spoil you with lavish dinner parties, but I can give you my word and keep it. I can give you trust." He cupped her face and caressed her cheek.

Claire's eyes searched his. They seemed hopeful and yet afraid of what he was about to say.

"And when the time comes," Will continued, "I'll be by your side, protecting you until my very last breath, just like I did before. You're the only reason I'm alive. You're the reason I was born."

Claire didn't lean forward as he did. She pulled away and slipped her hand from his. "If I'm being honest, then I should tell you that I've decided to help Serus."

Rejection ripped Will's heart from his chest. He knew it was wrong to feel this jealousy, but he couldn't help it. "You're staying here with Aven."

"After my dedication."

Will dragged a hand down his face and started pacing. Aven had abilities too. Will didn't know if he had been experimented on; all he knew was that he couldn't trust him, or Vincent for that matter. Not until he got answers.

What if we were brought together because it's not just Aalok I need to protect her from? What if Aven keeps her from fulfilling her destiny? Sophie had been so close to giving in because of Serus.

"Sophie didn't help him in the end," Claire continued cautiously, "but I still have a chance to."

"You're not the only one who made a promise," Will reminded her. "I'll go. You're not safe with Aven. He'll manipulate you again, just like he did in the first aeon."

"He'll only listen to me. You know that."

"Then why did Aramis make me his brother?" Will asked, raising his voice. "Did you ever think that maybe it was because He knew it put you at risk? Aven's soul is not the only one that needs saving."

"Are you mad at me for wanting to help him?" she asked, coming to her feet.

"Yes."

"Why?"

"Because just like Sophie, you're letting your emotions cloud your judgment."

"I'm not!"

"You are!"

Claire pressed her lips into a thin line before she said, "Why are you acting like this?"

Will squinted at her in disbelief. "You can't tell by now how I feel about you?"

"You haven't exactly said it out loud."

"We have a past that goes back millions of years. No amount of time can change who we are or how we feel."

Claire's tense shoulders slumped and her mouth parted for the heavy breath he could hardly hear escape.

His gaze went to the floor as a thought came. "But I can only assume it's the same for you and Serus," he added. "I don't know what it is I feel for Aven. All I know is that I can't imagine him being blotted out because I didn't keep my promise," she said softly as she came to stand before Will. "You just told me that InfiniCorp is looking for you. If you go to Vegas—" She placed a hand on his arm that tensed at her touch. "Will, I don't know what I would do if anything happened to you."

Adrenaline still pumped through Will's veins. He wanted to punch something, wanted to bolt out of the room and run miles down the beach. But he didn't. Instead, he unclenched his teeth and looked down at her.

"I was sent to protect *you*," he said. "Not the other way around."

"This is his last chance. I have to do this. Alone."

Will bit his bottom lip as his nose burned. Tears pooled in his eyes, but he wouldn't allow them to fall. She was telling him she didn't want him to go, that this was her choice.

"Then I guess tomorrow is goodbye," he told her flatly.

"It's not goodbye," she reminded him. "It's only farewell for a little while. I'll come back in a few days. I want to see Bevol, I mean, Snow. I'd really like to go for another ride in the meadow with you."

Will relaxed his rigid body at her words and let his voice go soft. "Then I'll have the saddles ready when you return." He nodded a good night and headed toward his room. "See you in the morning."

"Will you paint something for me while I'm gone?"

A switch flipped in Will's mind in that instant. He had so many memories from this visit, so many beautiful portraits of Claire to brush on a canvas. But he didn't want to paint another memory. He wanted to hold one.

He turned at the threshold and shook his head. "No."

"Why not?" she asked.

"Because if I'm being honest," he said, taking controlled steps to her, "I don't want to paint one tomorrow or a few days from now."

There was a quiver in Claire's voice. "When I get back, then?"

He looked down at her, knowing he should walk away, that he should go to bed with wanting, but the desire to touch her was too strong.

"No," he answered softly.

Claire's chest rose and fell, a clear sign he was making her nervous. "Then when?" she asked.

Will steadied his breaths despite the hammering in his chest. He didn't know if he would be punished for what he was about to do, but he didn't care. He would face the consequences of his choice.

"You saw that painting in my studio? The one of the festival?" he asked.

"Yes."

"But none of the others?"

Claire shook her head. "No, why?"

"If you had," Will caressed her shoulder, "you would have seen just how long I've dreamed of touching you."

The rise and fall of Claire's chest quickened, and he could tell she was finding it hard to catch her breath.

"I painted four portraits those first seven years I was in hiding. The first," Will said, tracing her jaw, "I swept Naples yellow over your closed eyes." He combed his fingers slowly through her long tresses. "Soft strokes of raw umber for your hair, and a viridian hue for the sea. "

Will swallowed hard. "The second, Indian red for a crackling bonfire." His thumb rubbed hard across her knuckles and he furrowed his brows. "Lamp black for Serus's trespasses. Flake white for Bevol's coat." His fingers trailed like a feather up Claire's arm. "The third, titanium white for

your faint aura, a waterfall backdrop of French ultramarine."
He fixed his gaze on hers. "Your eyes"—a faint smiled formed
on his lips—"terre verte with dabs of emerald green."

Will brushed his thumb over her birthmark keeping the
fourth a secret. One day he would show her the painting. One
day she would see that she had been all he'd always been in love
with her.

"I painted every moment, every single instance I held
back from telling you how I felt." He said softly. "I prayed for
the day I could fulfill my vow. Because you're my destiny." He
leaned in, cupping her face. "Because I am yours," he
murmured against her lips.

Will kissed Claire softly, then again with eager lips. At
her soft moan, he slid the thin straps of her camisole down and
pressed her closer. A noise rose in his throat as their skin
touched and he lifted her into his arms, wrapping her legs
around his waist. He fixed his wary gaze on hers and held it for
a long aching moment.

"What's wrong?" Claire asked.

"It's been a long time," he admitted in a husky voice. "I'm
not sure how gentle I'll be."

"I'm not as fragile as I look, Guardian."

"I know." Will grinned. "Just thought I'd give you a
warning."

Claire woke, finding herself cradled in warmth. She
nestled into Will's chest, inhaling his scent. He pulled her in

closer, and she let out a soft sigh, listening to the steady drum of his heart. Her heart wasn't steady. It was racing. The more she thought about how they made love last night, the harder it pounded.

Will's gaze had been fixed on hers with each roll of his hips. He had moved so achingly slow that at times it had been absolute torture. Claire needed their bodies moving to a rhythm of their soft song again, for him to kiss her neck, for him to tangle his fingers in her hair, and for her to slip into a vast ocean and be carried away by wave after wave of utter ecstasy.

The replay of their lover's psalm vanished the moment Claire's eyes flew open. She knew the knock wasn't coming from Will's door but across his room from hers. Her eyes roamed Will's beautiful face before she moved his heavy arm, snatched a robe from his bathroom, and slipped through the adjoining door.

Claire's eyes lit with surprise, not seeing Levi as she expected, but a bellboy in the hall, standing behind a cart.

"Hello, miss," the bellboy greeted with a tip of his hat.

"Oh, I'm sorry," Claire said, "but I didn't order breakfast."

"It was requested by the gentleman."

Confusion crinkled the corners of Claire's eyes, but she thanked the bellboy, and he nodded and left. Rolling the cart into her room, Claire's shoulders slumped when she spied the white rose in a tiny vase. She looked at Will sleeping soundly in his bed and quietly lifted the lid of the covered dish to quash her suspicion. But the origami note was there, lying on a stack of chocolate chip pancakes.

Claire's nose scrunched in disgust, as if the note were a dead roach. She didn't want to touch it, let alone read it. Aven was trying to ruin her happiness, butting in on her and Will's last day together. But she quickly reminded herself that she had made up her mind last night. She would counsel him after her dedication. She would tell him she knew who he was, who they had been. It was the only way to be free of the nightmare. It was her only chance of saving him. And Will. She wouldn't let anything happen to him either.

I am yours.

And you are mine.

They were soulmates, and their bond could never be broken. Their destiny could not be prevented. Not by Aven. Not by InfiniCorp. Not by anyone. With trembling fingers, Claire unfolded the note scribbled with calligraphy.

In the words of Poe,

From ev'ry depth of good and ill
The mystery which binds me still—
From the torrent, or the fountain—
From the red cliff of the mountain—
From the sun that 'round me roll'd
In its autumn tint of gold—
From the lightning in the sky
As it pass'd me flying by—
From the thunder, and the storm—
And the cloud that took the form
When the rest of Heaven was blue
Of a demon in my view—

Claire, give me one last chance to tell you what is true.

An alert that a driverless cab was waiting for Claire outside the hotel dinged from her phone. Again she glanced at Will who still slept soundly in his bed, but when the image of Aven's face flaking off in ash invaded her thoughts, she quickly dressed and left the chocolate chip pancakes, and the man she loved behind.

FORGIVE ME, YOUR GRACE

WEDNESDAY, 5:35 A.M.
OAHU, HAWAII

AVEN stared at the streaks of the pink and blue horizon, thinking up different scenarios of how the next few hours would play out. His chest was tight, heavy, and prickling with anxiety. He wished he could see the future. He wasn't sure if what he was about to do was a mistake. But Mal's instructions had been clear. There's only one way to save his soul.

He knew before Claire knocked on his door that she had arrived. He could sense when she was close from the peace and warmth that always relaxed his tense shoulders. Strength filled his weak legs, and he stood tall with his chin lifted high. He would keep this princess safe. He would kneel and vow it.

"Aven?" Claire said, looking around his spacious villa. "I got your note."

Aven watched her for a moment, standing in the full two-wall opening. He would have given her a tour of the five-bedroom home, pointed out the forty-foot ceilings, asked her to swim in the pool, sip a mimosa, but he wasn't the rich bachelor right now. He was a desperate man with everything to lose.

"I didn't think you would come," he said, slipping his hands into his white linen pants.

Claire eyed his defined torso, revealed by his unbuttoned matching shirt.

"I want the truth," she said finally.

"Then I'll tell you everything."

Claire glanced at her phone. "I only have an hour."

"Have somewhere you need to be?"

"The moment you give me a line, I'm gone."

"Fair enough," Aven said and gestured for her to follow him down the steps of his lawn to the beach.

They were only a few feet from his home before Aven began telling a haunting story about his pitiful past.

"I was ten when Will's father killed mine," Aven began. "After his funeral, I went to live with my uncle, who had a son close in age."

"Vincent?"

Aven nodded. "My uncle Jimmy groomed us to take over the business and led us in the ways of the Circle. Time seemed to blur by throughout the rest of my childhood and young adult life. Too much money. Too many parties. I was devastated when my uncle died suddenly; we had been close, but I didn't have much time to grieve during my studies abroad in Britain. On my twenty-first birthday, Vincent held an initiation ceremony; the money from my father's will was added to my bank account. So after the transfer of a little over six million dollars, I got piss drunk, bought whatever my greedy heart desired, and painted the town red until I received a text message to see the Oracle."

"An Oracle?" Claire asked, bemused. "Like a medium?"

"Before the night of your initiation ends, you are to consummate with one. So I went to the address given. It was the first time I met Bree. She was just as stunning back then as she is now. Having been a young man, I was overjoyed to be taken to her bed. She explained what would happen, the pleasure that was to come, but before anything could happen, we would have to do a spell that would summon a spirit guide. Not only for the pleasure, but for the enlightenment after."

"The succubus."

Aven nodded. "The *act*, as I'll call it, was nothing like I had ever experienced. But it came with a price. At the time, I didn't realize that the spell would curse me." Aven stopped and pulled his unbuttoned shirt to the side, revealing a tattoo. "Or brand me for life."

Claire furrowed her brows, studying the symbol. "What's it mean?"

"'Do thy will," Aven informed her, now knowing it wasn't his will signified, but Nehia's.

"I don't remember seeing a tattoo on your chest."

"Well." Aven smirked. "You were a bit preoccupied the last time I was naked."

"I think I know this symbol," Claire said, tracing the wings.

"That's because you've seen it before. You know this is Aalok's symbol, a mark of an Outcast."

Claire straightened and her eyes widened. "You know?"

A wry smile formed on Aven's lips. "I know you're still a stubborn princess just like you were before. That my name was Serus, and yours was Sophie. You were a Truth Keeper, and I was a rebel without a cause."

Claire's lashes fluttered before she squeezed her eyes shut. "How do you know all of this?"

"I've had visions of my past and my future. That's why I came here, Claire. I had a vision of you. A bad one. I had to make sure you were alright, that Will wouldn't . . . "

Claire's shoulders tensed at his silence. "Wouldn't what?"

"You drown, Claire. I saw Will holding you down. Your face was under the water. Your eyes were open, wide with panic. You were struggling to come up for air."

"No." Claire shook her head and backed away from him.

"I know it's hard to believe Will is capable of something like that. But I know what I saw."

Claire placed a hand to her head. Her eyes darted back and forth before they lit up as if a thought had made everything clear. "You saw the ceremony," she said.

Aven tilted his head. "What ceremony?"

"My dedication to Aramis. Will has to hold me under for three seconds. I'm supposed to be on the beach right now meeting him and Levi." She slipped her phone from her pocket and looked at the time. "I have to go. They'll be waiting for me," Claire turned to go back the way they came.

"My hour's not up," Aven called out. "You said you wanted the truth, and I have many more sins to confess, Truth Keeper."

PROPOSAL

EVERYTHING Aven had admitted, everything he had bared with complete vulnerability had been the absolute truth. Claire knew by his voice, by looking into his eyes that he hadn't lied.

Aven had told her about Nehia, the succubus, and her possession, how it was the reason he was forced to take so many women to bed. He then told Claire about a girl, Alex Anderson, and how she had died by Aven's own hands. Claire tried to reassure him it wasn't his fault, but Aven only kept shaking his head, saying it still haunted him. He had taken Claire's hands then, told her that he couldn't bear to have those images of her face in his mind and that he had said all those harsh words to protect her. He had cared enough to let her go.

Aven then went on to admit his feelings for Kitten, told Claire about the visions of her and him. He explained how guilty he felt for sleeping with Bree, but that in doing so, she had released him from his curse. He was finally free of Nehia.

Spilling his truth had taken well over an hour, and now, Claire was late to her ceremony and left with nothing but more questions and a swimming head. She hadn't even had a chance to talk about his redemption.

"Aven," Claire began, but a notification from her phone vibrated her back pocket.

W: Are you okay?

"He worries about you," Aven noted.

He should. After all, I'm here with you. How you acted last night. That's all it was. An act. All of it. Aven cares about you. And you care about him.

Only because of our past connection. Only because of my promise.

"Did you tell him you were meeting me?" Aven asked, breaking her from her thoughts.

Claire shook her head and messaged Will an apology, letting him know she would be back soon.

"How unlike you, Sophie," Aven teased.

The wave of déjà vu snapped Claire's gaze to Aven's.

"Do you have a book? Is that how you know everything?" she asked.

"No. I told you. I had visions and dreams," Aven reminded her. "I can show you them if you like."

When Aven placed his warm palms against her cheekbones and thumbs against her temples, Claire froze.

"Tell me instead," she said, taking a step out of his grasp. She didn't want to go through more hypnosis.

"It's not something I can simply explain," Aven said, furrowing his brows. "I'm not going to hurt you, Claire. We've Mind Walked before when I cured your fear of heights. Although, this is a Memory Lapse. But they are much the same."

Everything Will had told Claire last night shot through her brain like a bullet. Her breaths grew shallow as she stared at Aven in horror. Serus had manipulated Sophie, and Claire was sure Aven had been manipulating her all along. All the "truths" he told seemed full of holes now, twisted in his favor to make her feel sorry for him.

"Mind Walking," Claire breathed. "That's what it's called."

"What did Will tell you?"

"He said InfiniCorp used it to make super soldiers. They were forced to kill each other. How could you do that? How could you murder his little brother? "

"Lower your voice," Aven hissed. "Before you get both of us euthanized."

Claire swallowed and looked around for any sign of cameras or recording devices. They could have been in the trees or the rocks nearby. They were always well hidden. But it didn't matter. She and Aven had been talking about demons and possession. She wasn't about to stop with conspiracies now.

"You asked me if Will has given me a reason to trust him," Claire said, "and he has. He's been honest with me. But you–" She was breathing hard now, boiling with anger. "I don't know if I can forgive you for what you did to him."

Aven's brows rose. "What *I* did to him?"

"InfiniCorp. You own the company, don't you? You've been experimenting on people, manipulating them."

"Claire, let me explain."

"Then explain. Stop treating me like some crystal ballerina that sits on a wobbly shelf."

"I can't until we're married. It's one of the Circle's rules. But when we're married, you can ask me anything you want and–"

Claire's heart stopped. "Married?" She took a step back as her upper lip curled in disgust. "What makes you think I would marry you?"

"I was going to do this much different," Aven said. He ballooned his cheeks and blew out a breath before he got down on one knee.

Claire shook her head, not believing what Aven was doing. He had told her about Mal, how the fallen angel had paid him a visit, had explained about the bonding. Claire didn't think Aven had actually considered it. Not until now.

"Don't say it," she bit out.

"Claire–"

"Don't, because the answer will be no. You haven't changed. You're still thinking of yourself. You've only ever thought of what you could gain."

"Then forgive me," Aven pleaded. "Purge me of my sins."

"I can't. Even if I wanted to. I don't have that power."

"You do," Aven said, coming to his feet. "You're a Truth Keeper."

"Aven, all of your trespasses, everything you've done in this life can only be forgiven by the Creator. Not me and not anyone else. Only. Him."

Aven's eyes narrowed to slits. "Says who?"

"I should never have come." Claire turned to storm off, but Aven appeared in front of her out of thin air. She stumbled back, in shock, but he snatched her up and spun her into his arms.

"The end will be here soon," he said in her ear. "You can see the red planet." He pointed to the sun over the horizon. "It's like a shadow of the sun. When it crosses, hell will be unleashed on Earth."

Claire squinted, finding a faint reddish circle northwest of the bleeding sun.

Two suns. Will's vision.

"The earthquake was the first woe, the next will signal Aalok's arrival," he explained. "We only have until the harvest moon to get away before Vincent—" Aven cut his words short. "Claire, I need you to trust me."

"Vincent?" Claire twisted out of Aven's grasp and stared at him. She thought about Abby, about the shadows the little girl saw. "What does he have to do with this?"

"I swear, I wasn't involved with Aaron's death or what was done to Will, and I'm going to make damn sure the person responsible pays for what they did. Just please." Aven took Claire by the shoulders and pleaded with his eyes. "Marry me. Let me show you the world before it crumbles. Let me give you the life you always dreamed of. I can distract you from the chaos. When it's all over, you and Will can live happily ever after in the afterlife. All I'm asking is for the time we have left here on Earth. All I'm asking for is redemption. All I'm asking for is a second chance."

"If you know who I am, then you know what I have to do. I can't just hide away in some penthouse watching the world burn."

"Don't be stupid. You can't stand up to Aalok. He'll convince you to turn and then both of our souls will be damned."

"You're no different now than you were before," Claire snapped. "Even if I say yes, even if I spend every single day with you until the end, it wouldn't matter. It didn't then and it won't now."

An alert dinged from Claire's phone.

W: Did you change your mind?

Claire assumed Will found the cart with the chocolate chip pancakes. She would assure him that she loved him, that it was her Guardian she would choose again. But she wouldn't tell him in a text, she would say it face to face.

"I have to go," she told Aven and turned to go up the villa steps. Yes. She had made a promise, but she wouldn't fulfill it. Not like this.

"Sophie, wait."

Claire came to a halt and tried to swallow the thorns in her throat. She battled with the dream of Aven turning to ash, battled with choosing her destiny over a soul she had vowed to help save. But in her heart, she knew Aramis would find a way to help Aven if He could.

Turning slowly, she dared to look into Aven's eyes, now full of fear. "That princess you knew, the one you're still holding onto," she said, "she died so that others could live. I'm not the one to save you, Serus. Not anymore."

Aven blew a breath through his lips and watched Claire climb the steps to his villa, run through his house, and rush out his front door.

She's going to tell Will about your desperate attempt to steal her away from him. Kitten's going to give you hell. And then . . . you're going there when you die.

A few strides from the sandy steps of his home, Aven stood at the edge of the surf, thinking of how he could fix this. At least he knew Claire wasn't going to die. She would be at the ceremony soon. She would be dedicating her life in service to the Creator.

She made her choice, and for the second time, it wasn't me.

Part of him was proud of her. In a way, he had hoped she would deny him.

She's not hopeless anymore, but it appears that I am.

He watched the waves roll over his toes, then pull back, but the bubbling surf didn't return.

Aven followed the tide drawing out to sea, finding a hazy scene before him. A vision.

Claire was in the shallows with Will. An old man across from them signed with a gloved hand.

The book. Vincent will still want her to read it. You should have told her.

But telling such secrets means death. No questions asked, just a bullet to the head.

You're going to die anyway. You saw it. Why not die with some sort of dignity?

Telling his inner demons to shut up, Aven continued to study the mirage.

A little boy and girl ran to the surf, squealing with joy. A yellow umbrella was swept up in the wind. A local was strumming a ukulele. Waves drew away from Claire's ankles, drawing out to sea. Aven then saw his future self staring at the clouds expanding and rushing in over the ocean.

Not clouds.

There were seconds for Aven to decide, seconds to make a choice.

Save the Truth Keeper or save himself.

32

MAKING WAVES

WEDNESDAY, 9:03 A.M.
OAHU, HAWAII

AVEN stood a few feet from the shore, now dressed in black. His best suit seemed appropriate for this kind of funeral, but he hoped his visions were wrong. In his gut, he knew they weren't. He glanced around the beach, finding everything taking place just as it had in the haunting premonition.

A little boy and girl were playing nearby, squealing with joy. A yellow umbrella was swept up in the wind. A local was strumming a ukulele.

Creator, help me. Should I warn them now?
No one would listen. Wait until you see the waves.
If I wait, they die.

Vincent's voice echoed in his mind. *"Of their own stupidity."*

This was how it had happened in the vision. This was what he saw before the sea drew out and built wave upon wave with a watery wall of destruction.

Taking steps closer, Aven stopped at the surf, watching the waves roll over his dress shoes and roll back away. He focused on Will, Claire, and the old man, all of them out several feet in the shallows, and read their lips.

Claire promised to follow the Creator, to let him guide her path, no matter how rocky it may be. She vowed to keep the faith and to stand firm when the time came to stand before the fallen one.

"Praise be to Aramis and His will," the old man mouthed with a proud smile before he nodded to Will.

This is what you saw, Crey. This is how she dies. Warn them now.

As Will dipped Claire under, Aven held his breath for three seconds and then exhaled as she rose. He watched her eyes light up as she opened them, and the halo, the same white hue Aven had seen in the penthouse, encompassed her delicate silhouette. Even from this far away, he could feel her warmth. He would give up everything to have that peace. But he was damned. And if Claire wouldn't marry him, it didn't matter if he chose to side with good or not. Hell awaited him at death. And death could take him in a matter of moments.

"Now you have risen anew," Levi's gloves said. **"Devoted mind, body, and spirit to the king and creator of all. Go forth and walk in the light of his truth."**

Claire blinked the saltwater from her eyes and gazed up at Will a long moment. The sunlight kissed his face, making him appear as the warrior, the angel she had always loved.

This was where her new life began. This was where she took the first step toward her true destiny.

She hugged Will, then Levi, but a shudder beneath their feet drew her attention to the water.

A hand squeezed Claire's arm with a painful grasp. Her head snapped to Aven. "What are you—" she began, but he only tightened his grip.

"We need to get off the beach," Aven said to her. He looked at Will and Levi. "Head to the highest building you can find. Get to the top if you can."

Claire followed Aven's fearful gaze as he set it back on the horizon. The moment she saw the long line of waves in the distance, her mouth parted. She watched them build. They never broke formation but crested wider, taller. Though they seemed small and far off, Claire knew their true size. This was how it had started. This had been the beginning of Sophie and Alexander's end.

"Will," she whispered in a shaky voice.

A hard squeeze came to her arm again, and she watched Aven whip around and yell to the tourists. "Kai e'e! Kai e'e!" He then turned to Will and Levi. "Run, you idiots!"

Aven jerked on Claire's arm, cueing her to move her feet, but she pried his fingers away instead.

Aven planted a firm grip on her shoulders and twisted her to face him. "If you don't come with me, you die."

Claire looked to Will with pleading eyes, unwilling to leave his side.

"Go," Will urged. "I'll help Levi, even if I have to carry him."

"You can't," Claire said in a quivering voice.

"I can," Will said assured.

"Claire," Aven admonished as he tugged.

"I'm not leaving them!" Claire shouted at Aven.

"If I say the key phrase and put you under, you could drown," Aven hissed. "You have to come with me."

"Go," Will told her, caressing her cheek. "Aven will keep you safe."

Claire squeezed Will's hand, but he slipped from her grasp as Aven tugged her away.

As Aven and Claire ran, Will set his eyes on Levi and took a deep breath. "Ready?"

"To go home? Yes."

"No. Levi—"

"This is where I leave you." Levi took off his gloves and offered his hand.

The moment Will grasped his forearm, Levi's appearance changed. He saw Levi young, a captain of a ship, trying to sooth Alexander's rage.

"Zeruiah," Will whispered.

"May Aramis be with you, my friend."

"You knew this would happen."

"A thousand years here is only a day on the other side. I'll see you in a few moments."

Will's eyes pooled with tears as he slipped his hand away. "Farewell,"

"Farewell," Levi smiled sadly and walked toward the wave with open arms.

"Don't look back!" Aven barked. "Keep running!"

Claire winced as he tugged her. Somehow that pain, the stretch of her arm being pulled from the socket brought back a memory. It wasn't Aven that had been trying to protect her. It was Alexander.

Every decision that had led her to this moment raced through her mind. Her mother's death. Searching the attic. Finding the book. Her visit with Serena. Little Levi and his ominous assurance.

The knight can't save Paw Paw, but he can save you.

Without a second thought, she jerked from Aven's grasp and ran to her Guardian.

"Claire!" Aven cursed and ran after her.

"Claire, what are you doing?" Will yelled.

She slammed into him, wrapping her arms tight around his waist.

"Aramis will see to it we survive," she assured, burying her face in his chest. Bracing for impact, she squeezed her eyes shut, but they flew open again to a shout.

"Idiots!" Aven growled. "Faith can't save you!"

He took a stance and looked up at the wave cresting in his dark blue eyes.

"But maybe I can," he said, holding up his hand as if commanding the water to stop.

The raging current listened, slamming into an invisible shield in front of them. While water whirled with a fierce noise around the three of them, Claire and Will stared at Aven in awe.

After several hammering heartbeats, Aven's hand shook. He groaned and brought up his other hand, bearing all his weight against the opposing force.

Saltwater funneled past their invisible protection and plowed over the tourists and locals remaining on the beach.

The three of them were underwater now, protected by the bubble Aven had summoned, but his hands shook furiously.

He struggled to look at Claire, and then at Will.

Will nodded at Aven as if saying it was okay to let go.

Before Claire could protest, Aven wrapped his arms around her waist and the sea swallowed them whole.

A flash of a twinkling cave came to Claire's mind, then another image of her being sucked through a black watery vortex. Her lungs begged for breath as she tumbled, still wrapped in Aven's arms. After two more tumbles, the current ripped her away from his fingertips. She was rolling, shoved left to right by the black. Her lungs burned with fire as saltwater forced its way into her mouth. There was no escaping, no breaking the grip of the watery beast that wrestled her.

Stars filled her vision when something hard smacked into her head. Bubbles escaped her lips. Weightlessness filled her limbs. She floated gently down into a deep dark void, taking in water. There was no burning in her chest now, no sound sloshing in her ears, or any sight of blue.

Claire thought of Aramis, of how He had sunk in the dark with no hope of getting to the surface for air. And then, she closed her eyes, saying a prayer and thought of the family that waited on the other side of a curtain she couldn't see.

BEYOND

THE

VEIL

A TEARFUL

REUNION

WITH a flutter of her eyes, Claire woke to an aurora borealis above. It waved in purple, pink, and green, and past it, stars twinkled in a vibrant nebula-filled sky of blue-black.

She rested her head in the soft substance beneath her and ran her fingers through the warm grains of what she knew could only be sand. When the sound of waves filled her ears, she wondered if she was imagining the galaxy.

Am I still in Hawaii?

Sitting upright was easy, taking no effort at all, and she felt that if she had wanted to, she could float to the sky like a prayer lantern.

Am I imagining Sophie's favorite place to avoid the horror of drowning? Is my mind coping like it always does?

She glanced around her, finding a calm sea to her right. A forest of palm trees rustled to her left. She scooped a handful of sand into her palm, studying the pastel pink grains as they glinted. She glanced up again, finding no sun, but there was light. She set her gaze back on the pile of sand, zooming in on the particles. She could see every individual one, see the smooth roundness of one single grain out of the hundreds in her hand.

A lukewarm breeze caressed her skin as if beckoning her to stand. When she did, she looked down the beach, finding something like a mirage. It wavered, as if the air were blazing hot, and came closer, forming into that of a man.

Claire drew in a breath, but as she did, she wondered if it was in fact oxygen expanding her ribs. If she even had ribs. Being in this place, she wasn't so sure. Seeing the man clearly now, she could only assume she was Beyond the Veil. As he came to stand before her, Claire exhaled all at once.

"Hey there, Claire Bear," he said with a sweet smile.

"Dad?" she whispered.

She stared at her father, seeing how young he was. He appeared to be about the same age as her, about the same age she had seen him in the photograph she had taken to the worship center. Tears poured from her eyes as she wrapped her arms around his neck and squeezed him tight.

"I missed you so much," she cried.

"Shhh," her father said, taking a step back. "Wipe those tears."

"I'm dead."

"Yes, sweetheart."

"Where's Mom? Where's the white light we go into?"

"It's not your time. You have to go back."

"What do you mean 'go back?'"

"Your job isn't finished, honey."

Claire didn't want to leave. Not now, not ever. Everything Beyond the Veil was so perfect. She had no fear. She was full of peace and an all-consuming love. She was with her father again. She could be reunited with her mother, her brother, and her little nephew.

"You have no idea how many souls you have already affected over your lifetime, Claire, how many souls who will believe because of what you are going to do."

"Claire!"

She knew this far-off voice, felt the panic of the one it belonged to.

"Aven," she said under her breath.

"Please . . ." he pleaded.

Guilt flooded her chest. She never counseled him. She had chosen to turn her back on him.

"Where is he?" she asked her father.

"You need to go back," he replied.

Claire thought about her and Aven's walk on the beach. He had been asking for her forgiveness, begging her to help him change. He was a better person because of her. He had been willing to change the course of his life, but she let her anger get the best of her. She could have forgiven him. She could have asked him to go talk to Will.

"Answer me!" Aven screamed.

It's not over, Claire told herself. He's not dead. I can still make things right.

Claire felt the Creator's warmth before she turned. He was a towering bright figure before her. His power and might danced like the aurora borealis above, but in the whitest of white. She couldn't see his face, not past his brightness, but somehow she could feel him smiling down at her.

"Aramis," Claire said as her knees threatened to buckle under the weight of his unconditional love. She was ready to bow down before Him, to weep at His feet, but her father took her hand and supported her.

"It's your choice," her father said.

Claire's heart filled with hope at the words, and she nodded her head to the Creator, letting him know she was ready to fulfill her destiny. "I'm ready."

Aramis placed His hand on her shoulder, filling Claire's entire being with strength. She could feel herself fading, feel this place dripping away like the words on a page from a flood of tears.

"I love you, baby girl." Her father's voice was distant now. "I'll see you again soon."

A DESPERATE

PRAYER

Wednesday, 9:32 a.m.
Oahu, Hawaii

SALTWATER dripped down Aven's chin as he coughed up the sea from his lungs. He glanced beside him, seeing Claire a few feet away in the inlet they had washed upon. He ran to her side, but the instant he scooped her limp body into his arms, panic clutched his heart. Her lips were purple like the lavender of the meadow fields at Will's horse farm. No breath came from them.

No one did CPR anymore, but Aven was desperate, and he would attempt anything to save her life. Placing his mouth over hers, he gave his breath and pressed on Claire's chest.

Over and over he dug the heel of his palm. Over and over he exhaled past her cold lips.

Nothing. No response. Not a flinch.

"Claire!" He shook her and continued pressing on her chest, gave every breath he had no matter how dizzy he became.

"Please . . ." Aven begged, taking Claire in his arms. He swept her wet hair from her face and caressed her wet face. "I don't care about my salvation," he told her. "I don't care if you damn me to hell for all I've done," he said to the Creator. "Just please, don't take her from this world."

Nothing. No breath. No pulse.

His eyes burned as tears fell.

He screamed to the sky, "Did you do this just to punish me? Huh? Did you bring her into my life just to take her away again? She could go on to save others. Just bring her back so she can do that!"

No response. Not from Claire. Not from the Creator.

"Answer me!"

Claire spurted water from her mouth and coughed.

Relief spread through Aven as he helped her sit up.

"I died," she managed to say in a strangled voice. "I need–I need to tell you–."

Aven swept her up into her arms. "You can tell me at the hospital."

WASHED AWAY

WEDNESDAY, 3:07 P.M.
OAHU, HAWAII

WILL groaned and coughed, rolling onto his side as his lungs burned. Trees lay broken on the shore beside him; pieces of huts and splintered wood leaned on end as if a bomb had assaulted the beach. It didn't look like a beautiful tranquil shore any longer, but a sandy heap covered with a mangled mess of bodies and debris.

A war ground.

Will stood and forced himself to look around. He covered his mouth, finding the backside of a body, then another twisted, face up, and lifeless. His gut sunk to his feet, and he held back the sour bile stinging the back of his tongue.

Aven protected her. Claire's alive. She has to be.

A stab of guilt pierced his chest thinking of Levi. He had been washed away. Will could have saved him. But it had been Levi's choice. He was with his wife now and Will would see him again soon.

Trudging his way through the debris left from the flood, Will spied a hand peeking out from it. His stomach churned at its tiny size, and he made haste to dig the little boy out of soggy garbage. Regardless of his purple face, Will recognized this child as one who had been playing nearby with a little girl. There were no floaties on him now, but the yellow umbrella had somehow accompanied him with the other garbage. The little girl was nowhere to be found.

Finding a weak pulse, Will assured the child he would be okay and then called for help, from someone, anyone.

Locals coming from the street rushed to his side.

"He's alive," Will informed them and passed the boy off. He then looked to the blocked street. There was no way to get a car through, no passage to help people get the care the wounded needed. He joined a crew, moving the debris, working for hours to clear it. When dusk fell, he was given a ride in one of the ambulances to the closest hospital.

The beach, although it had looked like the aftermath of a war, was a peaceful sanctuary compared to the chaos of the hospital. Mothers and fathers screamed over their lifeless children, doctors hurried past, babies wailed with raspy cries. Every time Will passed a covered body, he prayed it wasn't

Claire or Aven. He prayed they were alive, that somehow they had survived this catastrophe.

Will checked every list, asked every doctor and nurse for a petite brunette with green eyes and a dark-haired male in a suit, but Claire and Aven couldn't be found.

Shock set in. Before Will realized it, he was wandering through the biohazard unit. It was quiet here. No nurses. No doctors. No dead. Just him. Alone.

He set his eyes on the word EXIT, feeling as if the red glow was a sign Aalok had won, that everything he believed in had been of his own delusion.

But those thoughts quickly fled the moment he saw the couple behind the glass.

It wasn't Aven's messy black hair that had drawn Will to the window. It had been the girl beside him in the hospital bed with long brown hair. It was like seeing his mother all over again; the IVs, the oxygen tubes. Will fixed his eyes on the machines. Even from this distance, he could see the tiny numbers on the screen and the steady spike of Claire's heartbeat.

He assumed Aven had paid to have this room because it was away from all the chaos. Will was glad he did. He could finally think about what he was going to say to his brother.

He gave a light knock on the glass.

Aven lifted his head. His shoulders fell in relief, and he kissed Claire on the forehead before he came out into the hall. He slipped his hands in the pockets of the scrubs; he had no doubt borrowed, and said,

"You look like crap,"

"How is she?"

"They said she'll be fine, but they want to keep her overnight."

Will let out a ragged breath and grabbed the door handle. "Good."

"You lied to me,"

Will drew back his hand slowly. "About what?"

"William Stryde isn't my brother."

Will held his breath.

"Carpenter," Aven teased. "The last name suits you better than the stupid 007 alias."

"How did you find out?"

Aven shrugged. "The cemetery."

"So you've known for a while, then."

"When I got back to Vegas, I did some digging. Found out about Aaron . . . your last 'mission,' how he was murdered, and how they dumped your body in the North Pacific. It's a miracle you survived the fall, let alone the shark-infested waters, with a bullet wound." Aven set his gaze back on Claire. "You should have stayed dead, brother."

A knot rose in Will's throat. "Were you involved in Aaron's death?"

Aven brought his gaze back to Will and narrowed his eyes. The look he gave made it seem like Will had taken a literal stab at him. "Do you know what they did to your brother when they brought his body back to the lab?"

Will swallowed hard. He didn't want to know. Not really. But he knew Aven was going to tell him.

"They dissected him," Aven continued. "Cut him up into little pieces and studied him. Is that what you want to happen to you? To Claire?"

"Claire?" Will shook his head. "She wasn't experimented on. Why would InfiniCorp want her?"

"Because somehow, without relation, you share the same gene. A gift from–" Aven traced A-R-A-M-I-S on the glass.

Will flinched at the name.

The book in Vincent's parlor. Can he read it?

"How do you know about–"

"The blood is the key to making the formula of Solace work," Aven explained.

Will remembered the commercials about Solace, the petitions that had been all over the newsfeeds in the hospitals. It hadn't been approved. But it was clear now that signatures were being scribbled as he and Aven spoke. They needed Solace to heal the world, to save them.

"I'll donate," Will said, rushing through his words. "He doesn't need her blood."

"He doesn't just want her blood," Aven said. "He wants her to read–"

"No,"

"He won't stop. He's obsessed with finding out what it contains. All he needs are the keys."

"The one that opens the lock,"

"And the other that unlocks the code," Aven added. "You need to disappear again. I can ensure Claire's safety if–"

"I'll go in her place."

"He doesn't want you to read it. He wants you dead."

"He's not touching her."

"This isn't the past, Guardian. You may have been her protector before, but right now, I'm the only one who can keep her safe."

Will gave Aven a wary look.

"I won't let him hurt her," Aven said softly, taking a step closer to Will. "Once she reads the book, he'll be satisfied."

"How do you know?"

"I don't, but I know how Vincent's mind works."

Will scoffed. "Cunning, deceptive. You can't protect her from a murderer. Even with what you can do."

The image of Aven holding back the wave came to Will's mind. He wondered if Vincent had the same ability and whether Aven could combat him.

"I can do much more than part the sea, I can assure you." Aven smiled with a wiggle of his brows. He then wet his lips setting his gaze back on Claire. "If you love her as much as I think you do, you'll do the right thing and disappear just like you did before. I can give her a life you can't. One in which she'll never want for anything. No harm will come to your counselor. I promise you."

Will couldn't believe they were having this conversation. "If you know who she is, then you know what she is supposed to do."

"I'll take her to Rome myself, see to it she's first in line when *He* arrives. When it's all over, I'll bring her back to you. But I can't promise she'll have the same last name."

Will looked at Claire through the glass. The muscles in his jaw tightened as he fought against his emotions. Everything inside him screamed to run into the room and whisk her away. But he didn't. This wasn't about him. It was about Claire and what she was meant to do. Maybe this was where their paths diverged. Maybe seeing her with him at the safe house had only been a hope. This angel had protected him from the demons of his guilt, and he had only imagined protecting her until the end of the world.

Tearing his gaze away from Claire, he looked Aven dead in the eyes. "If anything happens to her, I'll be coming after you. And I can promise you one thing: It'll hurt. A lot."

Aven smirked, and Will knew he was thinking of the first time they had met.

"I'll give you a free shot." Aven winked. "Just don't go for the money maker."

Will stared at the Truth Keeper through the glass. Aven loved her, and because he did, Claire was going to live. She would fulfill her destiny. He just wouldn't be there to see it. She had a new savior, and it wasn't him.

"How will you be able to convince her I'm dead?" Will asked after a long moment.

Aven furrowed his brows as if it were painful to speak. "It will be as if you were only a dream, all of it. Hawaii, Levi, your short-lived romance. Anything that would question our life together."

Will crossed his arms. "More hypnosis?"

"Something like that," Aven answered.

"She needs to know the truth."

"It's my way or the alternative."

Will's eyes darted to Claire as she stirred in her hospital bed.

"I have your word?" Will asked, offering his hand.

"You have my word." Aven shook it.

Forcing himself to walk toward the hospital exit, Will didn't look back.

"I'll be seeing you, brother," Aven called out behind him.

". . . No," Will said looking over his shoulder, "you won't."

Claire's eyes fluttered at the kiss on her knuckles. Her head was pounding. Her chest was sore. She thought about where she had just been Beyond the Veil. She had visited with her father, with Aramis. She didn't want to be back in her heavy body, but she had made the choice to come back. She set her gaze on Aven, knowing she had to counsel him.

"Hey there, Princess," he said with a small smile.

"Aven," she croaked, glancing around the room. The world seemed like technicolor compared to the crisp HD picture she had been looking at on the other side of the veil. Nothing could compare to the joy and peace she had felt being in that place. She could still feel it, but it was faint and too far away.

She set her blurry gaze back on Aven. "I have to tell you where I was. I have to—"

"Shh," Aven cooed. He leaned down and caressed her face. "Everything's going to be just fine."

Claire's chest ached when she saw the fear in Aven's eyes. She could feel a presence nearby, could feel it leaving with remorse. Will was alive, but she could feel a part of him dying.

As Aven warmed Claire's hands in his, pain ached in his chest, knowing what he must do. It was the only way to keep her safe, to keep his brother alive.

"Where's Will?" she asked.

Aven brushed her tears away gently and kissed her forehead. Two little words. That's all it would take. Just two whispered words to erase Will from her mind and replace the memory with a life in which he never existed.

Biding his time, Aven glanced at the IV line bleeding with black. Solace trickled through the tube much too slowly for his liking, but once it streamed past the tape on Claire's hand, he exhaled a shaky breath.

"Claire," he said, locking his eyes on hers. "I promise."

Claire's head sunk into her pillow, tilting slightly to the side.

Aven swept the hair from her face with sweet sentiment before quoting his favorite book that his mother had read to him as a child: "You should see the garden far better," he whispered. "If you could get to the top of that hill, and there's a path that leads straight to it—at least, no it doesn't do that—but I suppose it will at last."

PARAMNESIA

FEAR pounded at Claire's chest. She was drowning again, reaching for the surface with no hope. Someone was standing on the water above her. Aramis. She knew it had to be him. But when he plunged his hand into the water and drew her up, it wasn't her king. A mask covered this man's face. As he removed it, Claire saw Aalok, bearing a cunning smile like that of a serpent.

Jolting up in bed, Claire threw off the silk sheets.

A cool draft hit her body.

The stark alarm wasn't from finding herself naked. It was from the ring on her left hand that glinted.

Blinking away the haze of sleep, she stared at the diamond that sat snug between two onyx stones. The ring was breathtaking and by the size of the rock she could tell it had cost a fortune.

"Another bad dream?" a gravelly voice asked.

She tensed at the hand sliding over her thigh as her gaze snapped to the man beside her.

A pair of familiar sultry eyes stared back at her.

"What happened last night?" she demanded.

"I hate it when you forget how awesome I am in bed," Aven sighed, resting his head on his palm. "I can remind you if you'd like."

Claire tried to ignore how good he smelled, how her body went loose as his fingers trailed down her leg.

What am I doing? Where is Will?

She clenched her thighs and pushed him away. "Stop,"

"Usually there is a 'don't' in front of that 'stop'. Are you not feeling well?" He asked and kissed the back of her hand.

She jerked it away and held it up. "Why am I wearing this? We're not engaged." She watched Aven frown, rethinking her accusing tone. "Are we?"

"You don't remember?"

"Remember what?"

Aven gestured. "Hand me your phone."

"Claire got what she assumed was her phone off the nightstand and handed it over. She stared at it as Aven sat up.

The case was black, studded in diamonds. Black. Everything around her was black: the satin sheets, the décor, the floor, Aven's bed.

"I hate taking away screen time, but I can't have you calling the police again."

Claire shook her head. "Why would I—"

"What's the last thing you remember?"

Claire strained her mind. Her memories were blurry, scattered. "Hawaii. I was swept under a tsunami after you tried to hold back the wave with your superpowers. You're part fallen angel. Will . . . Will is my Guardian from a past life and I was—"

"A Truth Keeper?"

"You told me everything. About Mal, the deal you made, and . . ."

Aven's brows rose. "And?"

"Everything is blank after that. I-I don't know. I was in a hospital. I remember being in a hospital."

Aven let out a heavy sigh. "I hate this part."

"What part?"

"Claire," Aven said, taking her hands in his. "Do you remember the first time we met?"

"In Vegas. Laura and I were there for a bachelorette party. I met you at LAX."

"Yes, and after that?"

Claire thought she could remember seeing something about being saved from thugs, but when Aven squeezed her hands gently, it disappeared as if the picture had been blotted out with ink. There was nothing but a blank space.

Nothing but black.

"I-I don't know," she answered. She put a hand to her forehead as it throbbed. "It's all a blur."

Aven gently lifted her chin and made her look him in the eyes again.

"After our first night together at the Luxor," he said. "I took you to breakfast at Paula's."

I remember Paula.

"We spent the rest of the weekend together. Laura and your friends went home, but you stayed. I had made plans to take you to every place on your charm bracelet, took off work to take you around the world, but then my mother fell ill. We flew there. You held my hand during the funeral. That night, sitting at the piano, you told me you loved me, so I made love to you right there on the keys, and then you came back with me to Vegas for an event. I was there when you heard the news of the New York earthquake. I made every attempt to find your family."

"My mom, my brother, they're . . ."

"I went home with you when they had the vigil. You had an anxiety attack during the service, ran into the parking lot. I ran after you but—"

Aven's face pinched as if he was in pain.

"But what?"

"The guy didn't see you when he backed out. The doctors said it was a miracle that you weren't run over."

Claire squinted, seeing everything Aven was saying play out in her mind. Still, it didn't make sense. A face was still in the picture, flashing in and out.

Will . . .

Aven brought her face back gently to look him in the eyes. "Sweetheart . . . you can't trust your memories. Some of them aren't real."

Panic stabbed at Claire's chest.

He's lying.

"You were in a coma," Aven said.

Look in his eyes. Look for the truth.

Claire's breaths became short, shallow. "For how long?"

"A few days. When you woke up, your speech was slurred. I couldn't make out your words. You were upset about your family, but you were also talking about the tsunami that hit Hawaii."

Claire's eyes lit. "So there was a tsunami."

"Claire—"

"You held back the wave. I died. I went Beyond the Veil and came back. "

Aven cupped her face and made her keep eye contact. "This is what I mean about not trusting your memories. The doctors think you probably overheard the news of the wave while you were out. They say the coma changed your personality. They say your amnesia is permanent, that your mind is trying to help you cope with the loss. It created a dream that never existed while you were under. None of it was real."

"No." Claire shook her head. "Levi was real. I knew him as a child."

"You're right." Aven took his phone from his nightstand and scrolled through the photos before he gave it to Claire.

Claire stared at the photo of two tombstones with the name "Robinson" in the cemetery.

"He was buried with his wife a few days after your accident," Aven informed her. "I had someone take this picture and send it to me. I knew you wouldn't believe me otherwise."

"And Will?"

"Claire, you've never met my brother. You saw his picture on the mantle at my mother's before we went to the funeral. You asked about him, about Aaron."

You know that isn't the truth.

"They died in the war, seven years ago,"

No, he's not dead. He's probably looking for you. Aven's kidnapped you. You have to run away. Find Will. Find your Guardian.

The breath rushed from Claire's lungs. She set her eyes on the door as an ache swelled in her chest. Flashes of Will's face, of him standing in this very room protecting her from a drunk Aven swirled in her mind.

"Sweetheart."

Claire's chin was gently brought back so her eyes could focus on Aven.

"I need you to trust me," he said softly.

Pictures of Will in a Marine uniform invaded her thoughts, a scene of a boat with blue sails and strong hands guiding hers at a helm. Ruffling blond hair and a sweet smile faded, replaced by a weatherworn tombstone with the name "William Carpenter" and a date of his birth and death.

No.

"Don't strain," Aven said, squeezing her shoulder. "Don't fight to remember what's not real. Every time you do, it only gives you a migraine."

He's lying.
It's not real.
Don't forget the stars.
Don't trust your heart.

Trust the truth.

Claire pressed her palm to her hot cheek, then her aching forehead.

There's so many voices in my head. How can I be sure which one is mine?

Aven was right. It felt like her skull would explode right then and there from the pressure.

You can see in his eyes he's hiding something.

That's just the way Aven is.

Watch the way his mouth twitches at his lies.

Stop. Just stop talking!

Claire let out a whimper, cradling her head as it pounded.

"Claire."

A palm was out before her, offering a pill. It was black, chalky, and smelled like sulfur.

"It will make the headaches go away, and the ghosts."

"Ghosts . . ."

"The voices."

"Voices?"

See? He wants to help. He's trying to take care of you.

Don't take it.

Take the pill, Claire.

Don't.

"The doctors say you may never come back to me. But I don't believe that, and I don't plan on giving up. I need you to trust me. Let go of the past so we can move forward with our future together."

Claire thumbed the band of her ring. "Like our marriage?" she asked, looking up at him.

Aven smirked. "If you'll have me, Ms. Grace."

Claire stared at the pill a long moment before she threw it to the back of her throat.

Aven opened his mouth, a cue for her to do the same.

When she did, he said, "That's my girl," and offered her a bottle of water.

"Get dressed." He kissed her temple. "I have a surprise for you."

"I hate surprises," she grumbled and then glanced up with knitted brows, "don't I?"

"See? You're still you. I'll meet you downstairs, Princess."

A KILLER

"WELL, I've got good news and bad news," Jeremiah said, peeking his head into the storage room.

Will checked off the stock of rice on his tablet before leaving the bunker pantry and heading toward the kitchen.

The night Will had gotten back from Hawaii, he had packed his clothes, whatever food he could haul, and flew him, Blue, and Jeremiah to the snow-covered mountains of Montana. He couldn't stand being at his house or anywhere near his paintings. The fourth painting, the one Will never told Claire about, was out of sight but still hung in the living room of this bunker.

Jeremiah had set up his tech in the panic room and had kept tabs on Aven, but Aven had gone MIA the past few days, and that made Will nervous. He hadn't heard a word about

Claire or how she was doing. Will expected as much. Still, being able to know Aven's location had kept him somewhat sane.

"Can't find him?" Will asked Jeremiah, who was pouring a cup of coffee.

"No, I did, but . . ." Jeremiah took a sip from his cup.

Will paused from scooping the coffee grains to make a fresh pot. "But what?"

"I said there was bad news."

"Show me."

Jeremiah led the way through the hall and through a door leading into the panic room. Three monitors were on the wall. One was for the surveillance of the secluded land, another for the internet, and lastly, one that constantly scrolled an up-to-date newsfeed. On the screen, pictures and text were displayed with a familiar symbol.

"Remember how we connected everything about InfiniCorp?" Jeremiah asked, sitting down in a tattered leather-rolling chair.

"Yeah."

"A week ago Vincent visited Rome. We know the world government stuff is a ruse, that he's involved, but look who's right behind the pope."

Will studied the faces in the group shot. While Vincent shook hands with the pope, a familiar face behind him was scowling. Will knew that look, knew how the man's eyes narrowed with disapproval.

Aven.

"Son of—" Will cut himself off, remembering he and Aven's fight in Hawaii. "There has to be an explanation."

"He's been sipping champagne with the elitists while the rest of the world rots. What more proof do you need?"

"I don't see her."

"Your girl?"

Will had told Jeremiah everything about Hawaii, about how he felt about Claire, about Aven and what he could do. Jeremiah assumed Aven had been experimented. Will didn't bring up the fallen angel link, or anything about *The Book of Aramis* or the fact that he was Claire's Guardian. He only told Jeremiah it was purely a 'coincidence' she had been in Hawaii to see Levi. But Will didn't believe in coincidences. He could tell Jeremiah wasn't fully convinced either.

"If he was there, where was she?" Will asked.

"This photo was taken two days ago. And this"— Jeremiah tapped the touchpad and leaned back in his chair— "was taken yesterday."

Will stared at the picture of Aven on the front cover of *Time* magazine.

LAS VEGAS' MOST ELIGIBLE BACHELOR IS FINALLY GOING TO SAY 'I DO'

Will went back over his and Aven's conversation at the hospital in Hawaii. Aven promised he could protect Claire, but to keep her safe from Vincent, from the Circle, she had to change her last name.

Jeremiah sighed and put a hand on Will's shoulder. "Sorry, man."

"I knew it would happen, I just–"

"Didn't think it would be so soon?"

Will read the headlines on a new window.

SOLACE SAVES THOUSANDS

"That's not all I found," Jeremiah said as he brought up another window on the screen. "This is from five years ago."

Will looked over the document, finding it was from a morgue in Las Vegas. He studied a death certificate issued for a woman named Alex Anderson. On the bottom of a police document was the official statement of a murder case.

Suicide. Case closed.

Another screen popped up, showing a receipt for a very pricy casket, as well as a hefty life insurance claim.

"Vincent was the one who paid for the girl's funeral. But that's not what caught my attention. It was this one single fingerprint found at the crime scene. Jeremiah blew up the document, making sure Will saw the prints on the glass shard evidence and then another set of prints in another window screen.

At a tap of Jeremiah's finger, red dots lit around the lines of the prints, before blinking the word "match" and showing Aven's headshot.

Will dragged a hand down his five o'clock shadow. "Anything else?"

Jeremiah clicked on another window on the monitor and blew up an image. "This photo was taken the night before Alex Anderson was found dead. Aven was the last person seen with her after leaving the benefit."

Will rubbed his face, now flushing with heat. His heart fluttered with panic, making him pace the room.

"You left her with a killer, Will,"

"Where is he?"

"Vegas for now. But he booked a flight to the Maldives. It leaves tonight at twenty-three hundred hours.

"Still a no-fly zone there?"

"Yep."

"Call Caleb."

"What?"

"Call him. Do whatever it takes to get a hold of him."

"He told you never to contact him unless it was an emergency."

"I am pretty sure this qualifies," Will said and left Jeremiah to his search for the man who had created his Stryde alias.

ROSES RED

SUNDAY, 9:15 A.M.
LAS VEGAS, NEVADA

CLAIRE took cautious steps, letting Aven lead her with his hands over her eyes. She thought the surprise might be in a garage by the scent of gasoline, tires, and wax, but as he turned her, it was replaced by something sweet.

"No peeking," Aven teased.

Listening to the sound of a door whisk open, Claire fluttered her lashes as Aven uncovered her eyes. "I hope you like your surprise."

The sweet scent was undeniable now. There was a small trickling pond with white and black coy fish, white lattice lining the garden, and everywhere she looked, vines and bushes and trees with blooming white roses.

"It's beautiful," Claire said.

Aven took her hand and led her under a white arbor crawling with vines and more blooming white roses.

"I asked you to marry me under one just like this. I recreated the garden so every anniversary we could relive the moment."

Claire recalled being under a similar arbor, how Aven had kissed her, how fireworks exploded in the sky when their lips had touched, but one thing was off. "I thought the roses had been red," she said.

"Would you like me to paint them, your majesty?"

Claire gazed into his playful eyes, watched his charming smile spread. The gesture had been sweet, thoughtful, but too sudden. She took a step back, thinking of telling him she needed time, but he took her hand, now absent of her ring, and got down on one knee.

"Claire Evelyn Grace . . . before you, I had never met anyone with such honesty. You make me want to be a better man, and here I am, waking up every day, making sure that I can prove to you that I can be what you need, that I can be the man to protect you, to spoil you, to give you anything and everything your heart desires, to give you what you deserve. Be my light, be the sun always giving warmth through the darkness. Because no matter if you can't remember . . ."

Claire held her breath, seeing Will's face in her mind. For a moment she was lost in what she hoped was a memory.

"Even if I doubt, even if I lose my way, there's one thing I'll always remember."

"Aramis' words?"

"And that my knight in shining armor will come to my rescue."

"And if he's late again?"

Claire stared at her wrist.

Where is it? Where's my birthmark?

"I swear to remind you, every day for the rest of our lives, how much you mean to me," Aven continued. "Say yes. Say you'll stay. Don't leave me again to an alternate reality of your mind. Be my wife."

Claire closed her eyes and swallowed hard, pressing down the knot forming in her throat. Guilt swirled in her stomach as her chest squeezed so tight she thought it might burst.

She knew she loved Aven, knew from the way he was looking at her that he truly cared for her too. It was a desperate plea, a heartfelt request, but she didn't know if she could answer it.

As Aven stared up at her waiting, something happened, something magical.

A wind blew through the garden, carrying dancing white rose petals. They swarmed around her and Aven and froze as if waiting for her reply.

She recalled the tsunami again. Aven had been her savior. He had been the one in her dreams and visions keeping her safe. She knew by looking in his eyes that's all he wanted to do, and knowing this, she couldn't help but whisper "yes."

As Aven jumped to his feet and swept her up into his arms, the petals swirled into a tornado around them. Claire watched them in awe, letting the moment be joyous. But that joy soon faded the moment the rose petals bled red.

CLEAN SWEEP

SUNDAY, 7:05 P.M.
LAS VEGAS, NEVADA

THERE had been no answer when Kitten tried to call Paula's cell phone. She left several messages, apologizing for not coming in that morning for her shift. Although she was still hungover by late afternoon, she made another call, this time to the restaurant. It wasn't like Paula not to pick up the phone. Not even with a crowd. With no answer, she crawled out of bed and forced herself to put on a blouse and a pair of jeans.

It hadn't been the copious amounts of liquor Kitten downed or the voicemail Aven left that had led to her drunken-induced sleep. It had been the footage on the news, and seeing Aven next to Claire's hospital bed.

TSUNAMI SURVIVORS SAVED BY SOLACE

Since Hawaii had been bought back by Japan after WWE, InfiniCorp had bought a large shipment and had been secretly testing Solace there. Aven had informed her of that a few months ago. When Kitten saw the news pop up on her phone that a wave had hit, she knew the representative in Oahu had passed out the pills like candy. Aven had been in the right place at the right time. The poster child for InfiniCorp.

LAS VEGAS' MOST ELIGIBLE BACHELOR IS FINALLY GOING TO SAY 'I DO'

Kitten shoved her phone in her fuchsia purse and mumbled about Aven's voicemail.

"I wasn't exactly lying when I said I had to go out of town for work," Kitten mocked. "Asshole."

He had lied. Paula had been the one to tell her the truth when Kitten got the voicemail about his return with Claire. The truth was Aven had gone to Hawaii. He had been with Will and Claire. All Paula knew was that he had gone to apologize. He made Kitten stay behind because Nick wouldn't bother her at Paula's.

Speeding down the highway, Kitten went over her and Nick's argument the night before. She had gone with him to a party. He scolded her for working for Paula, told her she couldn't go to the worship center for Sunday service. She had already gone there for Wednesday night's potluck. That had been the first argument, Nick saying that his girl wouldn't be caught dead on that side of town with such—

Peasants.

That was the word that rubbed Kitten the wrong way. Nick had spoken of Paula as if she were a poor worker with no class or intelligence. Kitten said a few choice words of her own. In Kitten's eyes, Paula had more class than half the elitists she had socialized with at any event. Paula was wise beyond her years.

Because of the Words of Old.

Kitten had grown fond of their talks about the Creator, about Kitten's mother being with him, what a wonderful life her mother was living Beyond the Veil. During the worship center's Wednesday night potluck, Paula instructed Kitten not to talk about the Creator, to just listen to the message of the service, and sing to her little heart's content.

The message the worship counselor had given had been a good one, but it didn't hit home like her and Paula's heart to hearts. Kitten never felt more at ease, more welcome than when she was with Paula at the pancake house. The moment the word "Meager" came out of Nick's mouth, Kitten threw a drink in his face and told him it was over.

Red and blue lights flashed across the alley as Kitten rolled to a stop on Fremont Street. She watched the EMTs roll out the stretcher, wheeling a body bag to the open doors of the ambulance.

Oh no. Please no.

Kitten whiplashed the car into a faded handicap parking spot, and ran to the caution tape.

A cop with a poorly maintained mustache motioned for her to stop.

"What happened?" she demanded.

The officer placed a hand on his gun. "Ma'am, you need to leave,"

"I work here," Kitten explained. "The owner, Paula Benton, she's my boss, is she—"

"You work here?" the officer asked.

"Yes."

"Ma'am, I'm going to have to ask you a few questions."

"Was she in the body bag?"

"Ma'am, it's best if—"

"Enough bullshit! Tell me if she's dead!"

The shrill sound that came from Kitten's mouth surprised her. She was always one to keep her composure in public, but by the way the officer stepped back from her, she knew she was losing it.

"Please, Officer . . . Clark," she said coolly, glancing at his badge. "I just need some answers."

"I remember you." Officer Clark nodded, shaking his stylist pen at her.

Kitten's stomach rolled as he gave her a once over. "I don't think so."

Please don't be a past patron from Prancing Pony.

"You're Aven Crey's personal assistant."

Took you long enough, Mustache Man. It's not like I'm seen with Aven everywhere he goes.

"The guy's a hero. Not only did he save the woman he loves, but thousands of others."

Kitten narrowed her eyes at the back of the ambulance as it raced down the street.

"Maybe now the FDA will approve that miracle cure here in the states." The office gleamed.

"Paula Benton," She snapped. "The owner here. Was that her they drove away?"

The office gave her a look. "I didn't get your name, Ms. . . ."

"Katharine. Katharine Reece."

"Ms. Reece . . ." The officer said, scrolling through his tablet. "I don't see you listed as an employee."

Another officer came over and pulled officer Clark to the side. He handed officer Clark a marked bag of evidence and spoke in a hushed tone.

Kitten studied the item in the cellophane baggie as officer Clark held it up into the light of a street lamp. Inside, covered in blood, was a shiny gold cufflink bearing the initials N.G.

. . . Nick. Oh, Creator. No. Please no.

A *chime* sounded from the officer Clark's tablet.

"We've got a 10-202, people!" Clark ordered his team. "Wrap it up!"

He stuffed the evidence in his pocket and rushed to his cop car.

"Wait!" Kitten pleaded.

She watched helplessly as the police crew gathered up the crime scene markers and stripped the caution tape. All the cameras that had been taking photographs, the tablets documenting the crime, every piece of evidence was tossed into a barrel nearby and lit on fire. She glanced up at the surveillance cameras and then glared at the burning barrel. It was a clean sweep, and Kitten knew there was only one person who could have authorized it.

PRECIOUS PET

Sunday, 7:40 p.m.
Las Vegas, Nevada

KITTEN took swift strides into Vincent's mansion. She knew he had the footage. All she had to do was get into his computer and retrieve the past twenty-four hours. She went straight toward the parlor doors but slowed her steps, overhearing the argument in Italian coming from behind them.

"When Aven finds out, he's going to have it looked into," Vincent said. "You were reckless. Impulsive."

"She's *my* bitch," Nick seethed. "Not his."

"Language," Vincent warned.

"So what if Aven finds out? She was a Meager."

"She was like a mother to him."

Nick scoffed.

"It's apparent by your actions that you've changed your mind about the upcoming sacrifice."

"I offered one."

"You know that's not how it works."

"She's going to be my wife."

Kitten's heart raced as she peeked through the crack in the door.

Vincent rubbed his temples, clearly irritated over the conversation. "She's not of our breed."

Nick shrugged. "I'll get her fixed."

"You're trying my patience, Nicoli."

"Katharine is mine," Nick said with malice in his voice. "And I'll slit another Meager's throat if they try to get in the way again. And your brother's."

Vincent came inches from Nick's face. "Careful, cousin."

"Or what? You'll kill me? Like you did Jimmy? Seems you've made a habit of taking out your own kind to protect Aven. Why is that? What makes him so special?"

"Blood over benevolence."

"He's a half breed."

"He's valuable."

"Right. *The Book of Aramis*. He can't even read it."

"But he will bring us the one who can."

Kitten's breath hitched, and she watched Vincent walk to the Book under the glass case to stare at it intently.

"Aven took what's mine," Nick said. "I took what was his. We're even."

A knife flew across the room, stopping an inch from Vincent's eye. That eye darkened, pooling his irises black.

"Do unto others as they would do unto you," Vincent said, so calm, so unbelievably controlled that it turned Kitten's blood to ice. He tilted his head, and as he did, the knife flipped, flew across the room, and sunk into Nick's neck.

Kitten gasped and covered her mouth, listening to Nick choke on his blood. She pressed her back against the wall, holding back her whimpers as his body thumped to the floor. She panted for breath, fumbled with her purse, and grabbed her phone.

Please pick up.

Her stomach churned as Aven's playful voicemail greeting filled her ear. An ear-deafening beep followed.

"Av—"

The sting of a blade at her throat cut Kitten's words short. She knew by the fingernails digging into her arm, by the scent of the musky vanilla perfume, who this woman was before she even spoke.

"Naughty, kitty," Bree cooed in her ear.

THE GHOST

"ANY good memories sparked by dessert?" Aven asked. He wiped his mouth with his napkin and leaned back in his chair. When his phone rang, he frowned, silenced it, and then slipped it inside his suit jacket.

Claire studied the white chocolate raspberry cheesecake on the table. She had hardly eaten it, hardly had the stomach to put anything else in her twisting gullet.

She let her mind wander until an image of a toned body glistening in the sun came. She could feel the warmth of a hand. Will's hand.

One . . .

Two . . .

"Perhaps you should sit in my lap."

At Aven's silky voice, the scene in her mind went from a warm and vibrant hue to a dark night with blurring lights. She saw herself with Aven on his motorcycle, sitting with him at a bakery, a white room so bright it made her squeeze her eyes shut, but the moment she saw a house fire, she shook her head.

"I remember," she told him, glancing up.

Aven seemed pleased as he stared, giving his charming smile until the waiter caught his attention for the bill.

Claire poked at a raspberry with her fork and scraped the creamy cake onto the prongs before slipping them into her mouth. Another memory of her at Aven's mother's house came. Kate. She had said something to her, something important.

Forgiveness. Serena. Levi.

"Ms. Grace."

The fork clattered against the dessert plate at her faltered grip.

". . . or shall I say, Mrs. Crey?"

Claire stood to shake Vincent's hand.

Aven's cousin, she noted to herself.

She glanced over Vincent's shoulder, seeing Aven behind him, talking to . . .

Bree. Aven's ex. She doesn't like me very much.

Aven appeared to be put off by their conversation.

"Ms. Grace?"

Claire snapped her gaze back to Vincent.

"Are you feeling alright tonight?" he asked.

"Yes," Claire replied, "my head's a bit fuzzy."

"No more headaches?"

Claire shook her head. "One this morning, but no."

"Good. I gave Aven another prescription. Seemed the one you were using wasn't sitting too well with your system. But not to worry. You're under my care now. I'll make sure no ghosts come to bother you again."

A chill ran down Claire's spine at Vincent's words, but she forced a smile. "Thank you."

"Might I have a word with you for a moment?" Vincent asked as Aven approached.

"Can it wait?" Aven looked at his watch. "The show starts in twenty minutes."

"It will only take a second," Vincent gestured to the bar.

Aven seemed to force a smile and kissed Claire on the cheek. "I'll be right back. Don't talk to any strangers."

A flash blurred by in Claire's mind.

The gala. A little who girl wanted to dance, but she was afraid of Vincent. Of his—

. . . Shadows.

An ache split through Claire's skull, and she shoved the images from her mind.

You're doing it again. Don't. It only makes things worse.

Will is real. He's alive. You need to find him.

Claire sat back down and watched Aven talk to Vincent for a moment before she glanced at her clutch. It was covered in a beautiful pattern of black sequin and lace. Claire never cared much for lace, even the kind as soft as this. She scrunched her shoulders, knowing the same lacy pattern was the only thing covering her bare back.

With another glance at the sequin bag, she sighed and took out her phone. She thumbed through the numbers, looking at the letter "W," but the name "Will" was not in her contacts.

Why would he be there?

She then messaged Laura, asking how Jenna's wedding went. Aven had informed her she missed it, being in a coma and all. Which didn't bother Claire much. She had hated the dress Jenna picked out.

"Claire," a familiar voice said.

She sucked in a sharp breath and held it.

"Don't turn around," it ordered.

Claire didn't. She leaned back against her chair and asked in a hushed tone, "Who are you?"

"So he did make you forget about me."

Her breath exhaled all at once. "Will?"

"Maybe not . . ."

"Why do you keep haunting me?"

An unknown number popped up on her phone with a message.

```
    I'm about to send you some
Intel. Don't react. Just smile and
act natural.
```

Claire glanced up and met Aven's gaze. She smiled, but acting natural wasn't something she knew how to do. With a gulp, she tapped a new message that arrived with a *buzz* against her palm. She covered her mouth when the images popped up. The photos were of a bloody crime scene. A young woman a few years younger than herself was lying on a bed, half-naked, covered in bloody handprints. Bile rose in her throat as she read the girl's name.

Alex Anderson.

Claire vaguely remembered a conversation with Aven about this girl.

Another message popped up.

You're in danger, Claire. I sent you a map of where to meet me. You can follow the GPS to the lit arbor just outside the hotel. Go during intermission. I'll explain everything when you get there.

"You're not real," Claire tried to convince herself. She laid her phone on the table and slid shaky fingers over her damp hairline to the hairpins stabbing her scalp.

A strobe light of images flashed in her mind.

A girl with blonde hair humming. The poke of hairpins. A red dress. Meeting with a fallen angel so beautiful she could hardly stand to look away from him. His anger. His black unfurling wings.

Stop doing this to yourself. Stop listening to the voices.

What if he is real?

What if he's not?

What am I supposed to believe?

A warm breath graced the back of her neck as the ghost whispered in her ear. "Faith, Claire. Take the leap."

Swiveling around in her chair, Claire found no one sitting behind her. Her gaze darted to a man in a tux with blonde hair leaving the restaurant. He didn't seem out of place, but when he ran his fingers through his hair, she knew deep in her soul that the ghost wasn't a ghost at all.

MUSIC OF THE

NIGHT

SUNDAY, 9:33 P.M.
LAS VEGAS, NEVADA

INTERMISSION. Claire didn't wait for the announcement. She slipped from Aven's hand and rushed down the isle. Quivering, she braced herself against the wall outside of the theater and slipped her phone from her clutch. A light blinked on the map on the screen.

Will's waiting for you.

She didn't want to believe she was a hostage, but it was the truth. She knew Aven had been lying to her. Will wasn't a ghost; he was real, and he was here to rescue her.

"Claire?"

She shoved her phone in her clutch and snapped it shut. "Aven."

"Is something the matter?"

"No," Claire lied. "I'm fine."

Aven tilted his head, clearly unconvinced. "I'll get you a Cape Cod."

"Won't it affect the medication?"

"Of course not," Aven said. "Why don't you go freshen up?"

Claire tried to relax her brows, but the pain in her forehead scrunched them together again.

"I've seen that look before."

"What look?"

"The one you make before you're about to run away."

"Do I do that often?"

Aven's kiss felt cool against her hot forehead. "Five minutes."

She met his gaze and searched his eyes. In that storm of grayish blue, she found fear.

"Five minutes," she repeated.

"That's my girl," he said and seemed to force a smile.

Claire watched him head to the drink kiosk and withdraw his phone. It was clear by the way he loosened his tie, whoever he was calling, made him nervous.

Maybe it's not me. Maybe it's someone else.

"Katharine," Aven said into his phone. He glanced over his shoulder as he stood in line, watching Claire enter the ladies' restroom. "You called and hung up. Doesn't surprise me. I know you just love the silent treatment, but this isn't the time for it." He let out a long sigh. "Look. I know Claire being back is making you think things between us have changed, but they haven't. As soon as I know we're safe, I'll wean her from Solace. You have to trust me, just please, please call me back as soon as you get this."

Aven shoved his phone in his suit pocket, irritated that Kitten had resulted to childish games. He knew it was because he had explained in a voicemail what was going to happen on his way back from Hawaii. He assumed the mention of a false marriage had put Kitten over the edge.

When he had returned with Claire, he didn't call to ask Kitten to come and help him. It was something she didn't need to see. The first few days of Claire being on Solace were tricky. Claire would wake screaming, and he would have to put her under again. That's why he had to get the skin patch on her arm, that's why he had to erase his brother and their bond with the most intrusive Mind Walk he had ever attempted.

She loves him. They belonged together.

. . . And I belong with Kitten.

Soon they could be together. Soon, it would all be over.

Tonight will be the last ruse. By tomorrow, Vincent will be dead, and the truth will be revealed.

Standing at the bathroom sink, Claire scrolled through the map's directions. It was only a short walk to where the ghost was pinpointed.

You've lost it, her reflection said without moving its lips.

Claire glanced at her wrist, running her fingers over it. Somehow, she knew something should be there, something she always hated as a child, but now, wished more than anything would appear.

Where is it?

She waited impatiently for the soap dispenser to give up the foam and then scrubbed her wrist with her fingernails. She clawed at her skin until it was red, but no brown line appeared like she thought it would.

When a woman beside her glanced over, Claire shrugged, mentioned poison ivy, and washed off the soap and reached for a paper towel.

Something flashed in her mind—a bathroom, scratchy paper towels. Mascara smudged on her eyelids. An emblem on a white sweatshirt.

When the scent of fresh laundry and a mossy forest filled her nose, she blinked back to reality and braced herself on the sink.

Stop acting crazy, her reflection ordered. *Aven loves you. Don't do this to him. Let the ghost go.*

No matter how much she coached herself, Claire still wanted to claw at her wrist to find the little brown line she thought should be there. When the ladies' room was clear, she turned on the hot water and let it run until the steam wet her face.

Clenching her teeth tight, she held her arm under the scalding water, letting her skin burn, suffering through the wave of nausea as she scorched her wrist rose red. And then, as if it had been sewn on, her skin peeled back like a wet Band-Aid.

Claire gnashed her teeth from the pain. It was much worse than ripping off a Band-Aid. Whatever glue had been used to fuse this graph to her body wasn't going to give.

She kept her arm under the hot water again, bit her lip, and with one swift tug, ripped the skin graph away.

A yelp left her quivering lips, but her trembling fingers managed to turn the water to cold. She ignored the excruciating pain as she held her wrist under the stream and looked closely. There, past the blood and blistered skin was something she hoped she'd see.

My birthmark.

Tears fell in that instant, but at the sound of women entering, she choked them back and snatched a few more paper towels to cover her wound. She went into a stall, shoved the skin graph into her clutch, and stared at her marred skin for a long moment.

Why? Why would Aven do this to me?

Because it hid the truth.

She left the stall, ready to confront him, ready to make a scene.

Act natural, remember?

Peeking her head out of the restroom, Claire found Aven down the hall, still waiting in line for their drinks.

She then looked at the steps, knowing it was the only way out of the Coliseum Theater.

The beauty of free will is that you have a choice, a calm voice whispered.

Grabbing fistfuls of her gown, Claire shot off to the steps and didn't look back. If she were hallucinating, if she were truly being haunted, she would soon find out.

The marble arbor was lit like a beacon. It called to her with its beauty and the sounds of a fountain nearby.

The ghost stood with his back to her at the stone railing, but at the clacking of Claire's heels, he slowly turned, seemingly just as afraid to look at her as she was of him turning around.

His expression was full of concern as his gaze flicked over her shoulder. He took her hand and proceeded to look her over, sweeping her hair from her face.

"Mydriasis,"

"What?"

"Your pupils are dilated. It will take a few days for what they did to you to wear off. You'll have to detox."

Claire didn't budge as he tugged her hand.

"Tell me something only we would know, something that will make me remember," she said.

The ghost wet his lips, closing the space between them. He tucked her hair behind her ear and winced through a smile, as if her disbelief cut him deep.

"Orion," he said softly.

At the name of the constellation, Claire exhaled with eyes closed while a freight train of images raced through her mind.

They were of this man before her. At first, he sat at a table with her. Another man with white wool hair signed with gloves, talking to him, to her. She was then dancing with the old man, asking him questions about a dedication ceremony.

Next, she found herself jumping from a cliff, then dancing with Will, then sitting next to him on a beach, looking up at a starry night sky. She had never forgotten what he told her, what he asked her to do. It had been the only thing he ever asked of her.

"Take a leap of faith," she whispered.

"I'm real, Claire. Even if you can't remember, it's the truth." He stared deeply into her eyes a long moment, but then his gaze was on her lips, and his thumb softly caressed them. "But just in case."

Claire was ready for his kiss, ready for this dream to end and reality to begin, but as their lips brushed, a voice called for her.

"Ms. Grace."

Vincent stood casually with his hands in his pockets. Men in black suits and masked in sunglasses stood beside him, aiming the lasers from their automatic weapons at Will's chest and head.

"Don't shoot him!" Claire cried out.

Vincent's stare was hard, but his voice was as soft as velvet. "Shoot who, my dear?"

"Tell your men to stand down," Will ordered, pushing Claire behind him.

"Ms. Grace," Vincent said calmly, taking a step forward, "you need to come with me."

"Tell them to lower their guns!" Claire shouted, making eye contact with the tourists passing by.

They gave looks but didn't stop.

Vincent glanced over his shoulder. "Tell who?"

"Your men." Claire pointed. "The ones beside you."

Vincent looked to his left, then to his right, and back at Claire. "Aven is worried about you," he said. "He called me the moment he found you missing. I was already in the vicinity, so I promised I would bring you back to him. Safe and sound."

"Promised." Claire shook her head as a fog settled in her brain.

"You're having one of your episodes again," Vincent said. "You need to be home where it's quiet, where you belong."

Vincent's face blurred in her vision, and her head pounded with a dull ache.

"If the engagement party is making you nervous, we can reschedule," Vincent said.

"Tell her it's all a lie," Will demanded. "Tell her the truth."

Claire could feel Will's protective arm at her back. She leaned against him, breathing in his scent, trying to regain her focus, but when she looked back at Vincent, who seemed to double, she saw no men beside him.

The world tilted, and Claire stumbled forward, finding Will had disappeared too.

"Will?" she said, grasping air.

"You can trust me," Vincent assured.

The words drove nails into her skull. Claire pressed her palms against her temples and fell to her knees, moaning at the unrelenting pain.

"Claire," Will said as his blurry face came into view.

She could feel him again as his warm hands cupped her face. "You know I was sent to protect you. You have to believe. You have to fight it."

"You need to come with me," Vincent said calmly. He took a few steps closer. "Before you hurt yourself."

"Don't," Will warned Vincent. He helped Claire to her feet and backed Claire away from Vincent until her back was against the stone railing.

"He's not real, my dear." Vincent gestured for her to take his hand as he came closer. "Please. You need help. Your fiancé is looking for you."

What if he's right? What if I'm crazy? What if this is all just an illusion?

Exactly. It's all an illusion. Remember Aalok's tricks. Remember the book.

Claire pressed a hand to her head and stared at the ground, trying to pick apart every single moment since she had woken in Aven's bed.

The pill that smelled like sulfur. The skin patch. Her fuzzy memories.

"I can't," Claire whimpered as her knees threatened to buckle.

"Can't what, my dear?" Vincent asked.

At Vincent's words, a scene from *The Book of Aramis* sped through Claire's mind.

A fallen angel with a fake smile, her drinking from a cup of water, an illusion of a rose arbor, a demoted warrior adorned in armor of red. Vincent, he was holding back Sophie's Guardian with chains, burning him with his glove of electric shock.

Not just Sophie's Guardian. My Guardian.

Blinking, she saw Aalok grinning behind Vincent. His spirit was there, working behind the Veil. Vincent was his puppet, his hand to do his dirty work in this realm.

"Sophie, look into my eyes," Will said, gently bringing her gaze back to him. "What color are they?"

Commanding her sight to focus, Claire searched for the truth in that sea of endless blue.

Another vision from *The Book of Aramis* came, one of Sophie and Alexander on the beach before the wave hit and they became nothing but a vapor.

"Blue," she said with quivering lips.

"Remember the blue of the ocean that day we met," Will said softly, placing his forehead to hers. "Remember Bevol and your days spent in paradise. You will see it again. But you have to believe. You have to remember Aramis' vows. And ours."

Looking down, Claire found Will's hand clasped around her forearm and hers clasped to his. She glanced up, seeing him as Alexander, as the warrior Sophie loved, the warrior she had always loved.

"I am yours," Claire whispered, locking her gaze on him.

Will caressed a tear from her cheek as one trickled down his. "And you are mine," he said and kissed her.

Claire's memories, her true memories, came flooding back as Will held her close. Her past life, her present, all of it was crystal clear. She remembered. She remembered everything.

Will suddenly parted from her lips, withdrew a pistol from his suit jacket, and shot Vincent square in the shoulder.

Time sped up, and Claire watched Vincent stumble back but regain his footing as if the bullet had been nothing more than a paintball.

"Thought I'd return the favor." Will smirked.

Vincent growled, swiping the blood splatter from the hole in his suit, then looked up with a scowl. "Sparare," he ordered.

Claire's stomach flipped and the world turn upside down as Will swept her into his arms. She didn't have time to scream as they landed in the fountain below the arbor, evading the bullets ricocheting off the stone pillars.

Will snatched up her arm and tugged her beneath one of Poseidon's hippocampuses and over the fountain basin to a parked car to take cover.

Glass shattered in the passenger side window. Bullets assaulted a stop sign. People on the sidewalk ran screaming.

Will shielded Claire, returning fire as they crawled their way to the driver side of the rental car.

"Get in!" he ordered Claire, reloading the mag.

Claire's eyes went wide with panic. "You're not coming?"

"I'll meet you at the ramp," he said and tapped the "Autopilot" button on the screen.

"Please sit back and enjoy your ride," a robotic voice announced from the car speakers. "Automatic driver in ten, nine—"

Claire clung to Will's suit jacket, unwilling to let him go. "I can't leave without you."

"Six,"

Will kissed her despite the bullets flying. It wasn't a goodbye. It was a silent vow; a vow that he loved her.

"One"

"You're not," he murmured against her lips, and shut the driver side door.

FIRE FIGHT

AVEN ran toward the sound of gunfire and screams and saw Vincent standing at the railing. He watched as the getaway car sped down the highway and onto the exit, watched Will get on a street bike and follow it. He didn't know if the panic was guilt or that Claire was about to find out what he had done. Either way, she was out of his reach and there was no explaining now.

"Idiots," Vincent growled, walking under the stone arbor. He watched the car exit before he spun and tilted his head at his lackeys. "Sparare."

The men turned on one another and fired. Brains splattered on the concrete. Empty shells tumbled. Bodies thudded to the ground.

The last man left standing looked at the lifeless comrades at his feet, then gave a pleading look as he held his gun to his temple.

At the pop, blood sprayed the columns in crimson before the agent fell on top of the corpse pile.

"What the hell is wrong with you?" Aven spat at Vincent.

"I told you he was dangerous." Vincent faced him, situating his cufflinks, seemingly irritated at the blood on his white dress shirt.

"The only one that's dangerous here is you. Will's trying to protect her."

"Once she's far enough away, she'll remember everything you did to her."

Aven licked his lips. "Maybe she should."

"She'll never forgive you."

"She will."

"And what makes you so sure?"

Aven thought about Sophie, how she had been willing to forgive Serus for his trespasses. She was a saint. He didn't deserve her forgiveness, but he would get down on his knees and beg for it if he ever got the chance.

"Because she has before."

Claire watched the cars blur by as hers eased onto the exit ramp. Dread was a lead weight in her stomach. She left Will behind. She left him to die.

A thud startled her, and she was glad she didn't have control of the wheel. She watched a street bike skid across the highway in the side mirror. Her eyes then darted to the rearview where she saw Will.

His hair whipped back and forth as he clung to the back of the car. Behind him vehicles swerved to avoid the motorcycle's broken parts.

"Window," Will's muffled voice shouted.

Claire rolled down the driver side window and Will slipped through it.

"You-you jumped off that motorcycle," she mumbled, looking him over.

"You need fluids." Will gestured with his chin to the passenger console.

Claire blinked from her stare and took out a bottle of water.

They were on the open highway in the desert now, and although it was dark, Claire recalled a familiar scene.

Will asked me if I was okay after Aven's drunken show at his mansion. Aven was on his motorcycle. I was yelling at Will to stop the car before he hit Aven.

The whine of a crotch rocket filled her ears again, pulling her from the fuzzy memories.

Aven was on a street bike beside them, gesturing for Will to roll down his window.

Will yelled over the roaring wind at him, "This is your idea of keeping her safe?"

"Follow me," Aven shouted. "I know how we can lose them."

"Like hell," Will yelled back. "What makes you think I'll trust—"

Claire's scream cut Will's words short as glass shattered in the rear window.

"You don't have any other choice!" Aven yelled over the gunfire. "Do you want to save her life or not?"

"Please pull over. You are exceeding the speed limit. Please pull over. You are exceeding the speed limit," the dash alerted in its robotic voice.

Will ripped out the wires from beneath the steering wheel and silenced the autopilot. The car jumped forward, catching up with Aven as he zipped his street bike down the highway.

Will took Claire's hand that gripped the middle console and squeezed gently. "Don't worry. I have a place we can hide."

"What about Aven?"

"We'll figure it out. When we get to the cabin we'll deal with—"

Claire's seat belt snapped against her collarbone as tires squealed. Her head whipped back. With a low moan she looked to Will, who white-knuckled the steering wheel. She followed his wide-eyed gaze out the dusty windshield.

A figure blocked the way, wearing a red priestly robe. He unfurled his raven-like wings and stood with hands clasped in front of him. He didn't budge, didn't flinch as Aven's motorcycle slammed into an invisible wall in front of him. The robed figure slipped back his hood and smiled deviously as Aven's body sailed through the air.

Images of seeing this fallen angel sitting at a table in Aalok's throne room came to Claire. He had been the one with white hair dipped in red. He had been the same one she had seen in South Carolina before the Mustang crashed into the tree.

Claire watched Aven's body plow into the shoulder.

The rental car's engine revved. Her seatbelt locked.

"Stop!" she ordered Will. "We have to go back."

Will glanced in the side mirror, seeing Aven roll head over heels, but didn't slow down.

"We have to go back for him!"

"I'm pretty sure we're not invited to the family reunion." He said and pressed the pedal to the floor.

Aven rolled to a stop and groaned, favoring his ribs. They were broken. It was obvious by the way one protruded from his chest. He gritted his teeth and shoved it back in his torn flesh.

A black car with tinted windows pulled up beside him. Vincent exited and slammed the door shut. "You're trying my patience," he said, straightening his suit jacket.

Aven tried to stand, but his leg was broken. He used his fist like a hammer to snap his bone into place and crawled to a stand as his ribs mended on their own.

Vincent's brigade sped past them with their weapons aimed at the rental car.

"Tell them to back off," he ordered Vincent.

Gunshots rang out into the desert, followed by a car crash.

"Let them go!" Aven pleaded.

Vincent's cunning eyes gleamed as he said into Aven's ear. "Nevermore."

SHADOWS OF

REALITY

FRIGID steel bit into Aven's wrists as he rolled his head back with a groan. "Fucking hell."

He fluttered his lashes and tugged on the cuffs once more. The stench of bleach slapped him in the face. Something else sickeningly sterile made him scrunch his nose. It burned his watering eyes, but he commanded them to focus as he blinked.

White table, white chair, white—oh, shit.

"Dear, dear brother. Why must you always insist on going against your destiny?" Vincent's voice was an echo, as if it were coming from a speaker above, but Aven could feel his presence.

"Brother?" Aven croaked. He rolled his tongue to wet his dry mouth. Sand gritted against his teeth as he clenched them. A throbbing pounded against his skull.

The fall. Broken bones. Vincent smiling before he said—
Nevermore...

That was the last thing Aven heard before the darkness had taken him. It reminded him of something. A specific memory from when he was a boy.

Aven lounged on a couch in his uncle's study, reading a dark text, when a plume of smoke from the fire formed a blackbird flapping its wings.

"Having fun?" Aven asked it.

"Nevermore," the Raven squawked as it flew to sit on the mantel.

"Father said we are not to play mind games unless he is present."

The bird's red eyes glowed as it fanned its wings and squawked again. It flew to a rectangle glass case above the door, one that held a set of skeleton keys.

"Nevermore." It screeched.

"Or call upon the darkness to entertain us," Aven said.

"Nevermore."

Aven glared at the bird. "Take thy form from off my door."

The bird's form vaporized at Aven's words, and Vincent stalked into the room saying, "Quoth the Raven, nevermore."

Aven let the book fall onto his finger, marking his place. "Bored, dear cousin?"

"It would seem." Vincent smiled. "Let's play a game."

A game. One with the mind.

Jackson had been prepping the boys to learn how to Mind Walk. They had only been practicing a few months and had yet to figure out one another's keyword to trigger submission.

"You want to practice before practice?" Aven asked, placing the book to the side. He crossed his arms over his chest. "Father forbids Walking without him."

"Afraid you'll lose?"

"I fear nothing."

"So you think. I hear you screaming in your sleep, little blackbird. I know what you fear."

Aven stood to his feet, coming inches from Vincent's smug face. "Do it then. Put me under. I doubt you have a word to do so."

Vincent glanced down at the book and then at Aven. "Quoth the Raven . . ."

Aven blinked from the memory with an aching head.

Nevermore . . . that's his keyword.

"I never told you the truth." Vincent's voice still echoed in the white room. "Perhaps if I had, you wouldn't have followed in the footsteps of our uncle."

"*Our* uncle—wait." Aven squinted his eyes. "Jimmy wasn't your father?"

"He was a mutt. Just like you. That's why he took you under his wing. But he was a mistake, a bastard. You, on the other hand, you were designed. Our father had a plan for your purpose."

"What psychotic nonsense are you babbling about?" Aven asked.

"I deleted that part of the file,"

"That's why you let me take it."

"Vinny, our grandfather, had one request: keep the seed line pure. But even Grandfather broke his own code. He mated with a whore who brought Jameson Crey into the world. To keep face with the Circle, Vinny killed the Meager mother. Lucky for him, both Jackson and Jameson had been born on the same day. Vinny forged the birth certificates to make it appear as if they were twins. When the boys were of age, Jackson was required to bring forth a son to carry on the lineage."

"Let me guess. You?"

"One of pure blood, but another from the line of the Truth Keepers. As I said, you were designed, a request from the gods themselves."

"Why? Why breed with someone impure?"

"That's just it. The Truth Keeper line *is* pure. The purist there is. Their very own genealogy descended from the Creator himself. He breathed life into his Chosen. Taught them, walked with them. That was, until the day Aalok, our king, came to seduce the mother of them all. Seems Aramis has always hated our kind. He showed his favoritism when He banished our first ancestor from the first garden of Earth."

"He murdered his own brother,"

"It is true that our kind was once uncivilized. Over the years we have risen above the barbaric ways of our ancestors, but the search has never ended."

"That's what the wars have been over?" Aven asked. "Searching for some priest to torture so they'll read the text?"

"Making you was the answer to avoid such ways,"

"I can't read the book."

A sly smile spread across Vincent's lips. "The day our grandfather came to this conclusion he named you a mutt, denouncing you as one of us. But you *are* one of us, dear brother. As you are one of them. And being one of them makes me wonder." Vincent stooped down and took Aven by the chin. "If you have you been lying to me this whole time."

Aven jerked away. "Fuck you and your redemption. Where's Claire?"

Vincent stood and clasped his hands behind his back. "In the facility."

"She won't do it."

"She will"—Vincent tipped up his head—"for the one she loves."

"You're shit out of luck." Aven chuckled. "She doesn't love me. Not like that."

A cruel smile formed on Vincent's lips. "I know."

Aven's heart stopped. "Where's Will?"

Vincent turned to a framed mirror Aven hadn't noticed before. "In the other room."

The chains around Aven's body fell with a clink to the flawless white floor.

"Ms. Grace is down the hall. You have thirty minutes to convince her to read the book." He turned to Aven. "If you can't, I'm afraid I'll have to resort back to the cruel ways of our ancestors."

MENTAL

CLAIRE'S eyes fluttered open to a splitting headache that blurred her vision. She strained to glance at a bag of clear fluid on an IV pole, but her vision doubled. She leaned her head to the side and puked, coughing and gagging. Her vision started clearing, at least enough that the room wasn't spinning. She looked down at the steel poking in the back of her hand and then at the connected tubes of black.

Was I in a Mind Walk?

It was the bile Claire wiped from her cheek that she smelled first, and then the familiar stench of embalming fluid. She held back the urge to vomit again as her stomach rolled. Looking to her left, she found several gurneys in a neat row with sheets covering what she knew could only be bodies.

A stab of panic clutched Claire's chest. She fought her heavy torso and sat up. The room spun. A draft flew up her hospital gown as she flung back the stiff sheet. She no longer wore a black evening dress, but instead, a paper-thin hospital gown.

A whimper escaped her lips as she peeled back the tape and slid the needle from the back of her hand. She rubbed the sticky residue from her tender skin and glanced around the still wobbly room searching for a door, but there wasn't one. There was nothing other than her terrified face reflecting back at her in a framed mirror.

She fell off the gurney, and a hiss escaped her lips when her kneecaps banged painfully against the white tile. An attempt to support her weight against the rolling steel did no good. It slammed into the other gurneys, bouncing the bumpy masses beneath the sheets.

A lifeless pale arm fell.

Claire gagged and held her breath from the smell of vomit and embalming fluid.

A morgue. I'm in a morgue.

Holding back the acid rising in the back of her throat, Claire crawled across the icy tile and clawed the white wall to stand on shaky legs.

She stared at her blurry reflection, trying to regain focus.

Why would anyone need a mirror in a morgue? Unless—

If it was a one-way mirror, she could call for help. She could escape if only they could see her, hear her.

"Let me out!" she pleaded, although it wasn't a scream like she had intended. She could hardly hear her own voice, could hardly raise a hand to slap her palm against the glass.

"Let me out!" she managed again as her breath misted the mirror. Another raspy cry came from her throat, a little louder this time, and even louder as she finally found her strength. She pounded the glass with all her might, screamed until she went hoarse.

Something slammed behind her, something heavy like metal. It shook the walls and the mirror.

"Claire."

That voice. She knew it. Had loved it but now hated it.

Turning slowly, she struggled to breathe.

Aven was standing at a door that hadn't been there before.

"Stay away from me," Claire ordered.

Defensive hands were out before him as he took cautious steps toward her. "I'm here to help you."

"Help me?" Claire snapped. "You lied to me! You messed with my head!" Her eyes burned, but no tears came. He betrayed her. He had done things she would have never imagined he would do.

Aven cautiously put her arm around him. "Come on. I'm going to get you out of here."

Somehow, from the adrenaline or fury, she managed to shove him away, waving a heavy hand to slap him in the face.

Aven caught her wrist. "Claire, stop," he said, catching her other. He twisted her around into a bear hug.

"Where's Will?" Claire screamed, wrestling to be free of his hold.

"Stop fighting me," Aven grunted.

"I'm not going anywhere with you!"

"Do you want to find Will or not?"

"Let me go!" Claire screamed, but it was cut short as she went hoarse.

"I never wanted to hurt you," Aven said. "You have to believe me."

"You're a liar," Claire rasped.

Tears streaked down her cheeks as she went limp in his arms. She couldn't fight him anymore, couldn't gather enough strength to fuel the fire of her rage.

"I can't trust you," she strained to say.

"You don't have to," Aven said softly and scooped her up into his arms, carrying her out into a glaring white hallway.

"Mr. Carpenter."

Shoot to kill.

That voice, eerily unmistakable, was speaking again.

"It's been a long time, old friend."

Will blinked open his eyes, squinting as a bright light burned his retinas. The darkness gave relief, but a glaring white stung again.

Seeing a hanging light bulb swinging back and forth, brought back a familiar memory of torture.

Chained to a chair. A swinging lamp above. An electric shock.

He wasn't sure if it was from Alexander's memory or his own. He wondered if he was somehow in a dream, hoped it was. Dreams could somewhat be controlled.

He forced his head up, and waited for the light to swing back and reveal his captor.

A black suit. A black tie. A sinister smirk.

Vincent.

"Where is she?" Will croaked.

"With her beloved, of course,"

Will bowed his head as dread filled his chest. He had left Claire in Aven's care.

Clearly a mistake.

He squeezed his eyes shut at the throbbing in his head. When he opened them again, the room was no longer black but filled with light. The memory training flipped through the pages of Will's mind. He saw how he was tortured, tested, and conditioned to be a super soldier.

"Look familiar?" Vincent asked.

Will fought to break free of the frigid chains around his wrists, but at a shock, he bowed back.

Chains. My steel chair kicked into a tub of water. The pain. My screams that couldn't be heard.

"Do you remember telling me that you wanted to take the mission? That if it would keep your brother from being sent overseas, you would do whatever was required?"

The fire blazing through Will's skin eased, but the tingle of heat in his nerves itched every inch of his flesh.

"You volunteered, Mr. Carpenter. You chose this."

"It was you," Will rasped. "You made Aaron kill our unit, then you ordered him to kill me. Why? What did you gain?"

"A revelation," Vincent said as he stooped to Will's level.

Will narrowed his gaze on Vincent's smug face, attempting to be free of his bonds.

As if Vincent could read his thoughts, the chains fell, clattering against the steel chair and the floor.

Will shot out his hand, reaching his fingers toward Vincent's throat, but Vincent disappeared, and Will stumbled over his feet. He held out his hands to catch his fall, but his body froze, leaving his nose only inches from the ground.

Vincent reappeared and crouched. He waved a finger and tsk'ed. "My mind, my rules."

The air holding Will gave way and his cheek slammed against the hard ground. "Your mind?" he grunted, struggling to find the strength to stand.

Vincent slipped one hand into a pocket of his slacks and gestured to the white wall behind him. "Let's see what's in yours, shall we?"

The white background fell like a curtain.

Will's heart raced when he saw a moonlit desert before him. He shuddered at the two shots that rang out into the stillness of the night.

"You wanted the truth," Vincent said. "And the truth shall be revealed."

Will gulped down the knot in his throat and walked toward the sand, following the boot prints that led to the haunting memory he had suppressed.

"Son of a bitch!" Aven slammed his palms against a dead end.

Claire looked behind her. There were no doors. No exit signs, just white halls of nothingness. It was like a rat maze and they had been walking in it for what seemed like hours.

"We can't get out," Aven said, rubbing his forehead.

"Why?"

"Because this place isn't real, Claire."

"Wh-what do you mean?"

"A labyrinth of white." Aven gestured.

Claire pressed a hand to the white walls. "But—"

"We're in a Mind Walk. And if I could guess, it's Vincent who has us under."

"Mind Walk. I still don't understand what it is. How were you able to cure my fear of heights?"

"The white room is like a blank space in your subconscious. The Guide, which was me, cues the Sleeper, who was you, to pick a door that leads to the deepest parts of the mind. Thing is, the Guide can't see the Sleeper's emotionalized thoughts, hopes, fears, or desires. They can only hear the Sleeper's internal thoughts during the Walk. The Guide gathers information and make assumptions."

Claire shook her head. "But you did see what I saw."

"I did."

"How?"

"I'm guessing only some with the gift can."

"And Vincent can?"

Aven nodded. "It appears some of us have practiced the art of mind manipulation enough to perfect it. But a Guide can't control the dream, only the Sleeper can."

Claire licked her lips. "So we're in his mind? He's controlling this place?"

"Yep."

"Who's his Guide?"

"I'm guessing Bree. By the way we've been wandering around in his subconscious, he's not completely under."

"I don't understand."

"An IV hook up with a steady stream of Solace was how I rearranged your memories after the wave. We're basically in a coma. Vincent's not. Bree can wake him up anytime he wants, but we're stuck here until someone takes out the needle or Solace drains dry from the bag."

"Where are we? Our bodies, I mean?"

"Well, I'd like to think we're sleeping comfortably in a room at his house, but judging by the one I found you in, we're lying on a steel plate in his testing facility."

"Which is where?"

"Under a mountain, hidden in Death Valley."

Claire's breath frosted as she exhaled shakily.

"Even if we somehow wake up," Aven continued, "we're in the middle of nowhere with no food, no water, no shade. Just miles of endless desert between us and the nearest road."

Claire clutched her aching chest with a trembling hand. They were trapped in a deep sleep without any chance of waking up. She stared at the ground, wide-eyed, unable to move.

"Don't feed the fear," Aven said, cupping her face. "He uses it as fuel. The more control you lose, the more he gains. Since he's invited us into his subconscious, we have some kind of control over what we can do. A person's mind can be manipulated, but no one can force free will."

"Like being in a lucid dream. We still have a choice."

"Exactly."

Claire's shoulders relaxed as Aven rubbed them.

"That's right, Princess. Slow even breaths."

She tried to let out a controlled breath, but it wavered as she clutched her chest and winced.

"Still feels tight?"

Claire nodded.

Aven kissed her forehead, and Claire didn't pull away this time as he took her hand.

"Where are we going?"

"To look for a door. Vincent's stalling for now, but when he's ready, he'll have one for us to walk through."

"Why is he stalling?"

"If I could guess, he's busy playing with someone else in his little game."

Claire slipped through Aven's fingers. "He's in here too," she said in a whisper.

Aven turned to her and studied her face until it became suddenly clear who "he" was. "Shit."

Will's stomach rolled as he approached the lifeless bodies lying in the barren desert. His heart pounded like a hammer as he passed each face, each pair of lifeless eyes staring into nothing.

He first saw Blake, remembering their many nights spent in the barracks playing darts to pass the time.

A bullet to the back of his head.

He then saw Duke, the strongest in their unit, and the biggest but the kindest, a few feet away.

A bullet to his forehead.

Will knew it wasn't real, knew that this was just an illusion, a memory, but it didn't matter. It still made him want to look away. This *had* happened, but he hadn't been able to stop it.

Will didn't want to watch a repeat of what he knew was going to occur next, but he followed his past self's desperate pleas and shouting around an outcropping of rocks.

"Aaron, put down the gun!" his past self ordered.

Aaron kept his aim, although his hands shook with the gun he gripped tight.

Will came closer and looked into his eyes. They were pitted with black, no longer the color of crisp autumn leaves before the first snowfall.

"Aaron," Will's past self said, calmly taking cautious steps forward.

Aaron's ghost shoved the nose of a pistol into his past self's bulletproof vest and bared his teeth.

"Aaron." His past self placed a hand on his shoulder. "It's Will. It's your brother."

The pooling black cleared at his touch, at his words. The gun lowered slightly, but only for a second before Aaron screamed and covered his ears. The black pooled into his eyes like ink, and madness screwed up his face as if he had been possessed by a devil.

Will watched the past play out again, watched Aaron stop fighting, lift his head, smile, and pull the trigger. Again, Will felt the sting of the bullet at the pop of the gun. He stumbled back at the impact before he gained his footing and watched his past self lunge forward, twisting Aaron's arm and restraining him in a hold.

Aaron screamed, thrashing in his grip like a wild animal while Will's past self tackled him to the sandy ground.

"Take it out!" Will yelled at them.

"Aaron stop!" Will's past self ordered.

"He can't!" Will shouted over the sounds of the illusions wrestling. "Take it out!"

Aaron's ghost wiggled out from underneath his past self's hold, climbed on top of his older brother, and wrapped his hands around his neck.

Will clutched his neck and choked as his past self gasped for breath and kicked.

"The voices," Aaron wept. "I have to make them stop. I have to make them stop."

"Take out the COM!" Will screamed.

Will's past self reached out his hands for Aaron's uniform, gripped it, and rolled on top of him, pinning him down.

The moment Will's past self jerked the COM from Aaron's ear, his little brother froze. Light filtered back into Aaron's wide eyes and he lifted his brows, looking up at his older brother with recognition. "Will?" he croaked.

Will's past self pulled him up and held him by the shoulders to make direct eye contact. "It's me," he assured him. "You're gonna be okay."

Aaron glanced around the desert as if he had no idea where he was or what had happened before looking in the direction of Blake's and Duke's bodies. He stared at them for a long moment before he covered his mouth and broke down into tears.

"They're dead," Aaron blubbered. "I killed them." He looked at Will's past self with pleading eyes. "I couldn't stop, Will. You have to believe me. I couldn't stop. The voices. They told me to. They were so loud. I couldn't stop. I couldn't—"

"Shh," Will's past self soothed.

As Will's past self took Aaron in his arms and hugged him tight, Will fell to his knees, letting his own tears trickle down his dusty cheeks.

"I'm going to get you home," Will's past self assured Aaron.

No ... you won't.

This time Will could see the camouflaged soldiers that came out from their rocky hiding places. He watched them helplessly, unable to move, unable to scream a warning. Time slowed and Will cringed at the impact of the bullet beneath his past self's shoulder blade.

Another blast echoed in the desert, and Will watched in horror, unable to close his eyes, unable to look away, as a bullet punctured Aaron's neck, spraying blood onto his past self's cheeks.

Time sped up again, allowing Will to let out the war cry that had been silenced. It burned his throat as he ran to take vengeance on the soldiers who had shot him and his brother, but the moment he lunged to tackle one of them, he slammed into nothingness.

Will groaned as pain sliced through the back of his skull. He blinked, now seeing a ceiling of white and four walls. "Bastard."

"I told you," Vincent said, standing over him. "My mind. My rules."

"Why?" Will growled, coming to his feet. "Why did you do this?"

"Why do you think?" Vincent grinned.

Will racked his brain, going back over the painful memory. He and his team had walked Death Valley for hours, picking up no sign of explosives on their scanners. There had been static over their COMS, something like a strange silky whisper. Will had ordered his unit to change the station, but they didn't respond. It was the two gunshots that had rang a reply.

"It was a test," Will said with sudden realization.

Vincent tipped his chin up. "And all but one failed it."

"Aaron was the only one to listen to your command,"

A knowing smile formed on Vincent's lips as he waved his hand and the white walls disappeared as if made of thin air.

"The brain," Vincent circled Will, "is an interesting organ. Most humans can only access ten percent of its capacity. But you're not like most humans, are you, Mr. Stryde?"

The white floor melted away from Will's combat boots like snow, revealing a rocky ground beneath. Will stood, gripping something with a handle. He glanced at his hand, now seeing a long and heavy sword lit with an amber fire. He grasped the weapon tight, and it hummed a steady resonance like that of a hummingbird's wings in flight.

Across from him was Vincent, no longer in his formal attire, but in a heavy suit of armor adorned with a breastplate of jewels and a familiar rebellion emblem etched in his gauntlet. His black hair hung to his shoulders, and his eyes reflected the crimson of a fiery battle axe that he held in his black-gloved hand.

"Recognize this place, old friend?" Vincent asked.

Will could see Aalok's fortress not too far off through the falling ash. He knew where he was by the description of it from *The Book of Aramis*. This had been the chapter where Alexander fought his way to save the Truth Keeper. This was where he had lost the duel.

Will fixed his eyes on Vincent. "Caius."

"So you do remember."

"Why are you creating this illusion? How are you doing it?"

"Fascinating." Vincent smiled. "He put you in charge of protecting the Truth Keeper again, although you failed last time."

"Where is she?"

Vincent tapped his temple. "Safely locked away." He tilted his head, bearing a cunning smile. "For now."

Will glanced down at his suit of armor. "Why repeat the past?"

"How about another match? You win. She goes free. I win. You die."

Will's shoulders tensed. "This isn't real."

"It's a form of reality. And in reality, the only thing that remains immortal is your soul. Death in the mind is death, nonetheless. Bow before me, vow to convince Claire to read the book, and not only will I let you live, I'll let you keep your precious Truth Keeper."

The words Alexander had spoken to Caius came from Will's mouth the same as they had before. "I bow to no one but my king."

Vincent took his stance. "Shall we begin?"

46

BLANK SPACE

"DEAD end," Claire huffed. "Why do we keep walking? There's no way out."

"You're right." Aven sighed. "We might as well sit tight. Wait for Vincent to finish whatever he's doing."

"Which is?"

Aven slid down the wall to sit. "Whatever amuses him."

Claire mirrored him on the opposite side of the wall and wrapped her arms around herself. She didn't know what Will was going through, what Vincent was doing to him. She hoped he wasn't wandering a maze like she and Aven had, but then again, that would be better than being trapped in a morgue.

There was silence for a long moment until Aven lifted his head. "I'm sorry."

Claire could tell he meant the apology by the tone of his voice, by the pain darkening his eyes—now the color of a weathered tombstone.

"I was just trying to protect you."

"Protect me? You made me think I was crazy. You used it against me knowing it was the one thing I hated about myself. But I wasn't crazy. Everything you told me was a lie."

"Not all of it." Aven's throat bobbed. "I do care for you, Claire. Deeply."

"Then tell me the truth. No more secrets. No more lies."

Aven let out a long breath and bowed his head again. He stared at the white floor for a moment before talking to it. "Will is a super soldier. Vincent experimented on him during World War E. He wanted him back. That's why he's here. And you. He wants you too."

"Why me?"

Aven met her gaze. "Aramis chose you."

"How does Vincent know that?"

"Devils whisper half truths. They told him. Not to mention there is a huge file with documents and writings dating back to the beginning of time, well, since we were all incarnated."

"Someone translated *The Book of Aramis*?"

"Most of the story, in Aalok's favor, of course. It's the end that was never written. The last few chapters of how it all turns out."

"So you've known this whole time I was a Truth Keeper?"

Aven gave a slight smirk. "When I first set eyes on you at LAX, time literally stopped, Claire. I saw us as Serus and Sophie in a vision, only I didn't know who we were then. I only knew that in the deepest part of my soul, you were someone special, that you meant something to me."

"If you cared about me so much, then why did you take away my memories? Why try to convince me that Will was dead?"

"Because I knew you wouldn't have married me otherwise, not after seeing you cling to his side, ready to die beside him. I wasn't going to keep up the ruse. I planned to fly you and myself out of town before our engagement party. I was going to wean you off Solace and tell you everything, but you ran. Hopefully no idiot drank that poisoned bottle of champagne. Not that it would've worked, maybe made Vincent sick enough for me to get you somewhere until I could figure out another way to kill him. I gave Will my word I would keep you safe, and that's one thing my mother always taught me—us, to be a man of your word. Guess you could call me a liar for breaking that pinky promise."

"Wait." Claire held up her hand for Aven to stop talking. "Will knew?"

"Don't be mad at him. He was doing what he thought was right. Seeing the wave, seeing what I could do, he knew you had a better chance with me, well, at least we thought you did. We didn't add a fallen angel into the mix."

"So the fallen are here?"

"Yep,"

"And Aalok?"

"He'll arrive after the red planet crosses."

"Do you know when that will be?"

"Soon. Vincent wants you to read the book before it happens. He says it's the only way to save the world."

"Do you believe him?"

"I think the unseen entities are filling his head, whispering the greatest lie of them all."

"What's the lie?"

"That you can save yourself, that you don't need the Creator's forgiveness. Vincent is simply trying to prolong his fate . . . and mine."

Claire's dream of Aven turning to ash came again. She wanted to tell him, wanted to warn him of what she saw. But she couldn't bring herself to do it. He knew what was going to happen. He had chosen his path in his previous life, just as she had chosen the one Aramis set out for her. But they still had a choice. It wasn't too late.

"I forgive you," Claire whispered. "For everything."

"Of course you do. It's in your blood. Counselor, healer, saint. I never deserved you."

"I'm not a saint, I've made mistakes."

"In the flesh, it's impossible to be perfect. But you come so damn close. That's why I fell for you, Claire. That's what made me fall for you before."

"I'm only reflecting Aramis. I'm only following His ways. Without Him, I don't know if I could ever make the right choice. He's always led me. He's always been there to make sure I don't mess up."

Aven nodded slowly and bit his lip. "I see that now. I see that everything you are, everything I admire, is part of Him."

"Then why do you keep pushing Him away?"

"You know me, Princess." Aven leaned his head back against the wall and sighed. "I've always been a rebel without a cause. No point in picking a side now."

"You protected me despite what you wanted."

Aven rested his arms on his knees and leaned forward. "There's always been a part of me, a part of who I was from before that's been selfish. I was still getting what I wanted. And what I wanted was you."

Claire frowned.

"Every time I'm with you this calm washes over me. It's a peace I can feel but know I don't deserve. I've never felt it on my own because I haven't changed. So don't make me out to be the good guy, because we both know I'm no knight in shining armor sent here to protect you."

Claire scooted across the floor and sat in front of Aven. She took his hands in hers and looked down at his palms, brushing her thumbs over them. She didn't know how he had power in those soft hands, but it was a power he had wielded out of selflessness.

"I care about you, but Will and I—"

"It's okay," Aven said, drawing back. "You don't have to explain why you love him more."

"And yet, I can't see myself living a new life in which you don't exist."

Aven gave a charming smile. "Feeling's mutual."

Claire smiled back.

"Kitten's right." Aven sighed. "I am a stupid boy."

"What do you mean?"

"I'm not ready to let go of you. Not even for her."

"You love her."

"That I do."

"Does she love you back?"

Aven gave a light laugh. "That girl has loved me since we were kids. And I've always broken her heart. Especially when I played house with you. Leave it to an Outcast to make one stupid mistake after another. Always the fool."

"You said she was Aerith?"

Aven nodded.

"Do you think she believes in Aramis?"

"I hope so. I had her staying with Paula while I was in Hawaii. I hoped that maybe since Paula knew the Words of Old, it would rub off on Kitten. I wanted her to have a chance at redemption. Even if I can't." Aven let out a sharp exhale, looking to the ceiling. "Tell me, wise counselor. How the hell do I fix this one?"

Claire scrunched her shoulders. "Ask for forgiveness?"

"From Kitten or the Creator?"

Claire smiled. "Both?"

Aven pursed his lips, studying Claire's hopeful expression. His mouth parted, but the second he thought to ask her to pray about his damnation, to ask forgiveness, not from her, but from Aramis, the ground shook beneath them.

"What's happening?" Claire asked as Aven took her in his arms. "I feel strange."

"It's okay, I've got—"

Aven grasped air, and the convulsions ceased the instant Claire vanished.

"Claire?" Aven called, jumping to his feet. "CLAIRE!"

The lights went out all at once, and Aven found himself alone in a pitch-black nothingness.

"Touch her and I'll kill you, you son of a bitch!"

A DREAM
WITHIN A
DREAM

CLAIRE gasped a breath as she woke on a steel gurney. She tossed the sheet to the side, finding herself in the same clothes she had chosen for her dedication ceremony. They were still slightly damp, as was her hair, which was tangled in stringy seaweed.

Is this real or another Mind Walk?

She glanced around the room. There were no gurneys with bodies covered in sheets like before. She was alone, breathing in air absent from the stench of embalming fluid.

Sliding off her cold bed, Claire exhaled in relief that her feet and not her knees hit the icy floor. The ground seemed to bend as she took a step. Perplexing as it was, she didn't try to understand why it did.

She looked away from the one-way mirror and took steps toward the door, waiting for Aven to come through. When he didn't, she took the handle cautiously and walked into more white. Goosebumps covered her flesh as she took steps down the hallway. She took a left turn, then a right, disheartened that she was again in the never-ending maze.

Turning a corner, her brows lifted when she saw the glow of a neon exit sign. She hesitated a moment, standing at the door, unsure if she was ready to face what was on the other side. If Vincent was done toying with Will, she was next.

Aven's eyes flew open, and he shot up from a couch. He surveyed his surroundings, noting he was in Vincent's parlor. He wasn't sure if he was still in the Mind Walk, or if somehow this was where Vincent had placed him after the keyword. The room looked very similar to the memory of Vincent taunting him as a boy. The fire crackled in the fireplace. Edgar Allan Poe's book of poems lay in his lap.

He went over the last thing he remembered. Speeding down the highway on the motorcycle, ready to lead Will and Claire to safety. The angel that had come down like lightning flashed in his mind. That was the last thing he had seen. The unfurling of black wings, the glinting armor, the white hair with tips dipped in blood.

Zarak.

With a groan Aven stood, pressing a hand to his sore ribs.

Maybe this is real.

But it always seems real.

Glancing around, he found everything where it should be, but when he fixed his gaze on the empty glass case where the book once sat.

"Shit."

He's going to make her read the book.

Squawk.

Aven's head snapped toward the doorway. Above it, a raven sat. It fanned its wings, squawked again, and then flitted through the doorway. Aven followed the bird into the foyer of Vincent's mansion, wondering if he was still under. Either Vincent was playing with his head, or Mal was guiding him to Claire.

The front door swung open on its own accord, and a cold gust of wind ruffled the perched bird's feathers as it squawked, "Nevermore."

Crackling flames and a hum of weapons buzzed in Will's ears as he pushed off Vincent's axe.

"Where is your king now?" Vincent taunted.

Will spun on his toes, blocking the axe as it cut through the air.

Vincent countered, but a moment too late as Will's sword slashed open his wrist.

Vincent hissed and his axe clattered on the ground.

Will pointed the tip of his blade at Vincent's chest. "Let. Her. Go,"

"Choose Aalok and you can keep your precious Truth Keeper."

Caius's words from the past rang clear.

"I'd rather die."

Vincent smiled. "So be it."

The moment Vincent's glove lit with flames, Will thrust his blade into Vincent's stomach.

A taunting laugh echoed off the rocky walls around them, and Will took a step back, watching Vincent pull the sword from his middle and toss it to the side.

"You said you could die in this reality."

"I am the Creator, and therefore"—Vincent held out his hands—"I am god."

Will looked at the edge of the cliff behind Vincent.

Maybe a fall would wake him. Maybe taking Vincent down with him would break his skull and break Will free from this nightmare.

A growl rose from Will's throat as he charged, but Vincent disappeared.

Will clawed the air as he fell, then slammed into the ground. Stars against a black backdrop flickered in his vision. He blinked, struggling to open his eyes, hoping that hypnosis worked the same as it did in dreams. But when he found the damp rocky ceiling above him, he wasn't so sure.

He had seen this place in a memory, had read it in Alexander's story. Only this time, he was without the nagging Truth Keeper. He would have to find the door to the outside on his own, but first he would have to find his way through the rocky cave maze.

There were no tables covered with portraits, no people laughing and drinking. There were no children on the stage playing Beethoven, and no Aven or Will standing in the ballroom. Claire was alone, and it was dark, except for the dimly lit chandeliers above her that seemed to brighten when a voice spoke.

"How do you like your wedding gown?" Vincent asked as he slunk from the shadows dressed in a fitted suit.

Claire looked down, now seeing the glittering gown trailing with ostrich feathers behind her. "The engagement was a lie."

"It was," Vincent said, slipping his hands into his pockets.

"And you knew. You knew Aven wasn't going to go through with it."

"I did."

"Then why put me in this?"

"Because you still have a chance to save him."

More figures came out from the shadows.

The fallen Seraph.

"Join us," Vincent said as the Seraph made a circle around them. "Give Aven his salvation."

Claire swallowed. "Only he can make that choice."

The fallen Seraphs shook their heads and disappeared, and Claire wondered if they left to report Vincent's failure to Aalok.

"As you wish, Truth Keeper. But if you want to wake from this never-ending dream, I need you to do something."

"What?"

The book, just like the one Claire had read in Hawaii, appeared in Vincent's upturned palm.

"Read," he ordered.

"You're not supposed to know what's in it."

"And why not?"

"If Aramis wanted you to know, if he wanted you to have that information, then you could understand it. But you're of your father and his father. You are of the blood of the fallen. It's in your nature to be evil. To want only what you want. You don't think of others. You're selfish. That's why you can't read it. That's why you don't understand."

"Because I'm not chosen."

"No," Claire said. "That's just it. Anyone can read the book; they just choose not to. They reject Aramis' grace, and because of it they are blinded from the truth."

"Lies."

Claire racked her brain to remember the line, to recall the Words of Old. She couldn't quote the verse verbatim, but she quoted it all the same.

"In the words of Aramis himself," she said. "'Though seeing, they do not see; though hearing, they do not hear. In them is fulfilled the prophecy. But they are never hearing, never understanding, never perceiving. For their hearts have become calloused, they hardly hear with their ears, and they have closed their eyes. Otherwise, they might see with their eyes, and hear with their ears, to understand with their hearts and turn to me. And if they do, I would welcome them with open arms, but they deny me and the cup that overflows with truth at my table. For they only have to believe upon me, they only need call upon my name, but they are silent—except for the times they call upon their father to betray me. There is only one true father, one true king, and I alone am He.'"

"Read or die," Vincent told her.

"You can kill me but never my soul. That belongs to my king. As does yours, and he will do with it what he will."

Vincent's jaw tensed as he took a step forward. At the snap of his fingers, a spotlight behind him showcased Bree holding a dagger to a girl's throat.

The breath from Claire's lungs left all at once. "Kitten."

"Are you so careless with others' lives as well?" Vincent asked.

"Let her go!" Claire ordered. "It's me you want."

"Bree?" Vincent said, still glaring at Claire.

Bree pressed the blade into Kitten's neck.

Kitten cried out as blood trickled down her chest.

"Don't hurt her." Claire pleaded.

"Read the book," Vincent demanded.

Claire stared at the emblem on the cover of *The Book of Aramis*.

Even if I read it, will Vincent understand the parables?

Taking the book in her hands, Claire flipped through the pages to the beginning, but Vincent stepped forward.

"Read the end," he demanded.

The tome flipped across Claire's thumb until she found a line that she had never forgotten, that had given her the reason to believe.

"By grace, you have been saved," Claire said. "By faith you—"

"Not that one," Vincent growled.

"You can't stop what's coming," Claire told him.

A door at the stage flung open, and Aven shot through it. He took one look at Claire and then at Bree and Kitten below.

Bree jerked Kitten's hair back and dug the knife into her flesh.

"Stop!" Aven demanded with an outstretched hand.

The knife flew from Bree's grasp.

Bree lunged for it, but Aven slid it out of reach.

The ropes around Kitten fell, and she soared into the safety of Aven's arms.

"Are you okay?" he asked her.

Kitten nodded and hugged him, weeping.

Vincent snapped his fingers and Claire disappeared, only to reappear in the chair Kitten had been in. The ropes snaked their way around her legs, abdomen, and arms, binding her to the chair.

Bree took her place behind the chair and placed her fingers at Claire's temples. "What is it you fear, Truth Keeper?"

Will stood at the door as it hummed. It looked the same as it had been described in *The Book of Aramis*. He knew by the story it had been Aerith who helped Alexander and Sophie get the key to escape. But she wasn't here.

I'm alone.

Never, a voice whispered.

Falling to his knees, Will bowed his head and clasped his hands tight.

"You will never leave me, you never have. Not in the desert, not now. I know Aaron is with you. I know I'll see him again. I'm ready to let go of all I've harbored. All of my resentment. This was my path. I accepted this mission long ago. I took the vow to protect the Truth Keeper. Help me now. Help me fulfill my purpose."

The hum went silent, and Will opened his eyes to see the beams of electricity had disappeared.

Drawing in a deep breath, Will rose from his knees and went to the door, ready to face what was on the other side.

"Get out of here. Hide!" Aven ordered Kitten.

Kitten ran toward the stage to exit out the door he had come through, but as she took a step to climb the stairs, she slammed into an invisible wall. She turned to go another way, but it too was blocked by nothing.

"Vincent! Let her go!" Aven commanded. "This has nothing to do with her."

Vincent smiled viciously and set his gaze on Claire. "Bree?"

"What is it you fear, Truth Keeper?" Bree whispered in Claire's ear again. She pressed her palms to Claire's temples and tilted back her head, drawing in a deep breath. "Not that. Too easy. Ah . . . there it is."

"Enough!" Will shouted.

Aven and Kitten turned to find Will standing in the ballroom doorway with fists clenched tight.

Vincent glared at him. "I locked you away."

Will smirked. "I found the key,"

"Scars," Vincent said. "A painful reminder of what we try so hard to forget."

Bree forced Claire's hand onto the arm of the chair, lifted the dagger, and stabbed the blade through the raised skin on her palm.

Claire screamed, and as she did, the room shook and the ceiling gave way.

Will ran to Claire as debris fell, but it landed in front of him, blocking his way. He waved his hands in the air to clear it, and as it did, he found himself in the woods.

Claire's screams were distant now, but not far off.

He ran toward them, smelling smoke, hearing the wails of a fire truck. When he made his way to the backyard of a house engulfed in flames, he saw Aven looking up at Claire, who dangled from the gutter of a roof. Red from her cut dripped down her arm. He didn't know how she had cut her hand, but seeing the broken window above her, he could only assume it had been the glass that injured her.

"The mind," Vincent said in his ear, so close it tickled, "such a dangerous place."

"Stop! You're going to kill her!" Aven shouted.

"Tell her to read the book," Vincent called out.

"If she falls, she dies!" Aven argued.

"Tell her," Vincent said, slow, with meaning, "to read it."

"She won't," Will answered as he turned to face Vincent.

"I thought it was your duty to protect your precious Truth Keeper." He then glanced up at Claire as her bloody fingers slipped. "I wonder how long she can wait for you to save her this time."

Will ran to Aven's side and glanced up at Claire as she struggled to hold on. "This is a memory of hers?" he asked him.

"This is where she took me in our first Mind Walk," Aven replied.

"She was afraid of heights because of the fall."

A fire demon crawled out of the window and screeched. Claire screamed.

"Do something!" Will commanded Aven.

"I can't," Aven shouted. "Vincent controls this."

Will's eyes darted back to Claire. "But we're in Claire's mind, right?"

"I don't know."

"How did you cure her?"

"I woke her up."

"How?"

"If she's under by Solace, it won't matter. Not unless I'm awake. You're going to have to give Vincent what he wants."

"No."

"If you don't, she dies, and the purpose of her life, my life, everyone's damn lives she's touched will be in vain."

Claire's cries for her father made Will's stomach turn. He didn't know what had happened to her. They never got to talk about their past fears. But seeing her, seeing the fear in her eyes, listening to her scream about a fiery monster that was going to eat her father alive made up his mind. He knew what he had to do.

"Claire," Aven shouted. "Let go."

"I can't!" she called down in a shaky voice.

"Claire, I'm going to say the words," Aven called over the roaring flames as Will walked away.

"I'll do it," Will shouted to Vincent. "I'll read it."

"Well, well, well," Vincent said as Will approached him halfway across the yard. "Isn't this a wonderful surprise?"

At a snap of Vincent's fingers, the book fell from the sky, and as it did, Claire slipped from the roof with a scream. But she didn't fall down; she fell up, along with everyone but Vincent. He grinned wide watching the world turn upside down.

Will landed hard into a chair as a desk appeared before him, and *The Book of Aramis* slapped the surface. He glanced around, gathering his surroundings as the fog in his mind cleared. He looked to the couch where Aven was waking. Kitten was in his lap, waking too.

Claire sat in a leather chair, slumped to the side. An IV pole was beside her, and a fluid dripping down from the line bled black into her veins.

As Aven stood, Will raised a brow at him, asking a question.

Aven's eyes darted around the room, and Will knew he too wasn't sure if they were in another dream.

Will surveyed the room, letting his photographic memory pick apart the parlor. Nothing was out of place, or so it seemed. When Aven pulled back the curtains, Will noticed that there were no windows.

Glancing back at Claire, Will understood the trick Vincent had pulled. It had never been about that Truth Keeper, but another.

"You wanted me to read it," he said. "Not her."

Vincent's lips drew to one side.

"My memory," Will continued. "You knew I could quote every single word exactly as it was written."

Vincent narrowed his eyes and spread his hands across the desk. "Clever fellow. She tried but failed that test. As did another Truth Keeper."

Will's mother.

"You put us in here, made this illusion, to get me to quote it word for word."

"Tell me how it all ends, Mr. Stryde."

Will looked down at his chest as a chain jingled. On it was his dog tags and Aaron's, and with them, a skeleton key.

Will jerked the chain from his neck, looked at Aaron's tags with sentiment, and then unlocked the book. Opening it, Will licked his lips as the blank pages filled with words. "In the beginning, there was the word. And the word was—"

"The END," Vincent growled. "READ THE END!"

"Let them go first." Will glared at him.

At the snap of Vincent's fingers, Claire and the IV pole slid across the room and into Vincent's arms.

A letter opener appeared on the desk, and Vincent snatched it up and pressed the pointy end to her abdomen.

"Vincent!" Aven shouted.

"A life for a life." Vincent grinned. "Insurance our brother does as expected."

"What is he talking about?" Will asked, confused.

"Vincent's my brother," Aven said.

"Half brother," Will noted.

Aven nodded.

"I'm waiting. Impatiently," Vincent growled, digging the point into Claire's side.

Will took one glance at the blood trickling down her white gown and flipped to the back of the book. He took a deep breath, licked his lips, and read.

"And when it was time, the last of the Truth Keepers were delivered to Aalok, to give a testimony, to be a vessel for the king. And before the hour ended—"

Will paused, knowing that this part of the book was important, that this was the last stand Claire would have to face. If he were to read it, if he were to tell Vincent why Aramis had sent her, he could stop her.

"Go on!" Vincent poked the tip of the knife deeper into Claire's abdomen.

Will slammed the book shut and shoved it toward him. "Read it yourself."

"Oh, Will. You know he can't," Aven teased.

"That's a shame," Will mocked. "I guess he won't know how it all turns out."

"Choose wisely, Guardian," Vincent seethed.

"I already have." Will glared at Vincent, but then his eyes shifted to Aven, who stood bare-chested behind Vincent, swinging his shirt around his brother's neck.

Vincent dropped the letter opener and stumbled back, clutching the fabric choking him.

Claire fell to the floor, but Aven didn't let go, twisting his shirt tighter.

Will ran to Claire's side and took her in his arms, but as she woke, Bree appeared behind Kitten and ran a blade through her abdomen.

"No!" Aven cried out.

Vincent collapsed and Aven watched in horror as Kitten held her stomach, trying to keep the blood inside. She stumbled to the couch and fell back on it.

Rage filled Aven's eyes as he held out his hand, as if an invisible tin can was in it, and crushed it.

Bree gasped, clutching her throat.

Aven used his mind to slam her against the wall and slide her up it. Her feet dangled, her eyes widened.

"Aven, don't!" Will shouted.

"A dream is not reality," Aven quoted from *Alice in Wonderland*. "But who's to say which is which?"

When Bree fell unconscious, Aven dropped his hand and ran to Kitten's side.

Bree thudded to the ground.

"It's not real, you know it's not," Aven said to Kitten, cradling her. "You're not dying. She didn't stab you. You're okay. You're okay." He focused on the wound, ordering it to heal, but it wouldn't.

"Stupid boy," Kitten managed to say as blood trickled out of her mouth.

"Sore loser," Aven countered playfully as tears streamed down his face.

"I love you," she managed.

"Katharine."

Her eyes rolled back.

"Stay with me!"

Kitten went limp in his arms.

Aven leaned down and kissed her bloody mouth as she exhaled her last breath against his lips. His tears wet her cheeks as he wept over her, stroking her hair, kissing her forehead. He drew back and closed her eyes gently before he held her to him and screamed.

The canteen of whiskey and glasses on the bar shattered into a thousand pieces. The room shook so fierce that the walls wavered.

Bree regained consciousness as glass rained onto her. She managed to get to her feet, went to take a step toward him, but she appeared to be stuck in place.

Aven lifted the letter opener from the floor as he stood. He let it twirl in the air above his fingers as he tilted his head to get one last look at her.

"Aven, wait!" Will shouted.

"Misery loves company," Aven told him, never taking his eyes off of Bree. "I'm already going to hell, why not have someone join me?"

With that, Aven unfurled his fingers, willing the letter opener to slice through the air and into Bree's chest.

"Take that, you heartless whore."

Bree stumbled back against the wall, looking at her wound before she slid to the floor and fell limp.

"Aven."

Aven didn't turn to Will's voice. He only stared at Bree as she bled out, knowing he would be judged for what he had done. But he didn't care.

"Aven," Will shouted. "Where is Vincent?"

Aven glanced to where Vincent had once lain, but he was gone. "Shit."

Time slowed and Aven watched Will and Claire slowly fade into thin air.

Vincent reappeared before him with a wretched smile and a long dagger in his hand.

A grunt slipped past Aven's lips at the stab. Another thrust of the blade came, then another and another.

Vincent whispered the same words Aven had heard so many times in his recurring nightmares.

"Thy Kingdom come."

Blood poured from Aven's lips, and he listened to the slick sound of his muscles squishing against the dagger as it slowly withdrew. This had once been Nehia's way of torture, but now he knew, she had only been showing a dire warning of his deadly future.

48

I PROMISE

AVEN coughed up blood as he woke from Vincent's Mind Walk. He blinked, listening to crackling flames, and voices he recognized but couldn't understand. The words from Claire and Will were muffled, jumbled.

Black smoke curled on the ceiling, and Aven cleared his throat, now seeing Will's and Claire's backs to him. When Aven turned to his left, his heart sank.

Kitten stared aimlessly at the ceiling with her mouth parted. Her dry lips had yet to turn blue. Red spatter was on her cheek and a trail of blood was drying, making a direct line down her neck. The dark crimson had pooled in her hair, staining it in a shade Kitten had never dyed it before.

Aven recalled how he held Kitten in his arms and had kissed her bloody lips as she took her last breath.

"Don't look," Will's voice came.

A sheet was drawn up over Kitten's stiff body and then over her pale face.

"Will, it's really bad." Claire's voice was so shaky, so filled with nerves. Aven knew she was about to lose it when she reached a trembling hand to his face to comfort him.

"Damn," Will said as he came into view.

"I'm fine," Aven managed to say regardless of the blood in the back of his throat.

The pain in his abdomen burned like hell, and Aven gritted his teeth, trying not to puke. He attempted to sit up, but there weren't enough muscles there. At least not yet. He could feel them stitching back together, but it was taking too long. It wasn't only that. Something was pressing him down, holding him back.

"Look for a key," Will instructed Claire.

Aven pressed his chin to his chest to look at his body.

A steel straight link chain was wrapped around his chest, his hips, and his legs, holding him flush against the medical table. Aven could feel it now, feel the weight of grade 70 cold steel. It was the kind truckers used to haul heavy loads, the kind he had seen Vincent keep in a drum in his parlor. Aven thought it had been just for looks, but now he knew: Vincent had used it to torture his disobeying lackeys. The rust and crusted blood on them was proof.

Claire disappeared from sight, and the room blurred in Aven's vision as he watched her. He blinked again, forcing his eyes to focus on Will's face as he met his wary gaze.

"There's nothing but tools and gauze," Claire said, "Do you need gauze?"

Aven could only assume she had been searching the medical room for a key by the slam and clatter of drawers and cabinets.

"We're going to get you out of here," Will said.

Aven watched Will strain to break the chains with his hands. With each groan, his brother's teeth bared. The chains tightened, squeezing Aven tighter. Aven growled and bit his lip at the pinching pressure.

"There's no key!" Claire said with a frantic voice, appearing again.

The steel chain around Aven's chest clinked together as Will cursed. "I'm not strong enough," he said and swiped the sweat beading at his forehead.

Aven could see the blood on Will's fingers now, could feel his stomach closing up the holes. That's why Vincent had stabbed him. He hadn't left a key. Vincent had known Aven could heal, wanted him to suffer, wanted him to lie there with no hope of survival.

"You have to leave," Aven told Claire and Will.

"No." Claire gave Aven a stern look. She then glared at Will. "We're not leaving him again. We can wheel him out."

Will's brows pinched together and his eyes shut tight. "It's not a gurney, Claire. It won't collapse and it sure as hell won't fit through the door."

Claire tugged on the chains at Aven's ankles, twisting his feet, trying to slip them beneath the steel binding.

Aven considered telling Will to snap every bone in his body, but before he could part his mouth, an alarm sounded.

"EMERGENCY FIRE PROTOCAL INITIATING IN TEN SECONDS," a robotic female voice warned.

"Get her out of here," Aven yelled over the noise.

"TEN," the female warned.

Will grabbed the chains at Aven's chest again and grunted. A vein jutted from his forehead, and his face turned red, then paled the instant the chain snapped between his hands.

Claire put Aven's arm over her shoulder, and Will took Aven's other arm to help him to his feet.

"SEVEN," the female sounded.

"Run or you're not going to make it," Aven growled. "Leave me behind!"

"No!" Claire told him, holding him tighter. "You'll burn alive!" She hurried, and Will matched her strides.

"If you don't, we'll all suffocate," Aven grunted.

Although they were only a few feet from the open doorway, Aven knew the glass security door would close within seconds. They would all be trapped. They would all die.

"SIX," the female voice warned.

"Leave me!" Aven demanded as he refused to move.

Will slipped his arm from Aven's back and spun, swooping Claire up over his shoulder.

Aven fell to his knees and watched Claire's wide eyes recognize what had just taken place.

"No!" Claire screamed. "Let me go! WILL STOP! STOP IT!" she screeched, pounding at Will's back as he rushed her out of the room.

Aven crawled toward the door, blood streaking behind him. He knew he wouldn't make it, but it didn't mean he wouldn't try.

"TWO."

"WILL!" Claire screamed as he held her against the wall. "HELP HIM!" She pounded at his chest, but he wouldn't budge.

"ONE."

A loud *beep* sounded, and the transparent armor shot across the doorway, locking it in place.

"DOOR SECURE. FIRE PROTOCAL INITIATING," the robotic voice announced.

Claire fell to her knees and pressed a hand to the impenetrable surface. "No, no, no," she mumbled.

Aven leaned against the bulletproof glass and took in a few deep breaths, knowing the air would soon be thin.

"It's okay, Princess," he assured her and glanced up to say goodbye to Will, but Will was gone.

Pressing his face against the glass, Aven searched down the halls left and right.

A feral roar echoed, and Will appeared again, slamming a body in black tactical gear against the wall.

It was a black op super soldier. One of Vincent's mind-controlled lackeys.

He knew Aven would make it out, or maybe, he wanted to make sure Claire and Will didn't.

Claire ignored the brawl behind her. Her head was bowed, her eyes were shut tight, and her mouth spoke something like a prayer.

Aven had heard some of these words before, remembering Paula quoting them many times.

Claire was praying for help, praying in the name of Joshua for Aramis to aid them.

At the sound of gunfire, Aven's gaze darted back to Will as he shielded himself with the first agent against a second agent on the opposite side of the hall.

The second the second agent aimed his handgun at Claire, Will charged him, and Aven watched as a tussle ensued.

"Claire!" Aven shouted, banging against the glass. "Get out of here!"

She flinched but didn't open her eyes and squeezed her hands tighter.

At a loud *pop*, Aven's head snapped up to see blood on the wall and the second agent unmoving.

Will squeezed the trigger once more, sinking a bullet right between the eyes of a third agent coming around the corner. "Claire, we have to go," he warned and searched the lifeless agents for more weapons.

Aven knew Will was right. There could be more agents swarming the building once Vincent knew these had been unsuccessful. He was most likely watching the show from a safe distance, giving the orders.

"Claire," Aven said, pounding the glass again. He ignored the vents turning on behind him, sucking up the smoke, but also, the very gas he needed for his lungs to function. Soon there would be no breath, no way to speak any words.

Claire lifted her head and pressed a sweaty hand to the glass. "I'm not leaving you. I'm to fulfill my promise to you."

Aven's eyes burned as he held back his tears. She was willing to die for him, to save his soul from hell.

"You already did." Aven smiled, holding back his tears. "Now go. Go do what you were sent here to do."

"We'll figure this out." Claire wept. "We can get you out. We can still save you."

Will grabbed her arm, but she wrestled away.

"No!" she shouted, keeping her fixed gaze on Aven. "There has to be a way to open the door."

The desperation in Claire's voice made Aven's heart ache.

"Don't ever give up, Claire. Always be strong. Always fight for what you believe in."

Aven shot a glance to Will, telling him with his eyes he was going to make this easier on him. He was ready to be the bad guy, ready to take away Claire's choice. He couldn't make his brother do it. He couldn't make Claire hate him. There was only one thing to do now, and Aven was the only one who could do it.

A muscle tensed in Will's jaw as he nodded.

Aven gulped a breath of thin air. "Claire."

"Please," Claire cried, pressing her palm flush against the glass. "Please, don't say it."

It was all Aven could whisper, all he could manage as his chest tightened with sadness, with lack of breath. But he would say the words. He would make sure that the last thing he did in his life would be dignified—not for redemption, but for the Truth Keeper he had *always* loved.

Pressing his hand to hers, Aven whispered his goodbye. "I promise."

Will stooped swiftly and caught Claire in his arms as she fell unconscious. He lingered at the door and gave a smile, though his forehead seemed wrinkle with regret. "I'll be seeing you, brother," he told Aven.

"No," Aven rasped as he grappled for the last air left in the room. "You won't."

"Aven, I'm—"

"Keep her safe."

"You have my word," Will cradled Claire close, jogged down the hall, turned the corner, and was gone.

Sliding his bloody hand down the glass, Aven forced himself to stand. He stumbled left to right, knocking over beakers and tubes on the counters as he made his way back to where Kitten's dead body lay. He supported his weight against her gurney and pulled back the sheet.

Even in death you're beautiful.

He swept his clean hand down her face, closing her eyes before he took her hand and kissed the back of her cool knuckles.

I hope you're not where I'll be shortly.

Heavy eyelids beckoned him to sleep. Every sharp breath he took was useless. The vents had shut off. The flames had been put out. He was growing woozy, but he wouldn't let go of Kitten's hand. He would hold it as long as he was conscious.

At an exaggerated nod, Aven slipped from Kitten's fingers. He landed hard on the floor of scattered glass, but he could hardly focus on the pricks and stabs against his skin. He could hardly sense anything but the dark tunnel as it closed in. He lay in Kitten's pool of blood, staring at the ceiling. It would be soon. Any second, his dark demise would surely come.

Two fighting heartbeats later, it did.

Aven was dead, but still so very conscious. He felt his immortal body slip from the husk of his heavy flesh. It floated with ease above his corpse, looking down at it from the ceiling. But it didn't stay there. It was sucked swiftly down a crumbling rabbit hole in the floor, and into a tunnel of a never-ending void

DEEP SLEEP

WITH his head bowed, Will prayed to Aramis, listening to time ticking away. Three days he had waited for Claire to come out of her hypnosis. Three days he had paced the floor. He hadn't left her side, had hardly eaten, hardly slept. He only stared, watching, waiting.

Lifting his head, Will focused on the rising and falling of Claire's chest. She seemed at peace, but he wondered if she was still facing unimaginable horrors. The thought of it made him jump to his feet to pace the room again.

I used the keyword ... begged ... pleaded.
How did Aven wake her?

Will thought about the beach, how she had fallen unconscious. He clenched his fist thinking of how he had treated Aven. His brother was dead, and Will couldn't help but think if he had stayed just a few moments longer, they could have figured out a way to get him out of the room.

He sat back down beside the bed and stared at Claire, shaking his leg with growing anxiety.

She was lying there in the sand. Aven and I were fighting, and she just—

"Water."

Will ran into the kitchen and filled a glass full. He ran back into the guest bedroom, dipped his fingers in the cup and flecked Claire's face.

Nothing.

Tilting Claire's head back on her pillow, he poured the water on her forehead and smoothed back her damp hair. "Come on, Claire. Wake up,"

No response.

Water ... waves ... saltwater.

Will's gaze traveled to the bathroom before he rushed to the garage and grabbed a bag of salt he had stocked up on for the cabin. He poured several bags into the tub and turned on the faucet, correcting the temperature to lukewarm. He rushed back into the guest bedroom, gathered Claire's limp body in his arms, and held her, waiting for the water to fill just a few inches from the brim.

It could kill her, a voice hissed.

It's the only way, a softer voice pushed.

Staring at Claire, Will bit his bottom lip. He had been so hasty, so desperate to see if this idea would work. But would it? It was risky. It was stupid.

What am I doing?

Saving her life.

He kissed her head and laid her in the bath. A shaky breath left his lips, and he took in another as if he was taking one for Claire. He pinched her nose shut and pressed a hand to her chest, forcing her body beneath the water's surface.

The seconds ticked by as Will counted silently.

Fifteen . . .

Sixteen . . .

Seventeen . . .

Fear consumed him the longer he held Claire down.

She'll wake, a calm voice assured softly.

You're killing her, another snickered.

Will kept holding his breath and withdrew his fingers from Claire's nose. He watched the bubbles rise to the surface, felt the taps of her heartbeat begin to race at his palm.

His lungs burned. His head throbbed.

You're drowning her! a hiss warned.

Wait a little longer, a whisper requested.

His lungs screamed. His heart pounded.

Aramis . . .

Twenty-two . . . please . . .

Twenty-three . . . please . . .

Tears jeweled Will's lashes as he held Claire under but he kept praying to Aramis to wake the Truth Keeper he so dearly loved.

Tick . . . tick . . . tick . . .

THE

OTHER

SIDE

50

ASHES

TICK...tick...tick...

Aven gasped for breath, jolting up in his bed. He patted his body and checked for the wound that had been bleeding out. A sigh of relief escaped him. No wound. No blood. He glanced at the clock, finding the minute hand frozen, and patted his jean pockets.

No phone.

There was no pain in his limbs as he would expect from a hangover. No aching head. It was quite the opposite. He felt feather-light, full of energy.

He bounced from his bed to the window, surprised to find it shot out, shattered by . . .

A bullet from my gun.

The memory of Will and the letter from his mother and playing guitar for Claire came.

It was all a dream.

He glanced past the crack of the glass to view the outside.

It was dark, and the sky glowed with a reddish hue, appearing as if it were dusk.

The red planet. Has it crossed?

He needed to find Claire and Will. He needed to warn them.

No phone, he reminded himself again as he reached into his pocket to call Kitten.

Kitten . . .

An image of her lifeless body on a gurney made him sick.

His then saw the image of his own wounds.

Three deep gashes in my stomach.

Aven shook his head.

Nehia's mind games.

It wasn't real.

He rushed down the steps and into his garage, not bothering to put on a helmet, and squealed his blacked-out motorcycle down the street.

Something flaky, like snow, caught in his lashes as he zoomed down the empty highway.

Ash. He could smell it now—and sulfur. He curled his nose at the stench and sped up, only to come to a screeching halt at an impasse.

With a flick of the kickstand, Aven dismounted his bike and took careful steps to the edge of the ravine. The crack was

393

half a mile wide. There was a fog, something like smoke, blocking his view over the impasse.

More ash fell on his lashes, and Aven found himself in a blizzard of embers and dust.

Dry heat cracked his lips and burned his eyes, but he squinted at something coming from the other side that blinked on and off like flashing headlights.

He called to someone, anyone that may be on the other side of the chasm.

No answer.

"What the . . ." he said under his breath.

The lights flickered, and the smoke swirled around a bent metal frame as the dust cleared.

He knew the sign all too well, knew it should be welcoming him to Las Vegas, but it didn't. It was a salutation from another place entirely.

"Benvenuto all' Inferno"

Welcome to Hell

"Shit."

THE STORY
CONTINUES...

THE
AEON
CHRONICLES

BOOK IV

C O M E   S A Y   H I   T O   A P R I L
S H E   W O U L D   L O V E   T O
H E A R   F R O M   Y O U

 @April_M_Woodard

 @April_M_Woodard

 APRIL M WOODARD

 authoraprilmwoodard

Use these hashtags on
Instagram and Twitter!

#TEAMWILLSTRYDE
#TEAMAVENCREY
#TEAMCLAIRE
#TEAMKITTEN
#THEAEONCHRONICLES

ABOUT THE

AUTHOR

April M Woodard was born and raised in a small town in Virginia. She now lives in Georgia, near the big city of Atlanta, with her husband and three kids. She spends her days writing young with three kitties at her feet. Scratch that. Two kitties and a mogwai. When she isn't typing away on her laptop, she is sitting on her back porch, sipping sweet tea, and reading a good book.

Photo taken by SHANNONTHOMPSON ART

ACKNOWLEGMENTS

I want to give a big thanks to the amazing people that
I'm so blessed to have in my life.

TO MY READERS
YOU! Yes, YOU, are the reason I write.
To all the FEELS!

To my Betas
You ROCK! No. Seriously.
I LOVE YOU!

To my girl, J.M BUCKLER
My author bestie, my soul sista.
We're going back to Vegas after I publish book four.

To TIFFANY WHITE
My amazing editor
She waves her magic wand, and poof my books are polished gold.

To Shannan
My cover artist
I know you'll blow me away with book 4's cover.
I can't wait.

To Kristy
I wouldn't be able to keep my mind on the Creator's larger plan without
you reminding me. Thank you for sharing your NDE, and for answer my
questions on what it's like on the other side.

To my family.

Kiddos.
Thank you for letting your mama write. Yeah. Maybe one day we will get
that trip to Disney World if I can make it big.

To my supportive husband
You've always been my brooding knight and smirking sexy Outcast, all in
one.

www.ingramcontent.com/pod-product-compliance
Lightning Source LLC
Chambersburg PA
CBHW020910110726
47900CB00001B/94